I0598011

Also by Ray Hobbs and Published by Wingspan Press

Published Elsewhere

DAFFS IN DECEMBER

RAY HOBBS

Wingspan Press

Published in the United States and the United Kingdom
by WingSpan Press, Livermore, CA

The WingSpan name, logo and colophon are the trademarks
of WingSpan Publishing.

ISBN 978-1-63683-030-8 (pbk.)
ISBN 978-1-63683-976-9 (ebook)

First edition 2022

Printed in the United States of America

www.wingspanpress.com

This book is dedicated to Michael Bennett-Law and the Piccadilly Dance Orchestra, who ensure, through their superb performances and recordings, that the music of the Golden Age lives on.

RH

As always, I wish to acknowledge the invaluable assistance of my brother Chris in the preparation of this manuscript.

RH

Author's Note

As usual, I have tried to keep the use of musical terms in this story to a minimum, but some translation is probably necessary. I'll keep it as brief as I can.

Analysis in music is simply the breaking down of a piece into its component parts in order to explore the ways in which the composer has used them, also to pinch his ideas.

Aural Perception is ear training. It includes dictation, or hearing music and writing it down, and recognising harmonies and various characteristics as they are heard. It is most useful when we're damning someone else's efforts.

Keyboard Musicianship includes sight reading, playing various choral or instrumental parts simultaneously, playing music in different keys* from the original, harmonising a given melody, and generally showing off.

A Key* is the scale from which the notes of a piece are taken. It is characterised by the first note of the scale, which, for the purpose of this glossary, I shall call the *home* note. In other words, the music feels as if it wants to go home to that note and its associated harmony.

Before the Classical** Period, the word Sonata was used freely as a label for almost any kind of instrumental piece, but after the discovery of key-change, it was used more exclusively to describe a musical form that relies on that discovery for its dramatic quality, likewise the concerto*** and various forms of chamber music. It revolutionised the way music came to be composed, so it's all the more surprising that whoever discovered it was too modest to claim the credit.

Opus (literally, 'work'), is a word used in cataloguing a composer's output. As an example, if the first of his music to be listed was a group of, say, 5 studies, the group would be called 'opus 1', and each study would be numbered, so that the fourth would be referred to as 'opus 1, no. 4'. Be wary, however, of people who scatter opus numbers into their conversations. They only do it to impress.

An Arpeggio is a chord with its notes played one at a time, as on a harp (It: *arpa*).

The history of music is divided into eras, or periods: Medieval (up to the end of the 14th C), Renaissance (15th to mid-17th C), Baroque (mid-17th C to mid-18th C, Classical** (mid-18th C to early 19th C), Romantic (early 19th C to early 20th C), Twentieth Century (speaks for itself), and the twenty-first century is still open to suggestions, but we're hoping for something snazzy.

The Guildhall (School of Music and Drama) is a highly-respected place of education for musicians, actors and anyone involved in theatre, film and TV. They also do an irresistible scarf in black, white and red.

The Concerto is a piece for orchestra, usually with a guest soloist or group of instrumentalists. It is often the highlight of the concert; at least, that's what the guest performers hope.

Articulation is the actual business of hitting, bowing, plucking, or blowing the notes. Two important ways to do this are Legato (smoothly, joining the notes together), and Staccato (short and detached).

Colla Voce (follow the voice) is an instruction to musicians to ignore the conductor and second-guess the singer when he/she is singing *a piacere* (with total freedom), sticking to that often capricious performer like mud to a trainer. In fairness, singers are more disciplined nowadays, so the experience isn't the bronco ride it often was in times past.

Variations are simply diverse ways of treating a theme. Think of the humble potato and the wealth of appealing ways it can be served.

Timpani are drums with, at one time, copper shells, but nowadays, glass fibre has taken over as the new copper. They can be tuned, each to a different note, using levers that stretch or ease the skin, and the Pedal Timp can be tuned to two separate notes, the pedal being used to alternate between the two. Percussionists are clever people with a level of concentration that makes the rest of us feel like goldfish, and who can play the whole range of percussion instruments and count phenomenal numbers of bars when necessary.

Just one more thing before I leave you in peace to read the story:

About twelve years ago, I was accused by a published novelist of writing about a kind of music that 'no one had ever heard of'. The manuscript in question was of my first novel *Second Wind*, and his observation troubled me for some time until I reached a conclusion so obvious that only my bruised sensibilities at the time had caused me to overlook it. The fact is that the music is there to be heard, and the advice I have to offer any reader who is unfamiliar with the Golden

Age is simply to download the music. Explore the dance music of the 1930's and the great bandleaders, such as Ray Noble, Ambrose, Lew Stone and Henry Hall. Then there are the band singers: Al Bowlly, Sam Browne and Elsie Carlisle, among the rest. The numbers mentioned in the pages that follow are available on YouTube, and I recommend one clip in particular. Oddly enough, it features an orchestra rather than a band, but I'm no purist – I find that people who exclude all but their favourite things tend to deny themselves a great deal enjoyment – and the number in question is of significant importance in this story. It is taken from a concert by the Boston Pops Orchestra, and it can be found listed as 'All the Things You Are/Rebecca Luker.' Tragically, Ms Luker is no longer with us, but her exquisite performance of the number lives on as a fitting memorial to her wonderful talent.

I end with a somewhat tongue-in-cheek apology. I'm sorry to say that there is no recording of 'You Make Ev'rything Better', as it exists only in my mind. Like Freddy Hinchcliffe, I have yet to write it down. One day, perhaps…. We'll see.

RH

1

Airedale College of Music

September 2011

It was Craig Townsend's first week at the college, and it had so far been one of surprises. His main areas of responsibility were Analysis and History of Music, but now he found he was required to teach piano, keyboard skills and aural perception as well, none of which worried him, but he did wonder about the integrity of the person who'd framed the advertisement.

He was currently engaged in an Analysis session with the first-year BA (Honours) students.

'Bear with me if you feel that you left all this behind with "A" level,' he told them, 'but we can't take anything for granted.' There was no argument, so he went on. 'Key-change was discovered in the early-eighteenth century. No one knows who was responsible or exactly when it was discovered.'

As if on cue, a student raised her hand.

'Yes, Melanie?' Fortunately, the new students were wearing name badges.

'I don't understand, Craig. I mean, J S Bach changed key before the eighteenth century, didn't he?'

'No, Melanie, he didn't. Brilliant though he was, and you'll find no more ardent a champion of Bach than yours truly, he never changed key in his life. He made transient modulations, but he never changed key. The texture of his music made that impossible.' He was attracting enquiring looks from the whole class, who were possibly wondering if this lecturer with the untidy, dark-brown hair and strange ideas might be not altogether sane, so he explained. 'Imagine two cars in a carpark. One is a Honda, the other a Volkswagen. Let's look at the Honda first. We can view it from the front, the rear or the side. By opening a door, we can look inside. We can do just the same with the VW, but – and this is an important "but" – the two cars will always be different. Similarly, we can explore a key, using any of its harmonies that take our fancy, just as Bach did with his modulations, but the key we are exploring will never be a different key, any more than the Honda will ever become anything other than a Honda. We can explore a key, or we can change to another key altogether, as composers do when they write in the structure we call Sonata Form. That,' he told them, 'is when we get out of the Honda and into the VW as seamlessly as possible.'

One student was busily drawing a map with roads and railway lines. Craig asked, 'May I see that?'

The student looked up guiltily. 'I was only doodling,' he said. 'I do that when I'm listening, and that was very interesting, what you said about the difference between modulation and key-change.'

'All right.' Craig smiled at his protestation. 'I know you were listening. I have to say, though, that the trains in your imaginary country have at least one remarkable property.'

'What's that?' The student, whose badge bore the name Jon Birchfield, looked puzzled.

'You've got two lines criss-crossed here,' he said, pointing to the anomaly. 'It's a clever train that can make a ninety degree turn.'

'I haven't drawn the turntable yet, Craig.'

'Okay, I'll concede that.' Curiosity led him to scribbled note at the top of the sheet. There was a date, a time and a reference to a TV channel. 'Don't lose that,' he said, handing it back to Jon. 'The note's obviously important to you.'

'It's the start of a drama series tonight. I don't know what it'll be like, but the music's by one of our neighbours, so I thought I'd give it a go.'

'Oh?' Craig's curiosity was aroused. 'Who's your neighbour?'

'Liz Frankland. Have you heard any of her stuff?'

'Yes, I have, and I knew her slightly when we were at the Guildhall. Whereabouts do you live, Jon?'

'Eskgarth.' Possibly because Craig was a foreigner from London, he explained, 'It's in Netherdale.'

'I know it,' said Craig. I've just moved into a house in Thanestalls.' He looked again at the map and said, 'Mind you, I haven't seen any turntables, yet.'

———◆◄———

The swimming pool at Netherdale Sports Centre was officially fifty metres long, but it seemed to Liz that each length she swam was longer than the last, and it was all because of the education system and its long school holidays. At ten, Carla was a competent swimmer, but Liz felt naturally constrained to keep an eye on her when they went to the pool together, and that limited her own activity. Now that the long summer holiday was over, however, and she suddenly had the freedom to extend her limits, they seemed to beckon from an ever-increasing distance; in fact, they didn't beckon so much as mock, and mockery was unacceptable, especially on a Monday morning. With that thought, she reached the steps at the shallow end and hauled herself out of the pool.

A voice said, 'It gets harder, doesn't it?'

Liz looked round, recognising the voice, and saw Leah Lowe. 'Hi, Leah,' she said in a tone that combined both greeting and unspoken agreement.

'Fancy a coffee?'

'Why not?' There was work needing her attention back at the studio, but she could spare twenty minutes or so.

'I'll see you in the cafeteria, then.'

———◆◄———

They took their coffee to a table by the long window that looked out on to the outdoor tennis courts, in which, at nine-thirty, keen players were already taking advantage of the September sunshine.

'What are you working on now, Liz?' As a recently-retired lecturer in dance and theatre arts, Leah was always interested in Liz's work.

'Original music for a drama series set in the Cotswolds.'

Leah wrinkled her nose and asked, 'Does anything dramatic ever happen down there?'

'Only the usual things. There's jealousy, envy, infidelity, violence, murder, depravity, incest, necrophilia, basic lust....'

'Is that all?'

'They're a pretty sober lot, by and large.'

Leah smiled. She was almost thirty years older than Liz, but they had become close friends five years earlier, when they had combined their skills to produce a dance presentation for Leah's students. They had much in common, although physically, they were very different. Leah's hair, usually held in place by an Alice band, was medium-brown, now flecked with grey, whereas Liz's hair was fair, almost blonde, and she wore it in a long bob. Her figure was slim but shapely. By contrast, a life of ballet had kept Leah trim and toned, but inevitably flat-chested.

Changing the subject completely, Liz asked, 'How's your mum coping? In fact, how are you coping?' Barely two months had elapsed since the death of Leah's father.

'I'm probably muddling through better than my mum. It was bad enough for Martin and me, but theirs was a fairy-tale romance, as you know, and now, most of the things she associated with him are gone.'

'But she still has you and Martin,' said Liz, squeezing her friend's arm in sympathy.

'For what use we are.'

'Lots, I imagine.' She could certainly believe it of Leah. She was less certain of Leah's brother Martin, whose early communication difficulties had eventually been diagnosed as Asperger's disorder.

'The things I'm talking about were his musical activities. He stopped writing shows some years ago, but he kept the Dalesmen going for as long as he could. My mum used to love going to their gigs. You know how she felt about dancing.'

'Yes, I do. She taught me the waltz and the foxtrot so that I could go along with you all and take part.' She stood up and asked, 'Shall we have another coffee? I'll get them.'

She went to the buffet and waited behind a man and a woman who couldn't decide which snack would most effectively bridge the gap between breakfast and elevenses. Meanwhile, she thought of Leah's mother, lovely, sweet-natured Sylvia, now having to adjust to life without her beloved Freddy. It was too awful.

Eventually, the couple made their purchase, and she was able to get two coffees, which she took back to the table.

She'd been meaning to ask, 'What's become of the Dalesmen since your dad had to give up?'

'He didn't give them up.'

'No?'

'No, he carried on, losing one and then another to old age and worse, until the band just… disbanded.'

'That's a rotten shame. I mean, the music's still being played, but….' It was of no help to Sylvia.

'The New Albion Dance Orchestra's still going strong, but that's miles away, in Cullington.'

'That's what I meant.' She asked, 'Would it be all right if I were to look in on her?'

'Of course it would. She'd love to see you again, Liz.'

'In that case, I'll phone her and make arrangements.' She stood up and picked up her sports bag. 'Must go,' she said. 'I have to call in on my mother and grandma.' Now ill and infirm, Liz's grandmother had given up her home and gone to live with her daughter. Elderly people had become very much a part of Liz's life.

———— ◂▸ ————

She worked on the score for the TV series until it was time to collect Carla, who always found the first day of a new school year exciting, and was likely to chatter about it for some time. Liz was simply thankful that she enjoyed school, and she looked forward to hearing about it.

Surprisingly, Carla's first utterance after greeting her mother was a complaint. 'Why do I have to sit in this thing? I'm in Year Six now.'

'Child seats are compulsory until you're either a hundred and thirty-five centimetres tall or twelve years old,' Liz told her, 'or is it twelve centimetres tall and a hundred and thirty-five years old? I can never remember. Anyway,' she said, 'you wouldn't want me to be arrested for breaking the law, would you? Can you see yourself visiting your poor old mum in the Tower of London? They have a special dungeon there for child seat offenders.'

'I don't believe you.'

'It's true. I can tell you exactly where it is. You enter through Coldharbour Gate, you cross Tower Green, turn left at the Beauchamp Tower, and you see the sign ahead of you. "Child Seat Dungeon. Abandon Hope All Ye Who Enter Here".'

'Mum, you're being silly.'

'And you're suffering from an attack of premature adulthood. I'm told there's always a danger of it in Year Six, but don't worry, I'll measure you when we get home, and we'll work out how long you still have to spend in a child seat. In the meantime, are you going to tell me about your first day in Year Six?'

In a different tone, Carla said, 'It was really good. I enjoyed it. I'm in Mrs Wheatley's class now.'

'Wow! And what have you been learning?'

'History.'

'Don't keep me in suspense. What are you doing in History?'

'The Victorians.'

'I don't believe it,' said Liz, turning right and driving the short distance up the lane to the cottage.

'It's true,' Carla protested. 'You can ask Mrs Wheatley if you like.'

'I'm not accusing you of not telling the truth, darling. The reason I said that was because we did The Victorians in Year Six as well, twenty… some… years ago.' A glance in the driving mirror told her that Carla was unconvinced. 'Then we did Road Transport.'

'Huh. We did that in Year Two.'

'That's a relief. I thought for a moment we might have fallen through a time warp.' She drew up and pulled on the handbrake. Carla remained quiet, no doubt reluctant to encourage further silliness.

Liz let her out and closed the door behind her. 'Now for the moment of truth,' she said. 'Let's go to the measuring wall.'

They went through to the kitchen, and Carla stood with her back to the vertical, graduated line.

'No standing on tiptoe. Shoes are allowed, but no stiletto heels, footstools or stilts.' She placed the flat of her hand on Carla's head and held it against the line. 'One hundred and thirty-one centimetres,' she read. 'You have just four more centimetres to grow before we can put the child seat on eBay. It won't be long now.'

'In an abrupt change of subject, Carla asked, 'What are we having tonight, Mum?'

'What would you like?'

Carla looked at her in alarm. 'Haven't you made anything?'

'Yes, but it's a secret.'

'If I could choose,' said Carla, cautiously relieved, 'I'd ask for sausages and mash.'

'I just thought you might say that. That's why we're having sausages and mash.'

'Yes!'

It was good when Carla occasionally reverted to normal childhood. Children grew up far too quickly.

'Have you got any homework?'

'Only maths, and I can't do it.'

'Neither can I, darling.'

Carla snorted. 'You haven't even looked at it yet.'

'That just demonstrates how well I know my limitations.'

'What does that mean?'

'My limitations? The boundaries beyond which I am ignorant and ineffectual, if not downright incompetent.' Guiltily, she relented. 'Let me look at it later, and I'll try to make sense of it. In the meantime, go and change out of your school uniform while I make a phone call.'

'Who are you phoning?'

'An old lady whose husband died recently. Leah's mum, actually. I want to make arrangements to go and see her.'

'That's really sad,' said Carla, adding, 'but you're good at that kind of thing.'

'Off you go, flatterer.' She found Sylvia's number and dialled it, hoping it wouldn't be an inconvenient time for her. The phone rang four times, and then Sylvia picked it up.

'Hello?'

'Hello, Sylvia. It's Liz Frankland.'

'Oh, Liz. How are you?'

'I'm fine, thanks, Sylvia. More to the point, how are you? I'm conscious that I haven't seen you since the funeral. I just didn't like to bother you at such a time.'

'Oh, I'm managing, Liz. Don't worry about me.'

'I won't if you'll let me come over and visit you.'

There was a pause; Liz's offer had evidently come as a surprise. Sylvia said, 'Oh, will you do that? I'd love to see you. When can you come?'

'Is tomorrow free?'

Sylvia chuckled a little sadly. 'Every day is free, Liz.'

'In that case, do nothing about lunch. I'm taking you out.'

'Really? There's no need.'

'I think there is. I'll be with you at about eleven-thirty.'

'Right. I'll be waiting for you in my best bib and tucker.'

'Good for you. Take care, Sylvia.'

'And you. 'Bye.'

'See you tomorrow. 'Bye.'

Liz put the phone down, wondering what Sylvia meant by her 'bib and tucker'. She was in her eighties, and she sometimes spoke the language of a bygone age.

2

Within a very short time, Craig was asked to report to the office of Harley Stewart, known to the irreverent multitude as 'Harley Davidson'. To anyone else, he was Dr Harley Stewart, PhD, MA, BMus (Oxon), FRCO, Principal of Airedale College of Music.

Craig had no idea why he'd been summoned; so far, he'd not fallen out with anyone and he hadn't been accused of anything untoward, but fate could be a fickle bugger, so he approached the *sanctum sanctorum* with some apprehension.

A traffic lights system operated outside the Principal's office. Red stood for 'Busy', Amber meant 'Wait', and Green was the invitation to enter. Surprisingly, Craig's ring prompted a green light, so he opened the door and walked in.

'Ah, Craig,' said Stewart by way of greeting, 'settling in all right, are you?'

The enquiry seemed somewhat premature, as the term was only two days old, but Craig said politely, 'Yes, thank you.'

'Good. You're probably wondering why I've sent for you, so I'll put you out of your misery immediately. The fact is that, so early in the term, it's very difficult to find students who are prepared to take part in a lunch-hour recital.'

'Of course.' It was hardly surprising, given one week's notice.

'The point is, can you help us out by doing a lunch-hour yourself?'

'In the absence of a fully-practised up student who's raring to go, yes, Dr Stewart, I'll do one. It'll have to be on the piano. I'm still bringing my trumpet back up to scratch.'

'Oh, that's fine. Don't stand in awe, by the way. Call me "Harley".'

'Okay, Harley.' Craig stifled the smile that came to him at the thought of his being in awe.

'Let Rosalyn know your programme as soon as you can, so that she can type it.'

'I can do that now, Harley. How long is a lunch-hour recital?'

'About forty-five minutes. It gives everyone time to get back to work.'

'Okay. Have you a pen handy, or do you want to leave it to your secretary?'

'The safest way will be to tell Rosalyn as you leave.'

Looking at the disorganised mess on Stewart's desk, Craig was inclined to agree.

'Thank you for being so obliging, Craig.'

'It's no trouble, Harley.'

He took his leave and knocked on the door of the next office. Not surprisingly, there were no traffic lights to control visitors.

'Come in.' The voice was cheerful enough.

Craig pushed the door open and saw a woman of forty or so. She looked as pleasant as her voice had sounded. 'Are you Rosalyn?'

'I am, and you're Craig, I imagine.'

'That's right. I have to give you the programme of next Tuesday's lunch-hour recital.'

'Oh, are you doing it? Thank goodness for that. We thought we'd never find anyone to do it.'

'I'm surprised.' He could only imagine that being new had placed him low on the list of those to be asked.

'What are you?' Her pencil was poised.

'On Tuesday, I'll be a pianist.'

'Oh, good. What are you going to play?'

'I'm going to start with two sonatas by Domenico Scarlatti.' He gave her the details.

'I've got that.'

'Then Beethoven's Sonata in C, opus fifty-three, known as "The Waldstein".'

'Excellent.'

'And I'll end with one of Rachmaninov's *Etudes Tableaux*, the opus thirty-nine, number one in C minor.'

'Lovely. Thank you, Craig.' She looked at the programme again and asked, 'How long are the two sonatas by Scarlatti?'

'About two minutes each, at the most. The word "sonata" was used quite arbitrarily in his day. The whole programme shouldn't occupy more than forty-five minutes.'

'Good.' She gave a sigh of regret. 'It's just a pity I shan't be able to leave my office to hear any of it,' she said. 'Just for a change, it's a programme of music that I like. At least, I don't know the Scarlatti pieces, but the "Waldstein" and the Rachmaninov are right up my street.'

'If you like, Rosalyn, I'll have it recorded.'

'Would you really do that?'

'With pleasure.'

'That's very kind of you. You know, we don't hear much music from the Romantic Period at this place. It's frowned upon by the organists and academics, and you playing the Rachmaninov will be like an inrush of fresh air.'

'It seems to me that the college would benefit from some fresh air, Rosalyn. Will you be a sport and cross out all except the Rachmaninov?'

She looked surprised, but nevertheless did as he asked. 'What do you have in mind?'

'Let's begin with two of Chopin's *Etudes*, the opus ten, number four in C sharp minor, and the opus twenty-five, number one in A flat.'

'Oh, lovely.' It was clear that she meant it.

'Then, Chopin's *Fantasy in F minor*, opus forty-nine. It's only twelve or thirteen minutes long, so we'll follow that with the fourth of Liszt's *Transcendental Studies*, which I've also played recently. That's eight and a half minutes long.' He considered the programme and confirmed it, by saying, 'I think we've got ourselves a Romantic programme, Rosalyn, and if no one else enjoys it, you and I certainly will.'

'Oh, yes.' Her eyes were shining, but then she asked anxiously, 'Will you be able to practise those things up before Tuesday?'

'Yes, it won't take a lot of work to resurrect them.'

'I'm glad you came to work here, Craig. It'll be lovely to hear something different from the usual fare. Would you describe yourself as a romantic?'

'Absolutely, Rosalyn. Died in the wool and completely beyond redemption.'

———◆◄◄———

Liz found the house without difficulty, having visited Sylvia and Freddy within the past five years, and she parked her car opposite the front gate.

She rang the doorbell, fully expecting to wait. Elderly people didn't move quickly, and nor should they. Most of them had earned the right to take their time. Sylvia must have been waiting, however, because she was at the door in what seemed only a matter of seconds.

'Hello, Liz,' she said. 'I was just getting my coat so that I was ready.' She was wearing a flowered, purple dress. Purple seemed to be her favourite colour, because Liz had seen her wear it on more than one occasion.

'Hello, Sylvia,' said Liz, kissing her on the cheek. 'Let me help you with your coat.' She held it, positioning the sleeves conveniently for her and pulling it up to her shoulders. 'There,' she said, 'you're all gathered in. I hope you've got a hearty appetite.'

'I don't know about that.' She locked the door and took Liz's arm. 'Where are we going?'

'I thought we might go to the Shearer's Arms. Leah recommended it to me.'

Have you seen Leah recently?'

'Yes, I saw her at the swimming pool yesterday, although I didn't know she was there until I got out of the pool. I must have been concentrating on my own efforts, because Leah's hard to miss when she's in the water.' She opened the passenger door for Sylvia.

'Why is that, dear?'

Liz waited until she was in the car before answering. 'Because she's the epitome of graceful movement. She dives and swims like a ballerina, and she puts everyone else to shame.'

'I should hope so after all that ballet training.'

'Sylvia, you're so funny.' Liz patted her hands before starting the engine.

'Am I?' She sounded surprised.

'Yes, but in the nicest possible way.'

They drove to the Shearer's Arms, where several of the patrons recognised Sylvia and greeted her.

'I'd quite forgotten what a friendly place this is,' she said.

'And you're very popular.'

'I suppose so.'

They found a table, and Liz asked, 'What would you like to drink?'

Sylvia gave the question some thought. 'Nothing alcoholic, thank you. I don't drink very often.'

'Maybe a fruit juice or a tonic water?'

'Orange juice would be nice,' she decided.

'With ice?'

'Yes, please.'

As Liz turned to go to the bar, Sylvia said, 'The first time Freddy bought me a drink, it was in the American Bar of the Savoy Hotel. He bought me a pink gin. It was very strong.'

'I imagine you weren't used to it in those days, Sylvia. I'll be back in a minute.' Liz went to the bar and ordered an orange juice and a gin and tonic, deeply conscious that Sylvia had mentioned Freddy for the first time. She had no way of knowing whether it was a good or a bad sign. She asked for the drinks to be put on the bill, picked up a menu and re-joined Sylvia at the table.

Sylvia said, 'Freddy always said I ran on goffers.'

'What does that mean?'

'I should have explained. A car runs on petrol, but I ran on soft drinks. "Goffers" is navalese for soft drinks.'

'Of course. You were both in the Navy, weren't you?'

'Freddy was. I was in the Wrens.' The distinction seemed important to her. ' "Join the Wrens and Free a Man For the Fleet", the posters said. Freddy said I'd done much more than that. He said I'd taken a broken man, put him together again and brought him safely home. He said it was having me to come home to that helped him survive.'

Liz blinked hard. 'I'm sure it was, Sylvia.' She opened the menu and asked, 'Would you like to choose something to eat?'

Sylvia eventually made her choice, and Liz was able to order.

'You don't mind me talking about Freddy, do you? I find that it helps me. When I talk about him, he doesn't feel quite so far away.' She reflected briefly and said, 'Wherever Freddy went, there was music.'

It was as if she'd just remembered it. 'I rarely went fishing with him. I got enough of that with my dad when I was young. I just left the two of them to enjoy their fishing together. They were great friends, Freddy and my dad. The things we did together, though, were always accompanied by music.' She smiled faintly. 'He'd always wanted to be a bandleader. He told me in his first letter from Poland that he'd played before the war with a band called the "Humber Rhumba Boys". He came from Hull, you see, near the River Humber.'

Liz nodded to show that she understood. Anxious not to stop the flow, she kept quiet and let Sylvia continue.

Sylvia seemed to be gazing into space, remembering. 'He sent me songs he'd written for me in the PoW camp.'

'What a lovely thing to do.'

'Yes.' She was quiet for a spell, no doubt enjoying the memory. Then, moving on, she said, 'The first Dalesmen were a motley collection, but he persevered with them until they were ready to start playing gigs. He had a way of getting the best out of people.'

Again, Liz nodded, hoping that the food wouldn't arrive just yet. It was clearly important for Sylvia to reminisce.

'His next venture was to write a musical for the Yoredale Players. After that, they just kept asking for more. He wrote the music, book and lyrics, as they say, and I choreographed and rehearsed the dances.' She looked directly at Liz and asked, 'Do you know what I miss most of all about his music?'

'No. Tell me.'

'At every gig I went to, he used to get the band to play a certain song, and then he'd hand over to someone else and he'd come down to the floor to dance with me. It became our song.' She smiled self-consciously. 'It's a hackneyed concept, isn't it?'

'Only because it's such a lovely thing that everyone claims it if they can. Don't apologise for it.'

'Oh, no. I'm not apologising.'

'Which song was it, Sylvia?' Liz had to know.

'He wrote to me about it from the prison camp. He told me it was his favourite song, and it soon became mine as well.'

Liz waited.

'He said it was the most perfect marriage of music and lyrics.'

14

She stared ahead in mute recollection. Then she spoke again, and her eyes were moist. On our first date, a friend of ours asked the band to play it for us, and we danced to it for the first time. It's by Jerome Kern and Oscar Hammerstein. It's called "All the Things You Are". I have a recording of it, but I'd love to hear it played again by a proper band. It's just a shame Freddy got rid of the arrangements when the band fell apart.'

3

Liz thought she knew the answer, but she had to ask, 'Have you got everything packed for school tomorrow, Carla?'

'Yes.'

'Had I better look at your homework?'

'Okay.' Carla took out her French exercise book and showed it to her.

Liz put her glasses on, found the latest piece of work and read it through. 'I see it's about shopping,' she said.

'Yes, it's important if you go to France.'

'I can't disagree with that. Isn't it ironic, though, that there are people in this country who can't wait to leave Europe, and you're learning French so that you can go shopping there?'

'What does "ironic" mean, Mum?'

'Irony is about the curious nature of opposites, and it can sometimes be humorous and sometimes serious. Learning French is a serious matter,' she said, opening the book at the evening's work. ' "*J'aime beaucoup la vert robe*",' she read.

'It means, "I like the green dress very much",' said Carla.

'So it does, but "*la robe*" is a feminine noun, so the adjective should be "*verte*", not "*vert*". Also, the adjective comes after the noun in French, and not before it, as it does in English.'

'It doesn't matter, Mum,' Carla explained patiently. 'We're only going to role-play this tomorrow. Writing in French isn't important at Key Stage Two.'

Liz closed the book and handed it back to Carla. 'It's important to me that you learn French properly,' she said.

'How do you know French properly?'

'How did I come to learn French properly? I went out with a Frenchman for some time when I was a student.'

16

'Oh.' It was a surprise for Carla. 'Was he nice?'

'Of course he was. I wouldn't have gone out with him otherwise. I've made the occasional mistake,' she said, thinking of Carla's father as a glaring example, 'but I've usually been quite particular in choosing male company.'

'Will you find someone new to go out with?'

'Not for some time, Carla,' she assured her. 'Now, if you do make progress with your French, when bureaucracy allows it, I'll reward you by taking you on holiday to France, so that you can use your French.' On reflection, she added, 'Even if the sceptics get their way, I suppose we'll still be allowed to travel to Europe.'

Carla narrowed her eyes, as she often did when confronted with a new concept. 'What's bur... what you said?'

'Bureaucracy is the power of officials to make our lives difficult. I was actually thinking about the way your curriculum is organised.' On brief reflection, she said, 'No, it's wrong of me to offer you something and make it conditional. I *shall* take you to France, and then you'll *have* to use your French.'

'Oh.' Carla looked at her thoughtfully and asked, 'Is that a promise?'

'No, but barring accidents, it will happen.'

'You never promise.'

'You're quite right, darling, I don't.' She wondered for a moment about the suitability of the topic for bedtime discussion, and realised she couldn't avoid it. ' "Promise",' she said, 'is a special word. I could promise you that holiday, and then walk out of this house and be run over by a bus, so that I couldn't take you to France or anywhere else.'

'Not in Hardacre Lane, Mum,' said Carla confidently. 'Buses can't get up here.'

'Well, outside the supermarket. Anywhere, in fact. The point is that if I never make a promise, I'll never break one either.'

'My dad's promised to come and take me out a week on Sunday.'

Liz had been afraid this might come up. All she could say was, 'Well, let's hope nothing happens to make him change his plans this time.'

'He always promises.'

'And sometimes he comes, and you have a lovely time together.'

'He shouldn't promise, though, should he?'

The conversation was becoming too judgemental for Liz's peace of mind. She put an arm round Carla and drew her into a bedtime cuddle. 'You and I can be as high-minded as we like,' she said, 'but we mustn't fall into the trap of expecting everyone to conform to our lofty standards. We must be prepared to make allowances.'

After a while, Carla's eyelids began to droop. Liz looked at the clock and said, 'Time for bed.'

'Okay.' Carla kissed her. 'Night-night.'

'Night-night.' Liz returned the kiss and removed her arm, which was now numb. 'Sleep tight.'

'Hope the bugs don't bite.'

'If they do, take off your shoe.'

'Hit them 'til they're black and blue.'

'Night-night, darling.'

It was a meaningless ritual observed by children and loving parents, and it was a shame Simon had mocked them for it, although Carla seemed to have forgotten the incident. Liz hoped he would keep his promise and come for her on Sunday.

———◆◀———

Craig had been aware for some time that his trouser waistbands were no longer as comfortable as he preferred them, and he also realised that he'd had little exercise that summer. The situation demanded a drastic remedy involving regular visits to Netherdale Sports Centre, which was reputed to have a fifty-metre swimming pool.

His first opportunity occurred that Saturday morning, and he entered the water with the composure and poise that virtue inspires.

He was so intent on completing as many lengths of the pool as he could, that he paid little heed to other swimmers, apart from allowing them generous space. It was a glorious feeling to be doing the right thing, and he felt inclined to push himself hard. He'd already swum further than he'd intended, and that alone spurred him on. He was a little tired, it was true, but he was going well. That was until a crippling pain attacked his right lower leg. He was in the middle of the pool, and he had to reach the side if he were to haul himself out, but in that basic action he found himself defeated. He was simply unable to swim, such was the paralysing effect of the pain. He knew the cause was cramp, and the way to deal with it was to stretch the cramped muscle, but present circumstances made that impossible. All his effort was going into reaching the side. Instinctively, he struck out with his arms only to find that the side of the pool remained horrifyingly out of his reach. Early training told him to lie still on his back and float, but the agony in his leg had a different agenda. His head was now beneath the surface. Blind panic made him thrash with his arms, and he surfaced once, taking a huge breath before the demon in his leg rendered him helpless again. His head went under water once more, and he flailed again with his arms, but with little effect. The awful truth was dawning on him that he was about to succumb to drowning, when he felt a hand cup his chin, and an unseen force propelled him to the surface. He heard a woman's voice say, 'You're okay. I've got you.' He felt the water recede from his face, and he exhaled and took another breath, making himself cough and choke.

With the relief from drowning came a reminder of the leg pain. Without being consciously aware of it, he must have cried out, because the voice said, 'What is it? Chest pain?'

He managed to splutter, 'No… cramp… right calf.'

Another woman's voice close by asked, 'Are you okay?' He heard his rescuer say, 'Yes, I've got him. He's got cramp in his right calf.'

The other woman said, 'I'll get out and help you lift him out.'

The hand that had cupped his chin now guided his hand to the steps. She asked, 'Can you manage if you grab the handrail?'

'Yes. Oh, shit!' Lifting himself, one-footed, out of the pool, he apologised. 'I'm sorry,' he said, 'but it's agony.'

Together, the two women laid him on the pool side, and one asked, 'Right calf, you said?'

'Yes. Hell's bells!'

She grasped his right foot and bent it into the walking position, proceeding to massage his calf with her thumbs. It gave him almost instant relief, at least from the pain, but he was still gasping and coughing after his repeated ducking, and the stench of chlorine still hung in his nostrils.

'Now,' said the woman who'd eased his cramp, 'stand up and put your foot flat on the floor.' Between them, the two women helped him to his feet.

They had attracted the notice of several swimmers as well as a life guard, who asked, 'What's all this?'

'He was drowning,' one of Craig's rescuers told him, 'but we got to him before it was too late. Where were you?'

The attendant muttered something unintelligible and asked Craig if he was all right.

'Yes,' he managed to say in between choking and coughing. 'Thanks... to these... two... ladies, I'm... okay now.'

'It was my friend who saved you,' said the woman whom he took to be middle-aged, possibly in her fifties. 'I only helped her pull you out and stretched your calf. You'll have to remember that in future. If you get cramp in your calf, stretch it by getting your foot into that position,' She pointed somewhat unnecessarily to his feet.

He resisted the urge to tell her he knew that already. Only an idiot would make such a clever dick remark after the ignominy of being fished out of a public swimming pool.

'My friend knows her muscles,' said the other, who looked considerably younger. 'She's a ballerina.'

'Used to be,' her friend said modestly. 'How long were you in the pool?'

'Nearly an hour. I'm trying to get... fit.' With a final bout of coughing, he relieved the irritation in his airway.

'You were trying to kill yourself. If you're unfit, that was far too long to be swimming.'

The younger woman was looking at him curiously. She asked, 'Were you ever at the Guildhall School of Music?'

'Yes, ninety-seven to twenty-oh-two. My name's Craig Townsend. I'm sorry. You have the advantage of me in that bathing cap.'

'Of course.' She pulled off her swimming cap and the shower cap beneath it, and shook her hair loose. 'I'm Liz Frankland, and the one giving you the well-deserved bollocking is my friend Leah.'

'I remember you, Liz, but I'm surprised you remember me. Anyway,' he said, 'I'm very grateful to both of you ladies. Thank you very much.'

'We're going to get changed now,' said Leah, 'and so should you.'

She surprised him by favouring him with a smile. 'Come and join us in the cafeteria for coffee afterwards, and I'll go easy on you. You've had enough punishment for one morning.'

———◂▸———

He was already in the cafeteria when they arrived. He asked, 'What can I get you, ladies?'

'Just two white coffees, no sugar, please,' said Leah, taking the seat beside Liz's. 'That was a neat bit of life-saving,' she said. 'Well done, Liz.'

'Thanks, but you're the expert on cramp. I wouldn't have known what to do.'

'You do now.'

Craig went to the buffet and asked for three Americanos with milk. While he waited, he watched the two women, who appeared to be talking whilst trying not to look at him. He was unsure whether he was the object of their pity or their amusement.

The coffee came, and he paid for it, taking it over to their table and claiming the seat opposite them.

Leah asked, What do you do for a living, Craig?'

'I'm a lecturer at Airedale College of Music. I've only just started there.'

'What do you teach?'

'Analysis, History of Music, and anything else they throw at me.'

'That's a coincidence. It's what my husband was doing at Nidderdale when we met, although his main thing was composition.'

'Nidderdale?'

'Yes, it was a college of performance arts before it was swallowed up back in nineteen seventy-six.'

'Seventy-six? That was before I was born.' As the words left his mouth, he regretted saying them, and they'd not gone unnoticed.

'That's perhaps not the smoothest remark you've ever made, Craig,' said Liz. 'How old are you?'

'Thirty-one.'

Leah shook her head. 'I'm in the company of children, and yes, Craig, I have a son who's only a few years younger than you.'

'Surely not.' He meant it. 'I'm sorry. I spoke without thinking, as usual.'

'Keep the compliments flowing, and I may just forget your little *faux pas*.'

'I think you've just redeemed yourself, Craig,' said Liz.

'I'm glad. After this morning, the last thing I want is to offend either of you. I'm afraid I do sometimes put my foot in it.' After a little more thought, he said, 'It can be a topsy-turvy world, can't it?'

Liz looked puzzled. 'Why do you say that?'

'You two saving my life this morning.'

'Oh, I see,' said Liz. 'You think it's a topsy-turvy world because two of the weaker sex saved you from drowning. Leah, did you realise we'd just pulled a male chauvinist out of the pool?'

'I didn't mean it like that,' he protested.

'If it bothers you that much,' said Leah, 'we can always chuck you back in. It's no trouble, but you'll have to wait until we've finished our coffee.'

'No, please don't take it the wrong way.' He couldn't bear the idea. 'I'm not a chauvinist at all, in fact, I've often been mocked for my old-fashioned… deferential… attitude towards women.'

'We won't mock you for that,' said Liz, 'will we, Leah?'

'Absolutely not. A bit of deference goes a long way in this imperfect society of ours.'

Craig felt himself squirming. 'It's embarrassing,' he said, 'and it's going to sound crazy, but I have to explain it to you. I owe you that, at least. You see, it has nothing to do with male domination or any of that nonsense. Well… not really. It's more to do with escapism.'

'Keep going,' said Leah. 'You've yet to make sense, but it's not quite ten o' clock. We've time in hand.'

'I hope so. You see, some time ago, in childhood, I adopted the values of a cosy world that most people would call a fool's paradise. In my exotic microcosm, hitches, mishaps and misunderstandings can all be resolved. Even the worst scenario can be put right and result in a happy ending.'

Liz thought she knew the answer to her next question, but she felt she ought to ask, 'Are you often disappointed?'

He nodded. 'More often than not, but you see, I'm beyond help. I'm an inveterate romantic.'

Leah had been following his explanation seriously. 'We sometimes visit your world, Craig. Liz is a composer, as you know, and my background is in dance, so we're no strangers to make-believe. In fact, the only difference between you and us is that we go home at the end of our visit.'

'Yes, I can see that. Maybe it all began for me when I didn't want to go home.'

Liz gave him a searching look, but simply said, 'Well, you've got a perfectly respectable job, so you can obviously cope with reality.'

'I suppose so,' he said, looking at his watch, 'but I must go home and do some practice. I have a lunch-hour recital at the college on Tuesday.'

'What instrument?'

'Piano.'

'What are you playing?'

'Two studies by Chopin, his *Fantasy in F minor*, Liszt's fourth *Transcendental Study*, and one of Rachmaninov's *Etudes Tableaux*.'

Liz's interest seemed to be well alight by this time. 'Which of the *Etudes Tableaux?*'

'The op. thirty-nine, number one.'

'Wonderful. Are the lunch-hour recitals still open to the public? I know they were when the college first opened.'

'As far as I know. I'll let you know, but if there's a problem, you could come as my guest. I'll get your email address from your website.'

Liz fumbled inside her bag for a business card, which she gave him. 'Phone me instead,' she said.

'Okay.' He stood up. 'At the risk of sounding repetitive, thank you again, ladies.' He shook hands with them both and left.

———◆◆———

'He's a lovely bloke,' said Leah, 'but he shouldn't be allowed out without his mum or a responsible adult in attendance.'

'I'm inclined to wonder about his mum,' said Liz. 'Something went sadly wrong with his home life.'

'It certainly sounds like it. Anyway,' said Leah, changing the subject, 'My mum was thrilled to bits when you phoned her, and she had a wonderful time with you, although she was afraid she might have bored you.'

'Bored me? What gave her that idea?'

'She talks a lot about my dad.'

'I know. She says it makes her feel that he's not so far away. It's obviously good for her.' She thought about their conversation at the Shearer's Arms. Sylvia had done most of the talking, but Liz had enjoyed listening to her. 'I saw what you meant about her missing the music,' she said. 'There was a special song, one that they called their own….' She tried to remember its title.

' "All the Things You Are",' prompted Leah. 'It's a beautiful song.'

'Yes, I remember it now. She said she had it on a CD, but it wasn't the same as hearing it played by a "proper" band. I think she meant a live band.'

'And a dance band, not a big band. That's important.'

'You sounded like your mum just then.'

'Oh, hell. Did I?' Leah bit her lip. 'Do you think I might be turning into her?'

'You could do a lot worse.'

Leah became serious again. 'I suppose I could take her to Cullington. Frank Morrison would do any mortal thing for her, but it would be an emotional experience, and I'm not sure she's ready for it.'

'One day, perhaps.'

———— ▶◀ ————

Craig phoned that afternoon. 'Liz,' he said, 'the lunch-hours are still open to the public, and it would be marvellous if you could come.'

'What time does it start?'

'One-fifteen.'

4

The Recital Hall at Airedale College was just as Liz remembered it, with tiered seating and a platform shaped in what was possibly a trapezium, although she had forgotten most of that stuff about geometric shapes since leaving school. Most importantly, however, the somewhat ordinary piano she remembered had disappeared, and a magnificent Steinway Model 'D' grand stood in its place.

At one-fifteen, the door opened, and the audience fell quiet as Craig, wearing a light-grey suit and a black roll-neck shirt, entered the hall and took the two steps up to the platform. He bowed to the audience and took his place at the piano.

The first of the studies by Chopin was infernally difficult. Liz remembered practising it when she was at the Guildhall. That was before she'd changed her first study to Composition, and the opus ten, number four might have been a contributary factor in that decision. It held no horrors for Craig, however, who was playing it brilliantly, and Liz couldn't help comparing him, with some difficulty, with the apologetic and embarrassed soul he'd been on Saturday.

He reached the end and took his applause from an audience that was bursting with enthusiasm.

The second of the studies was the one some people called the 'Aeolian'. The name was a nonsense, of course, like most of the popular nicknames given to pieces of music, but the study itself was sublime. Liz closed her eyes and let the gentle, rippling arpeggios wash over her until the insistent yearning of the music brought it to its ecstatic climax. Craig might well be the romantic he claimed to be, but he played exquisitely and without a hint of exaggeration.

Liz had not known what to expect. She knew that, to have been given the lunch-hour, Craig must be a capable pianist, but she was quite startled, partly by his electrifying technique, but more particularly by his feel for the music. The *Fantasy in F minor* was sheer poetry, and he treated it as such, expressing each nuance with total understanding but, again, without overstatement.

The *Transcendental Study* and the *Etude Tableau* were fiery, thrilling and compelling, so that, when Craig reached the end of the recital, the applause was ecstatic. He bowed to the audience and then held up his hands. When he had silence, he said, 'Thank you, everyone. There is time for a last-minute addition to the programme, and it's for Rosalyn, who'll be listening to the recording later. It's Rachmaninov's transcription of a piece by Nikolai Rimsky-Korsakov, "The Bumble Bee".'

Liz had no idea who Rosalyn might be, but she must have some special influence over Craig for him to include the piece in her name. The transcription was light-hearted, thrilling and entertaining, a perfect encore.

After the recital, Craig was surrounded by admiring students, but they had to return eventually to their studies, leaving the way clear for Liz to congratulate him.

'Magnificent, Craig. I'm breathless.'

'Really? That's very nice to hear. Thank you, Liz, and thanks for coming.'

'It really has been my pleasure. I remember you at the Guildhall, of course, but I never heard you play.'

'Oh well, I don't think I ever gave a recital there. I was usually too exhausted.' He looked at his watch and asked, 'Have you eaten yet?'

'No, I don't always eat lunch.'

'I haven't either. I never eat before a performance, but now that you've taken the trouble to come, will you let me give you lunch? I don't have to teach until four.'

Liz hesitated. 'I should be getting back,' she said, 'but after such a treat, yes, I'd like to join you. Where are we going?'

'The Beech Tree. Now that the students are hard at work again, it should be fairly quiet.' He led her into the foyer, where he offered her his arm.

'You really are unique,' she told him.

'I suppose we all are.'

'I mean, I can't remember the last time a man gave me his arm. It's such a lovely, old-fashioned thing to do.'

'As I told you on Saturday, Liz. I live in a lovely, old-fashioned world.' The sliding doors hissed open, and they stepped outside. 'My home is in the past, where they do things differently.'

'And why not?' Thinking of her student days, she said, 'The students loved your recital, but how will your Romantic programme have gone down with the academic staff?'

'Not at all well.' He chuckled. 'Most of the hierarchy work on the principle that if you don't look like Bach, you're ugly, whereas the remainder are firmly entrenched in contemporary music, but I didn't do it for their benefit. I did it for the students.'

They left the campus and crossed the road to the Beech Tree, where Craig's prophesy proved to be correct. There were no more than five or six people seated at the tables.

'What would you like to drink, Liz?'

'Oh, just a slimline tonic, please. I have work to do this afternoon.'

'And I mustn't drink alcohol when I have to face students, so I'll join you in that.' He ordered the drinks and asked for them to be put on the bill. 'Let's get a table,' he suggested, picking up a menu.

As they sat down, Liz said, 'Something you said earlier set me wondering. It was about the Guildhall and about being too exhausted to play in public.'

'Oh yes, I had to give up my night job in a filling station because I wasn't getting enough sleep. I had a succession of jobs,' he said, 'but that was the most exhausting.'

'What else did you do?'

'I worked in a fish and chip shop, but that was ruinous for the waistline, so I got a job in a sports club.'

'What did you do there?' She was fascinated, having only ever worked as a waitress during her holidays.

'Oh, handing out towels, cleaning the showers, manual massage, the usual things....'

'Massage?' She'd never thought of that as a student job, except in extreme cases, when 'massage' hinted at a great deal more.

'Yes, it's a good thing for a pianist to do. I helps strengthen the wrists and fingers, especially when you're working on some would-be Mr Universe with muscles like spring steel.'

'Fascinating.' Looking at the menu, she said, 'I'd rather like the mushroom quiche salad, if I may.'

'Of course.' He took the menu to the bar and ordered food.

'With all those jobs,' said Liz on his return, 'it sounds as if you spent more time earning money than you did working at your studies.'

'It felt like that at times,' he agreed. 'You see, my father left us when I was thirteen. It was a good thing and a bad thing, really.'

'Why?'

'Whilst my mother and I were better off without his drunken presence, my mother was left to keep house and bring me up on her modest income. She was very good, you know. She insisted that I went to the Guildhall. Fortunately, in those days, I was able to get a full grant, but I had to work as well to help my mother.'

'So that was the home you didn't want to return to.'

'Until my father left, yes.'

She thought of her own divorce settlement and Simon's reluctant part in it. 'Couldn't the authorities make your father pay something?'

'No, they never traced him.'

Recalling their conversation on Saturday morning, she said, 'I can't blame you for living in your cosy dream world.'

'It's a safe place,' he said. 'Everyone needs a safe place, real or imagined.'

She stood up to remove her coat and drape it over the back of her chair.

'What a lovely dress,' he commented. 'It looks so good on you.'

'Thank you.' It was a light-blue summer dress that she'd had for a while, but it was good that it was appreciated. 'I don't often wear dresses, but this is my going-to-recitals number,' she told him.

'With a figure like yours, you should wear them more often,' he said, 'although I have to say, I've seen you now in your bathing costume, jeans and a T shirt, and now a dress, and I think you look lovely in all those things.' He hesitated and said awkwardly, 'I shouldn't have mentioned the bathing costume, should I?'

She laughed, only a little embarrassed, and said, 'It was a shade intimate, but it was a compliment nevertheless, and I don't get all that many nowadays, so thank you.' She was a little puzzled, though. 'Are "bathing costumes" a part of your magical, retro world, Craig? I call mine a "swimsuit".'

'That's because American is the new English. They talk about swim caps as well, and sailboats and race cars.' With another apologetic look, he said, 'I made my remark about your… swimsuit… in all innocence.'

'I know.'

It was a convenient moment for the waitress to arrive with a quiche salad and a chicken salad. They assured her that they had everything they needed, and she left them, Craig to recover from another *faux pas*, and Liz to find a harmless topic.

'Leah's had an awful time recently,' she said.

'Oh?'

'Her dad died a couple of months ago. He left a big hole in her life and her mum's.'

'I've experienced that with my mother,' he said. 'Poor woman.' As if clarification were needed, he added, 'Leah, that is.'

'He was a lovely chap and very talented as well. Among his many interests and pursuits, he had a dance band.'

Craig's eyebrows rose immediately. 'A proper dance band? Not a big band?'

Liz laughed. 'You sounded just like Leah and her mum just then. Yes, a proper dance band that played music from the Golden Age.'

A dreamy look invaded Craig's features. 'Oh, Carroll Gibbons, Ambrose, Ray Noble, Geraldo, Lew Stone, Al Bowlly….'

'We're talking about the same thing,' she assured him. 'I wasn't sure you'd know what I was talking about, but it seems you're a believer.'

' "Devotee" is the word, Liz. I grew up with their music. My granddad's box room was an Aladdin's cave of seventy-eights. He'd almost forgotten they were there. They'd been my grandma's, you see, and when she died, they sat there gathering dust. He had a record player that played seventy-eights as well as LP's, and he let me listen to them whenever I visited him. They formed the music track of the cosy world I told you about.'

'Is your granddad still alive?'

'No, but when he died and we were clearing his house, I rescued the records. I still have them at my place in Thanestalls.'

It was Liz's turn to register surprise. 'Thanestalls? We're almost neighbours.'

'I know. One of the students, Jon Birchfield, tells me he lives not far from you.'

'Two houses away,' she confirmed. She looked at him quizzically and asked, 'How did he come to mention me?'

'He was doodling on a sheet of paper, and when I looked at it, I saw that he'd written the details of *Mum Alone*. He wanted to hear your score, and rightly, too. I was very impressed.' He adopted his awkward look again and said, 'I was going to mention it earlier.'

She couldn't help laughing at his discomfiture. 'It's all right,' she said. 'I'm not offended.'

'Oh, good.' He seemed to be searching for something to say that was neither about that nor about her scanty apparel at the pool, and she was about to help him out, when he asked, 'What's the situation with Leah's father's dance band?'

'It's defunct. It had been dwindling for some years – the musicians were all of a certain age group – and, when they got down to penny numbers, they gave in to the inevitable. It's very sad, and particularly for Sylvia. That's Leah's mum. It was a big part of her life.'

'A thing of beauty should be a joy forever, Liz.' He was suddenly thoughtful.

'I couldn't agree more, but what's on your mind?'

'The college has a big band, but the students have probably never heard of the dance band era, and I think they should be relieved of their ignorance.'

Suddenly, she was excited. 'Do you mean as part of the college curriculum?'

'No, the academics are stuffy enough about the big band. They'd be sure to put the mockers on anything else that smacks of popularity with the ignorant masses. I'm thinking in terms of something independent of the college, a band that can do as it pleases.'

'That's even better, but it'll need careful planning.'

He looked at his watch. 'Can we meet again?'

'I'm sure we can. My evenings are out, I'm afraid, unless you come over to us.'

'When?'

'Have you anything lined up for tomorrow evening?'

Without hesitation, he said, 'No, I'm free.'

'How do you feel about sausages and mash?'

'Reverential.' It was a simple, unequivocal response.

'They're my daughter Carla's favourite delicacy. Come over tomorrow evening and she'll share it with you.'

His expression told a whole story. 'She sounds like a generous girl,' he said. 'What time?'

'Five-thirty for six.'

'Fine. Where do you live?'

She took one of her business cards from her bag. 'You've lost the one I gave you on Saturday, haven't you?'

'No, I'd just forgotten about it for the moment. It's the excitement, you know.'

She smiled indulgently. 'You've had enough excitement for one day, Craig. You'd better calm down or you may not sleep tonight.'

5

Liz unwrapped the tissue sufficiently to find that Craig's offering was a bottle of red Bordeaux. 'Thank you, Craig. Come through and meet Carla.' Carla was packing her books for Thursday morning.

'Carla, this is Craig. We were at the Guildhall together.'

'How do you do.' Carla offered her hand as Liz had taught her.

'How do you do, Carla.' Craig took her hand with difficulty as it was so small. In the end, she settled for three of his fingers.

With the formalities dealt with, Carla asked him, 'Can you think of any famous Victorians?'

Craig thought. 'Prince Albert?'

'No, somebody ordinary.'

He thought again. 'How about Lord Lister? He was quite ordinary compared with Prince Albert.'

'I'm glad you came, Craig,' said Liz. 'I'd forgotten all about him. Take a seat and tell Carla about Lord Lister. She's learning about the Victorians at school.'

Craig nodded. 'As we all did.'

'True. What would you like to drink?'

'Can you manage a neat tonic water, Liz? I'm driving.'

'Neat tonic water it is. Ice and lemon?'

'Yes, please.'

She left the room to get it.

Carla was determined not to be side-tracked. 'What did Lord Lister do?'

'He was a surgeon, and when he started out, lots of people were dying from infections they'd picked up in hospital, so he started disinfecting his instruments with carbolic acid, washing his hands regularly and cleaning his patients' wounds.'

'Didn't people know to wash their hands?'

'No, they didn't. As a matter of fact, they used to laugh at Joseph Lister when they saw him washing his hands and brushing his nails.' He took a glass of tonic water from Liz. 'Thank you, Liz.'

'But everybody knows you get germs if you don't wash your hands,' protested Carla.

'They didn't know that in those days, and that's why so many people were dying, and why he was so important.'

'I'd quite forgotten,' said Liz. 'There was childbed fever as well. Midwives were taking it from one patient to the next because they never washed their hands.'

'I wasn't sure if I should mention that,' said Craig.

'Carla knows how babies arrive,' she assured him.

'Anyway,' said Craig, 'it was because of Lister that antiseptics came into use, so he was a very important Victorian. Are you making a collection of them?'

Carla considered the question and said, 'Yes, I am, really.' She finished packing her books.

'Go and get ready for dinner now,' said Liz.

Craig asked, 'Shall I open the wine and let it breath?'

'Okay, I'll find you a corkscrew.' She went to the kitchen and returned with a waiter's friend.

As he cut the foil and removed the cork, he said, 'I'm being nosey, I know, but I last saw you when you left the Guildhall two years ahead of me. What happened to you then?'

'For some reason that escapes me, I married a total plonker and became pregnant. It was a horrible nine months with one problem after another, although the actual birth wasn't too bad, but I've no reservations about it whatsoever, because Carla's the best thing that ever happened to me.' My only regret is my choice of husband, who, even now we're divorced, continues to blight an otherwise pleasant existence.'

'I'm sorry to hear that, Liz, but I shan't pry.'

'Oh, it's nothing more embarrassing than the fact that he keeps making promises to Carla and then breaking them.' She shrugged and smiled. 'Okay, that's my life dealt with. What have you been up to these past.... How long has it been?'

'Eleven years since I saw you, but nine since I left the Guildhall.

I've achieved very little, really. I worked as a session musician at first, but that wore thin very quickly. More than anything, I resented being treated as a servile artisan by a succession of self-proclaimed geniuses with neither charm nor ability, so I did an MA and got into higher education. Some students can be dickheads, but that's true of any collection of people, and there are always some who make the job worth doing.' He gave her the kind of apologetic look she'd come to recognise, and asked, 'Do I sound cynical?'

'Not cynical. Disillusioned, maybe. I must say, I do most of my recordings with professionals, so I don't have the problem you....' She broke off when the kitchen timer shrilled. 'That's what happens when you start filling in the years,' she said, going to the foot of the stairs. 'Carla,' she called, 'dinner's almost ready.' She went into the kitchen and stopped the timer.

Craig asked, 'Can I do anything?'

'I don't think so. I only have to mash the potatoes.'

'Let me do that,' he insisted, 'and I'll save you the effort.'

'All right, strong man,' she said, handing him a masher. 'Most of the children Carla knows,' she said, 'talk about "tea", meaning "dinner", so she sometimes gets confused, as she gets "dinner" at school, meaning "lunch".'

'Language can be a minefield,' he agreed, straining the water out of the saucepan, 'even without regional differences and the class system thrown in. Do you think I might have a knob of butter and a dribble of milk?'

'Certainly.' She passed a pack of butter and a knife to him. Taking a bottle of milk from the fridge, she said, 'Of course, being a posh Londoner, you won't have encountered the problem until now.'

'No,' he said bravely, 'but I can handle most things.' He dropped a chunk of butter and a splash of milk into the potatoes and proceeded to pulverise them.

'I can see you've done that before,' she said.

'I told you how I feel about bangers and mash. This isn't preparation as much as veneration. It has to be done properly and respectfully.' He seasoned the potatoes and continued to mash for approximately two minutes before inspecting the contents of the saucepan and pronouncing them ready.

'I just hope the other ingredients don't let the side down,' said Liz, carrying the gravy to the table.

'They look pretty good to me.'

Liz took two tureens from the warming drawer and dispensed mashed potato into one and peas and runner beans into the other.

'I'm even more impressed,' said Craig.

'Don't be. I only use these things when we have a visitor.'

'In that case, I'll just feel honoured.' He poured wine into two glasses.

'Take a seat, Craig.'

Carla looked at the mashed potato that her mum transferred to her plate. 'Thanks, Mum. It looks really smooth. How did you make it?'

'I relied on a special process that I've never tried before.' She smiled secretly at Craig. 'Have some peas and beans. They're nice too. Help yourself to everything, Craig.'

Even with the distraction of her favourite dish, Carla looked thoughtful. Eventually, she said, 'If you and Craig knew each other at the Guildhall, Mum, how did you come to meet him again?'

'Sheer chance, darling.'

'I moved from London to Netherdale last month,' explained Craig, 'and then, one day, I looked in the mirror and realised I was looking very unfit. I had to do something about it, and quickly, so I found out where the swimming pool was, and I went there on Saturday.'

Carla's eyes were bright with curiosity.

'Well, I'd been in the pool almost an hour, when suddenly I developed cramp in one leg.'

'What's cramp?'

'It's what happens when a muscle contracts... squeezes itself together,' Liz told her. 'It's very painful.'

'Very painful indeed,' confirmed Craig. 'Not only that, but I was at the deep end, and because of the cramped muscle, I couldn't swim. I thought I was going to drown, and then – guess what?'

'What?'

'Your lovely mum dived in and saved me from drowning.'

'She's a good swimmer,' said Carla, who seemed to regard the punch line as an anti-climax. After all, it went without saying that a mum who could do almost anything should be able to rescue a drowning man without much effort.

The two went on, however, to have a natural and grown-up conversation, with Liz making only an occasional contribution. For her part, she was still coming to terms with the seemingly nebulous student becoming an excellent pianist and a devotee of 1930's dance music.

Their conversation continued up to Carla's bedtime, when she said goodnight quite formally to Craig.

'I've taught her not to kiss goodnight on a first meeting,' explained Liz.

'Quite right,' agreed Craig. 'Very right and proper.'

Liz kissed Carla and they said their goodnights before parting.

'Before our conversation took place on Tuesday,' said Liz, 'and before I had any idea that you were keen on dance music, I spoke to Leah's husband. He's very knowledgeable about that kind of music. Unfortunately, though, he's far too busy just now to help us, so discovering you is like a.... I was going to say the answer to a maiden's prayer, but I'll change that to the prayers of two mature women.'

Craig smiled at the thought. 'I've been called a few things,' he said, 'but not the answer to a prayer.'

'Don't let it go to your head,' she warned him. 'There are things we have to decide. First of all, where are the musicians coming from?'

'That's easy. I have a captive and renewable source of musicians who'll do it for nothing until it looks like taking off, and even then, they'll do it for less than union rates.'

'How can you be sure?'

'They're all keen to earn my approval.'

Eyeing him with mock-sternness, she said, 'You know, Craig, for a self-confessed romantic, you can be downright Machiavellian.'

'All right. What's the next question?'

'Premises. Where will they rehearse?'

'In a school classroom. It shouldn't be too expensive.'

'It needs to be within easy reach for the students.'

'Okay.'

'More wine?' She picked up the bottle.

'No, you have it. I have to drive home.'

'I'll keep it under sentence until tomorrow.'

Apparently lost in thought, he made no response.

'A penny for them, Craig. That's what my grandma used to say, and still does occasionally.'

'The band will need a name.'

'Can't we make a decision about that later? It's not exactly vital at this stage, is it?'

'I think it is, Liz. The musicians will need to feel that they're a part of an identifiable entity. If it has no name, what can they call it?'

'I suppose "The Band" might sound rather prosaic after a while,' she conceded. 'Maybe you've got a point.'

After some thought, Craig offered the information, 'I have recordings by Jack White and his Astoria Ballroom Collegians. That was at one fifty-seven Charing Cross Road,' he added, as if he were planning a visit.

'Don't keep me in suspense, Craig.'

'Bearing in mind what students get up to when they're not drinking and… things, they could be called "Collegians". As a matter of fact,' he said, warming to his own theme, ' "The New Collegians" suddenly rings a bell. Can you hear it, Liz?'

'I can hear so many bells I feel like the Hunchback of Notre Dame.'

'Happily, you don't look like him.'

'Thank you, Craig. You do wonders for my morale.'

'I'm afraid I have to ration it tonight,' he said, looking at his watch.

'Are you expected home?'

'No, there's no one to expect me. It's just a little matter of preparation for tomorrow, references and that kind of thing. I work on the basis that an hour-long lecture should generate four hours of individual enquiry, so I need to make a few suggestions, to point them in the right direction, if only to begin with.'

'I've been meaning to ask you this, but by all means tell me to mind my own business….'

'I wouldn't dream of it. I'd just give you a silly answer. What's your question?'

'At your recital, you dedicated your encore to someone called Rosalyn. I'm just being nosey, but who is she?'

He smiled at the question. 'She's the principal's secretary, and she's fond of Romantic music, but she couldn't get to the recital, so I had it recorded for her.'

'What a lovely thing to do.'

'Well….' He shrugged modestly and then looked again at his watch. 'I must go,' he said.

'Well, thank you for coming. I think we have something here.'

'So do I. Thank you for your hospitality. I've had a superb meal with a lovely hostess, and the hostess's daughter was sublime.'

'You're very kind.' She showed him to the front door.

'Goodnight, Liz.' He kissed her cheek and said, 'It wasn't our first meeting, after all.'

'You're right. Goodnight, Craig.'

6

Liz joined Carla in the kitchen and said, 'Now, we need to address the subject of dinner.'

'Yes?'

'I had thought of doing roast breast of humming bird on a bed of Chinese nettles—'

'Yerk!'

'But I changed my mind and bought fishcakes instead.'

'Yes!'

A little later, Carla brought her English homework to show Liz, who was impressed.

'That's a very good essay, Carla, and only three spelling mistakes.' She closed the book and handed it back.

'Mum?'

'Yes, darling?'

'Why are you Elizabeth Frankland, but I'm Carla Tyersal?'

Liz took off her glasses and put them on the coffee table. 'It's because when your dad and I divorced, I reverted to my maiden name, but because you're his daughter as well as mine, you kept his surname.'

It was clear from Carla's expression that Liz's explanation had answered only part of her question. 'Why did you...?

'Revert?'

'Yes, to your old name?'

'I'd always worked as Liz Frankland, so that was how everyone knew me, but that wasn't all.' She would have to be as honest as she could be without actually damning Simon in his daughter's eyes. 'When people divorce,' she said, 'the ex-wife needs the ex-husband's agreement if she's to continue using his name. Your dad and I discussed it and decided against it, as there would be so many Mrs Tyersals that people would be confused.' In truth, Simon had told her, very much in anger, that if she was taking his effing daughter, she wasn't going to take his effing name as well. Liz vividly recalled telling him what he could do with his name.

Carla asked, 'Could I revert to my maiden name?'

Liz smiled at her innocence. 'Do you mean you want to change your surname to Frankland? That's something we'd have to consider very carefully.' Even so, she was strongly tempted.

———◆►◄———

Liz looked at her watch, inwardly fuming. Carla was at the window, looking out for her dad, as she usually did, but even she was looking fatalistic.

'I'll see if I can get him on the phone,' said Liz. As she went to pick it up, she noticed that the message light was glowing. She pressed the button and waited.

'Hello, Liz,' said Simon's voice. The message was timed at 10:42. 'I'm afraid something's, like, come up again, and I won't be able to call for Carla. Say sorry for me, will you?'

'Bastard,' she muttered.

'What, Mum?'

'I'm sorry, darling. He must have phoned when we were at the supermarket. I should have checked the phone for a message.'

'He promised,' said Carla wistfully.

'Yes, I'm afraid he did. Listen, darling, would you like to go to Betty's in Ilkley for afternoon tea?'

Carla's expression suddenly brightened. 'Yes, please.'

Her vulnerability made Liz gather her up and hug her for several seconds. The poor little scrap didn't deserve to be let down by a man who wasn't fit to be called her dad. 'In that case,' she said, 'that's where we'll go.'

———◆►◄———

Carla was thoughtful on the way to Ilkley, and when she did speak, it was to make a an observation on a sensitive matter. 'We went to Betty's once before when my dad didn't turn up, didn't we?'

'That's right. I try to vary these things, but an element of duplication is sometimes inevitable.'

Carla eyed her pensively and said, 'I think I know what you mean, but I'm glad we're going there, anyway.'

'You're quite a pragmatist, Carla. I've suspected it for some time.'

'What does that mean?'

'It means that, rather than getting bogged down with theoretical concerns, you take the practical approach. To put it simply, you leave it to common sense to guide your footsteps.'

'I just try to be sensible.'

'I know, darling. So do I, but I'm easily distracted.' She turned into Brooke Street carpark and found a place fairly close to the top. Then, having paid and displayed, they walked along the Grove with its beautiful columns and glazed canopies to the celebrated Betty's Café.

There was inevitably a queue for tables but, at least, Carla was able to read all the framed advertisements from the 1930's that lined the passage into the dining area.

Eventually, a young man showed them to a table by the window that looked out on to the Grove. He left them with the menu and apologised for the fact that wholemeal scones were no longer available.

'Oh dear,' said Liz. 'Now we'll have to be naughty and have white ones instead.'

Carla asked, 'Do we have to have scones?'

'No, the only thing that's compulsory is that you enjoy whatever you have. Look at all these things on the menu.' She turned it so that Carla could see it.

After detailed inspection, Carla asked, 'Could I have creamed mushrooms on toast?'

'If that's what you'd really like, how can I refuse? What would you like to drink?'

'Orange juice, please.'

'Consider it ordered.'

A waitress came to their table, notepad in hand. 'Good afternoon, madam,' she said. 'Are you ready to order?'

'Yes, I am. My young friend would like orange juice and the creamed mushrooms on toast. Also, I shouldn't be surprised if one of the cakes were to prove popular, but we'll see how it goes.'

'Of course, madam, and for you?'

'I'd like a ham and cheese sandwich and a pot of the Tea Room Blend, please.'

'Certainly, madam.' The waitress made a note on her pad and retired.

When she'd gone, Carla leaned across the table as far as she could, and said in a conspiratorial whisper, 'I think Hannah's going to have a baby.'

Hannah was Simon's new partner. In a matching whisper, Liz asked, 'What gives you that idea?'

'The last time I was up there with my dad, I passed the little bedroom and I saw a pile of dispersible nappies.'

'*Disposable* nappies, darling. Well, what a surprise.'

'Will she grow huge in front?'

'It's inevitable, I'm afraid. I was enormous when I was carrying you.'

'I don't believe you. I'm not that big.'

'Well, I felt enormous.'

Carla evidently felt that the argument wasn't worth pursuing, because she asked, 'Will the baby and I be related?'

'Only distantly,' said Liz, crossing her fingers under the table.

'I'm not keen on Hannah.'

'There's no reason why you should be.'

'In fact, I don't like her at all.'

'That's fair enough.' Liz couldn't think of a reason why anyone would like Hannah, and that included Simon, although he'd always been a mystery.

'When you have a baby, does it really hurt?'

'It can, but it's worth it in the end.'

'What actually happens?'

Liz hesitated. 'Do you really want to discuss childbirth at the tea table, darling? I'll gladly talk to you about it later, but it's not a fit topic for a mealtime.' She inclined her head towards the kitchen and said, 'Look, the waitress is bringing our order, and we want to enjoy it, don't we?'

———— ►◄ ————

Some things refuse to go away, and one of them was Carla's preoccupation with childbirth, so Liz summoned her nurturing instinct on the way home and gave her the description she wanted, being careful not to scare her in the process. The rest of the journey was uneventful, and Carla forbore to ask any further difficult questions.

Almost on cue, the phone rang at nine o' clock, and Liz knew the caller would be Leah.

'Hello?'

'Liz, it's Leah. How are things?'

'All right now.'

'Oh? Didn't they start too well?'

'No, Simon was supposed to call for Carla, but at least he's consistent. It was the third no-show out of the last three.'

'Oh, no.'

'I took her to Betty's as a consolation.'

'That was a good idea.'

Leah sounded strange, as if she had something on her mind. 'What is it, Leah?'

'Oh dear. I saw Simon this afternoon.'

'Where?'

'In the queue for some trashy film at Pictureville. We went to see *Tinker, Tailor, Soldier, Spy* as a means of prising Gavin away from his piano for a couple of hours. Simon was with what's-her-name with the scary eye make-up and pendulous boobs, and her two urchins. Also, to the naked eye, the signs are that she's more than a teensy bit pregnant.'

'I know. So that was the reason he failed to show up.' She explained quickly, 'I mean, the cinema was, not Hannah being pregnant.'

'Carla probably had a better time with you at Betty's. Did she enjoy it?'

'Yes, but she asked me all about childbirth.'

'No, really?'

'Simon and Hannah have been stocking up on disposable nappies, and Carla saw them the last time she was there. Now she's suddenly interested and inquisitive.'

'Oh, bad luck, Liz. Did it bring it all back to you?'

She laughed. 'It wasn't all that bad. The months that preceded it were the problem. I suppose it's different for each of us.'

'I wasn't impressed. "Push it back," I told them, "I've changed my mind. I don't want it now.'

'You should have thought about that earlier.'

'That's what the midwife said. If you don't mind my saying so, it's a silly thing to say. I mean, when it all seems terribly urgent and you can't get your clothes off fast enough, you don't think about the consequences, do you?'

'Don't you, Leah? I can't remember.'

'I'm sorry. I should be more sensitive.'

'It's all right. It's not a problem for me.'

'You're very brave, Liz.' Suddenly, she said, 'Oh, I've got a call waiting. I wonder who it is.'

'It's your turn to be brave and find out.'

'Okay, I'll be in touch. 'Bye.'

When Leah had rung off, Liz realised she still hadn't told her about Craig's idea.

———— ►I◄ ————

That night, after a serious talk with Carla, Liz waited until she'd gone to bed, and then phoned Simon.

Hannah answered, so Liz greeted her politely and asked, 'Did the boys enjoy the film?'

'How do you know about that?'

'One of my friends saw you at Pictureville. I'd like to speak to Simon, please.'

'Just a minute.'

Liz gathered that Simon was in the same room, because she heard Hannah say at her normal volume, 'It's your bloody "ex", and she knows about Pictureville.' It was typical of Hannah that she made no effort to cover the mouthpiece.

'Liz....'

'That's right, Simon, it's your bloody "ex", and in case you didn't quite catch the warning, I know about Pictureville.'

'You don't understand, Liz. I'd lost my diary, and I, like, got the dates mixed up.'

'And a cow jumped over the moon, but if the little dog laughed, it was more than Carla did. In the end, I took her somewhere as a consolation. Don't you realise that when you break a promise to her and make one of your feeble and transparent excuses, it's not forgoing the treat that's the problem for her, so much as the realisation that she means so little to you?'

'Oh, that's a bit strong. You don't know what problems I have to contend with.'

'I imagine you're about to invent a few.'

'For one thing,' he said, as if he'd found the perfect excuse, 'Hannah is pregnant.'

'I know.'

'How do you know?'

'The usual things, you know, swelling of the torso, swollen ankles.... One of my friends saw you with her and the boys.' There was no need to mention Carla's astute observation.

'The bitch.'

'It was a perfectly innocent remark, a damned sight more innocent than your behaviour, anyway.'

'The thing is,' he said, ignoring the accusation, 'we're, like, going to get married.'

'Don't tell me, let me guess. Her father's been on your doorstep with a loaded shotgun. Why, oh why didn't he pull the bloody trigger? Is there no justice in this world?'

'Don't mock, Liz. We're going to get married so that we'll be a cohesive family unit....' He stopped, offended. 'What's so funny about that?'

Liz controlled her laughter. 'Even if I explained it, you wouldn't get the joke. Listen, I'm making this call not just to hold you to account over your latest broken promise, but to ask you about something else.'

'What else, for goodness' sake?'

'It's about Carla, obviously, or I wouldn't be wasting my breath or my time on you. She wants to change her name to Frankland, so that people make the obvious connection between us. It's very important to her, but to do that requires your agreement.'

There was a hiatus of several seconds, and then he said, 'All I want is for Carla to be happy.'

'An aspiration you demonstrate so convincingly. Do you agree to her changing her name?'

'I've already said, all I want—'

'Just say, "yes".'

'All right, yes.'

'You'll need to sign a document. I'll bring it over to you.'

'Thank you.'

'I'm not doing it for your convenience. I'm doing it because I know from past performance that you're even less likely to turn up than Santa Claus on Midsummer's Eve.'

'All right. Any-bloody-thing that'll get you off my back!'

'Thank you, Simon. Carla will be very grateful.'

7

OCTOBER

Towards the end of the week, Liz phoned Craig with disappointing news. 'I've asked the local authority about the possibility of a weekly letting,' she told him, 'and the rent they want to charge is ridiculous. We'll have to think again.'

'Wait just a minute, Liz. I may have the answer.'

'What have you found?'

'It's only a possibility at this stage, but one of the staff here put me on to the Building Trades Club in Ickringill. It's on a direct bus route from Bradford City Centre, and they have a seldom-used upper room that may bear looking over.'

'We could go this weekend, if they're agreeable.' As an afterthought, she said, 'I'd have to bring Carla.'

'I'd be disappointed if you didn't. In any case, I have something for her.'

'I'm all agog.'

'Are you? I'd like to see that sometime. Anyway, I'll phone the steward and see if we can make arrangements to look the place over.'

'I'll wait to hear from you.'

———— ▶◀ ————

Liz and Carla drove, as arranged, to Craig's house in Thanestalls, where he welcomed them inside.

The interior of the cottage was, as Liz had suspected, furnished in retro Art Deco style, with reproduction furniture, a fabulous carpet, and even a candlestick telephone.

'I'd quite forgotten,' he said, 'that there's so much of the kindred spirit in this village. Musicians, I mean.'

'Have you met Adam Watkinson?'

'Yes. You've come across him, obviously.'

'Everyone knows of Adam. Anyone who's been in *Donkey Ride to Bethlehem*, anyway.'

'Were you in it, Liz?'

'I was one of the angels. I know Adam and Jenny quite well, as it happens.'

'Good. 'Bear with me a moment. I have something for Carla.' He went into the next room and emerged with something in a paper bag, which he handed to Carla. 'I was in Ilkley last weekend,' he said, 'and I found it in a bookshop.'

The book was called *Victorian Britain*. Carla asked, 'Is this to lend?'

'Borrow,' Liz corrected her.

'No, it's yours to keep. I hope you haven't already got it.'

Carla shook her head, still speechless.

'I think,' said Liz, 'that someone's so taken aback, she's forgotten her manners.'

'Thank you, Craig,' said Carla, 'thank you very much. It's wonderful.'

'I hope so.'

'Yes, thank you, Craig,' said Liz. 'That was very kind of you. Actually, if we'd known you were going to be in Ilkley, we might have joined forces. Which day were you there?'

'Sunday.'

'So were we,' said Carla.

'We went to Betty's,' explained Liz. 'It was a consoling treat for Carla because her dad was unable to keep his promise.' She raised her eyebrows as she spoke, and Craig nodded discreetly.

'I've never been to Betty's,' said Craig. 'It's not the kind of place a solitary chap frequents.'

'Surely, it won't be long before you find someone to make a visit possible,' said Liz.

'You could come with us, couldn't he, Mum?'

'Why not? We could reward your kindness, Craig.'

'There's really no need.' He looked at his watch and asked, 'Would you like coffee, or should we go?'

'I don't like to dictate, but I've quite a lot to get through before I go to London. If you don't mind, shall we go?'

'Okay, let's go in my car. Yours will be safe enough here.'

'I'm afraid we'll have to use mine, Craig. It has Carla's seat in it.'

'Of course.'

Carla screwed up her face in distaste, but followed the adults to Liz's car.

'It seems to me,' said Craig as they set off, 'that we're part of a musicians' colony hereabouts, with you, me, Adam Watkinson, and Jimbo when he's at home. Did you know Jimbo at the Guildhall, Liz?'

'Everyone at the Guildhall knew Jimbo. I wonder if he's grown up yet.'

'He pointed me in the direction of Thanestalls when I said I was moving north. He'd noticed that the cottage was for sale, and he told me about it.'

'Good old Jimbo. Generous-natured as ever.'

'How well did you know him, Liz?'

'Well enough.' She took her eyes off the road long enough to give him her 'not in front of Carla' look.

Changing the subject, he said, 'I suppose we should decide which of us is going to do the arrangements.'

'I suggest we share the job.'

'Okay, if you're happy you've got the time.'

'I'll tell you when I'm too busy, Craig. Also, I've been on the phone to Frank Morrison, leader of the New Albion Dance Orchestra in Cullington. He's an old friend of Leah's husband, and he tells me he has arrangements he can't use nowadays. The line-up of his band has changed so much since its formation that he's had to re-arrange much of the repertoire, so he's happy to let us have them.'

'That's a stroke of luck. Very generous of him, too. When can you get hold of them?'

'I said I'd go over on Wednesday, before I go to London.'

'Have you got a recording session?'

'Yes.'

'Mum,' said Carla, 'if you're going to London, where am I going to stay?'

'I hadn't forgotten you, you poor little waif. I'll let you know in good time.' Turning to Craig, she said, 'I used to leave her with my mum, but she's busy enough with *her* mum. I'll sort something out.' It would probably mean a phone call to Leah and Gavin.

Eventually, they joined the A658 and entered Ickringill.

'The Building Trades Club is about halfway along the main street. Coming in this direction, it'll be on the right,' said Craig.

'You know Craig, for a man who uses a candlestick to make phone calls, you're exceptionally well organised.'

Carla asked, 'Mum, what have we come here for?'

'To see if we can find a room we can afford, so that we can start up a band.'

'A rock band?'

Liz could hear the disbelief in her voice, and when she looked in her driving mirror, she could see it as well.

'Of course not. It's… well, it's an unusual kind of band nowadays, but it's very exciting, and I think when you hear it, you'll like it too.'

'There it is,' said Craig, pointing to a building about fifty metres away.

As Liz approached, she saw the sign for the carpark and turned right into it. The club seemed to have few patrons at that time.

They walked into a bar where two men sat talking with another, who stood behind the bar. He wore a T shirt, and his neck, arms and hands were covered in tattoos.

'Good morning,' said Craig. 'My name's Townsend. We've come to see the steward about the room upstairs.'

'That's me,' said the man behind the bar. 'I'll take you up there, but I don't know what you'll make of it. It hasn't been used for a while.' He had a knowing kind of delivery, reminiscent of a stage gangster.

He led the way up a staircase to a large room, of which maybe two thirds was covered in mainly threadbare carpet. The rest, however, was a modestly-sized, maple dance floor. As Liz looked around the room, she imagined she saw evidence of some of the floor's history, because in a far corner stood a dilapidated and abandoned drum kit that bore the name *Stan Robinson's Dance Band*. There was also an upright piano that seemed to crave love and attention.

'We're thinking in terms of Sunday mornings to begin with,' said Craig, 'but we might want a weekday rehearsal as well, later on.'

Looking at the dust-laden room, Liz could only marvel at Craig's vision for the band.

As if reading Liz's thoughts, the steward said, 'The room hasn't been used for a fair while. That's why it hasn't been cleaned, but if you want it, I'll get the cleaners in.'

'How much are you asking?'

'It'll include cleaning, so the Chairman says a score will do it.'

'Twenty a week?'

'Can't do it for less,' he confirmed.

'Of course not.'

Liz kept quiet. As she saw it, no one else wanted it, but they couldn't do it for less. However, it was still a lot cheaper than a school classroom.

'Okay,' said Craig, taking two ten-pound notes from his pocket. 'If you'll give me a receipt for that, I'll be obliged. Here's my card for the details.'

'No sooner said, Boss.'

Liz asked, 'Can I just try the piano?'

'Feel free, now you've paid.'

Liz surveyed the dusty keys and attempted a scale, but gave up, disappointed. 'We'll need to bring a digital piano,' she said.

The steward grinned and said, 'There's a limit to what you can get for twenty quid nowadays.'

'So there is.' They followed him down to the bar, where he wrote a receipt laboriously, finally handing it to Craig and asking, 'Will you stay and have a drink?'

'I'm afraid we have to get back. Thanks for your help.' He shook the steward's hand.

''Bye, then.'

''Bye.'

Once outside, Liz said, 'I'm glad you didn't want to stay for that drink.'

'I was game, but I knew you wanted to be away.'

'It wasn't the place,' she explained, 'it was him.'

'I could tell.'

'You know, Craig,' she said, opening her car, 'I can't fault you.'

'You know I'm not a brilliant swimmer.'

'I think we'll just forget about that. What I do admire is your ability to see possibilities where most people would give up.'

'There's no secret,' he told her. 'I just imagine things as I'd like them to be, and then I roll up my sleeves and make them happen. I reckon, when the cleaners have finished in that room, it'll be a different place, and if it's not, I'll be in there with my Marigolds on and my bum in the air until it is.'

'Mum,' asked Carla, 'will the music be like "All I Do the Whole Day Through"?'

'Of course. I was playing that last night. Yes, that's the kind of music the band will play, and if they don't get it right the first time, Craig will make it happen, won't you, Craig?'

'You can depend on it.'

———▶◀———

'Leah, it's Liz.'

'I know.'

'Of course you do.' Leah had one of those phones with an address book that told her who was calling.

'What's been happening?'

'Craig and I went this morning to look at the upper room of the Building Trades Club in Ickringill.'

'What on earth for?'

'To see if it would do.'

'Do what? Liz, you're talking in riddles.'

'It's lost in muck, but it's going to be cleaned, and it will become the rehearsal venue of the New Collegians Dance Orchestra.'

Leah sighed audibly. 'Have you been sniffing Brasso again? You know it makes you silly.'

'Listen, Leah. Craig is not only a brilliant pianist, he's also a devotee of the Golden Age. His house is a shrine to the thirties, and he uses a candlestick telephone. He's clued up about dance music, and he's going to form – no, that's not quite right – *we* are going to form a band.'

'Well, well, well. Do you think you can find the musicians?'

'Craig has what he calls "a captive and renewable source".'

'Do you think youngsters will take to the music?'

'Why not? You did, I did, and I'm fairly sure Carla has become infected too.'

'In that case, jolly good luck to you both.'

'Actually, mentioning Carla reminds me. I have to be in London from Thursday night to Saturday. Could you and Gavin possibly have her for me?'

'Of course we will. We'd love to, and it'll be ammunition as well.'

'What?'

'The next time Mark and Emma lecture their clueless mum about bringing up children, I can quote you as my referee. Also, if I remember rightly, Carla's quite fond of bangers and mash, isn't she?'

'She is, rather.'

'As is my other half. When we first met, we used to have lunch at a local café that sold healthy food, salads and so on. Gavin's favourite was pork sausages and baked beans on toast with a poached egg on top, and he's never grown out of it.'

8

When they arrived at the club the following Sunday, the tattooed man was absent from the bar. In his place was an older, comfortable-looking man with dark-rimmed glasses and, Liz was relieved to notice, no visible tattoos.

'We made arrangements last week to use the upstairs room,' she explained. This is Craig Townsend and I'm Liz Frankland.'

He smiled broadly. 'How d' you do. I'm Geoff Broadhurst, the new steward.'

'That was a quick turn-round,' said Craig.

'Oh well, the club had already appointed me when you came. Scott was working his notice when you met him, but there was an incident during the week, and he was asked to leave. I won't go into details, if you don't mind.'

'Of course not.'

'You'll be interested to know that the cleaners came in on Friday, but I was far from satisfied with the result of their work, so I sent them upstairs again to do it properly.' He corrected himself by saying, 'I actually sent two of them back upstairs. The third said something very rude to me and left, but I think you'll find the room more to your satisfaction.'

'Thank you,' said Liz.

'There's just one thing I should point out,' said Geoff. 'The little girl is very welcome in here, just as long as she doesn't come up to the bar. It's the law, you know.'

'Of course.'

'When the others arrive, I'll send them up to you.'

'Thank you. You're most kind.'

They climbed the stairs, wondering just what to expect, and when they reached the landing, Craig said, 'What a transformation. It's surprising what three cleaners and keen steward can achieve.'

'I like him,' said Liz. 'He exudes honesty, unlike his predecessor.'

'Let's set some chairs out. I'm expecting seven or maybe eight this morning.'

'Have we got a percussionist?'

'Yes, but I don't know whether she'll bring her own kit or use Stan Robinson's gear in the corner, there.' He nodded towards the superannuated equipment they'd seen on their first visit. It was now more recognisable as a drum kit following the removal of many cobwebs. 'I've told her about it.'

His query was answered sooner than he expected, when a diminutive girl wearing glasses in circular, tortoise-shell frames appeared at the top of the stairs and said, 'Hi Craig. Can somebody give me a hand with my drum kit? It's a folding one, so it's not massive.'

'With pleasure, Jessica.' He followed her downstairs to where her collapsible drum kit lay in its folded parts.

More students arrived, and Liz heard them greet Craig.

'Go straight upstairs,' she heard him say, 'and give Liz a hand to set the chairs out, please.'

When the unfolding and tightening of music stands was complete and the instruments had been warmed up, Craig called everyone to order.

'Let me introduce Liz Frankland,' he said. 'Some of you will have heard her scores on TV, and they'll give the first-study composers among you an idea of what you're aiming for. You'll have to work hard, though, because Liz is good.' He noticed that Carla was peering uncertainly at the gathering almost from behind Liz. 'The youngest one among us,' he told them, 'is Carla, and, like you, she's come to hear a live dance band for the first time.' He was rewarded when he saw Carla return the friendly smiles of his students. 'The first number we'll try today,' he said, 'is "All I Do is Dream of You".' He set about handing out the band parts. 'The arrangement isn't exactly right for our line-up, but we'll manage for now. Reeds and brass, play all cues, please. I'm afraid we haven't got a second trombone yet.'

A student at the back of the gathering looked at his part and said, 'I can play both parts, Craig.'

'Thank you, Tyler,' said Craig. 'Now we know we're in professional hands. Liz, would you like to stand in front?'

'No, you take this one, Craig.' She motioned him to carry on.

'Okay, folks, as it's a band arrangement, the intro is four bars only. Ready? A-one, a-two, a one-and-two-and....'

The first eight bars were enough to convince Liz that something very special was taking place, and fond memories of Freddy and the Dalesmen caused her to blink to prevent tears from forming. She looked down and saw that Carla's eyes were shining, and her face was a manifestation of wonder. Ninety years on, the music had lost none of its power to bewitch its listeners.

Craig, however, was being much more hard-headed. 'It's going well,' he said, stopping them, 'but, trumpets and trombone, that staccato at the end of the first phrase needs to be really tight. Ta-dat, ta dat-ta-duh,' he demonstrated. 'Let's try it again from the top, and when we get to bar four, remember what I've said.' He counted them in again, and a tighter, more polished performance emerged.

'Well done, everyone,' he said finally. 'Liz, I think it's your turn.'

'Okay.' She handed out a set of band parts for *Stay as Sweet as You Are*, telling them, 'Same as before, play all cues, but above all, enjoy it.' She counted them into the four bars of introduction, and if their expressions were any guide, they were heeding her advice.

A surprise came, however, with the first line, when Craig took up the vocal refrain: 'Stay as sweet as you are, don't let a thing ever change you....' He sang to the end and received an enthusiastic round of applause.

'Thank you,' he said, 'but I think you'll see, now, why I dropped singing and took up piano and trumpet instead.'

'You sang very nicely,' said Liz, 'but I'd like to run it again. Reeds, in bars five to twelve, I'd like to hear more from you. That yearning feeling that you get in the inner parts is very important....' She stopped and joined in their laughter. 'I'm sorry,' she said, 'that was an unfortunate way to phrase it, but, either way, I'm sure you'll agree that it's important.' They tried again, with immediate success. The only person not to see the joke was Carla, who enjoyed the music no less for that. They became aware, also, that they were no longer alone. Several club members had left the bar and were standing on the stairs and landing. One of them, an elderly man, asked, 'Are we bahn to be treated to this every Sunday morn'?'

'I'm afraid so,' said Liz. 'We're a permanent fixture.'

'Nay, don't apologise, love. It's champion.'

'Well, thank you. I'm glad you like it.'

'We thowt we were getting' one o' them rock bands. All shoutin' an' twangin' an' swearin', but this is real music. Anyroad, we'll let you get on.'

'Thank you.'

One of the clarinettists raised her hand to say, 'We've just been talking, Craig, while those men were here, and we like your singing, but we know two people you might like to listen to as well.'

'Thank you, Emilia. You know, "Don't call us, we'll call you" has never sounded quite so polite or less wounding.'

'I didn't mean—'

'I know you didn't. Will you ask those people to come and see me when we're back in college? I'd like to hear them sing.'

———•►◄———

After the rehearsal, Liz and Carla found a table away from the bar while Craig got the drinks.

Carla waited for his return before remarking on the law forbidding children to go to the bar. 'There are rules everywhere I go,' she said.

'That's how society works, 'said Liz. 'There have to be rules or there'd be chaos and uproar.'

'But nobody ever explains them,' she complained.

'The rule about children at the bar is quite straightforward,' Craig told her. 'No one is allowed to buy alcohol or drink it in a public place until they're eighteen.'

His explanation seemed to satisfy Carla only in part, because she was wrestling with another anomaly. 'And they don't allow pets at the swimming pool,' she said, 'but who would want to take one there, anyway?'

'I think I've missed something,' said Liz. 'I'm sure dogs would be unwelcome in a swimming pool, but how did this come up?'

'They have signs,' said Carla. ' "No heavy petting". It's a funny way to say it, but that's what it must mean.'

For the second time that morning, Liz was caught off-guard. With a sidelong glance at Craig, who was grinning, she said, 'That's not what "petting" means, darling. It has nothing to do with dogs.'

'Well, what's it about, then?'

' "Petting" is... oh dear.... It's couples... being affectionate towards each other. You see, not everyone wants to see it happen in public.'

Understanding dawned. 'Do you mean kissing and that sort of thing?'

'That sort of thing,' confirmed Liz, hoping the topic was now exhausted. 'Did you enjoy the music?'

'Oh yes, it's fantastic. Are we going to do this every Sunday morning?'

'If you want to come along, yes, we will.' It would obviate the need for child-minding. In any case, it was wonderful that Carla derived so much enjoyment from the music.

Several of the students got up to leave, and Liz imagined they would be using the same car. One of them said as they came to the table, 'It's criminal, that music not being heard, and for so long. I mean, those guys really knew their craft. Who's responsible for it all, Craig?'

'It was eclipsed by the big bands in the forties, Brandon. Then, in the fifties, rock 'n roll drove the final nail into its coffin. I'm glad you all enjoyed it, though.'

'We did,' confirmed Brandon, 'and the guys are up for more.'

As the students left, Liz said, 'It can't be the first time you've realised that you've done something momentous for their generation, Craig.'

'Not the first time,' he agreed, 'but it's not always been as dramatic as this.'

When the last of the students had left, Liz gave a twenty-pound note to Geoff, the steward. 'Thank you ever so much,' she said, taking the receipt. 'I'm glad you took over as steward when you did.'

'It's a real pleasure to have you here,' said Geoff. Several members echoed his sentiment.

Liz fastened Carla into her seat and took her place in the driving seat. 'It's a long time since I felt so much satisfaction,' she said.

'Me too.'

In the back, Carla made her feelings known by singing, 'All I do is dream of you the whole night through, ta-dat, ta dat-ta-duh.'

Craig smiled. 'She even remembered the staccato brass parts,' he said.

'What are you doing for lunch, Craig?'

'I haven't even begun to think about it.'

'Shall we all go to the Shepherds' Rest in Eskgarth? I'd like to do that after all your hard work, getting the band together.'

'I think I can stretch a point and join you in that,' he said.

———•••———

Leah was out all day, but Liz caught her at home, as usual, a little after nine.

'Well,' said Leah, 'how did it go?'

'It couldn't have gone better. The students loved the music, and so did Carla. She sang "All I Do is Dream of You" on the way back, the room has been cleaned properly, and the club members who were there this morning thoroughly enjoyed our efforts.'

'What kind of turn-out did you have? Gavin's bound to ask.'

'You'd better write it down, then. Ready?'

'Just a minute.' There was a pause. 'Ready.'

'Kit drums, two trumpets, one trombone, two clarinets and one alto sax. No piano or bass as yet, but there was so much enthusiasm, they're bound to wax evangelical when they get back among their friends.' Suddenly remembering, she said, 'Oh, yes, there are two singing students who may well join us. Craig provided the vocal refrain this morning, and he wasn't bad, but it's going to be a band of young people, so we need young vocalists.'

'You do surprise me, Liz. I mean, about Craig. Contrary to early indications, he seems to be turning into a good hand.'

'A good what?'

'Sorry, it's something my dad used to say. A "good hand" is a reliable sort of sailor, apparently.'

'Well, Craig's all of that and a romantic visionary too.'
'Liz?' There was mischief in Leah's voice.
'Yes?'
'Are you developing—'
'No, I'm not. Once bitten... forever shy.'

9

Craig was walking through the foyer, past the Recital Hall, when a student spoke to him.

'Craig?' She was pretty in a refreshingly wholesome way.

'Yes, Lauren?'

'Have you got a minute?'

Reading upside-down, he saw that she was carrying a copy of 'Bewitched', and he saw that as a clue. 'Yes, as many minutes as you need. I'm finished for the day.'

'Emilia Harrison said you'd like to hear me sing.' She didn't look particularly confident.

'Emilia the clarinettist? Yes, that's right.' He thought quickly. 'Come into the Recital Hall. You've got a beautiful song there, and it deserves the services of a Steinway.' He opened the door for her.

'I used to fancy myself as a Doris Day tribute singer, she said modestly, but you're playing music from a different time, aren't you?'

'Only by about twenty years,' he said soothingly, 'but I love Doris Day as well, so I'm sympathetic.' He took the music from her and put it on the music desk of the piano. 'Are you okay with this in "C"?'

Suddenly, she looked almost relieved. She asked, 'Can you transpose at sight?'

'If I can't, I've no right to be working here. What key would you like to sing it in?'

'"D" if you don't mind.'

'It's no trouble, Lauren. Relax and enjoy yourself.' He played the four bars of introduction and accompanied her to the end of the song. She was really very good, but he had one reservation. 'That was lovely, Lauren, but, if you'll take one little word of advice, you're trying too hard to sound like Doris Day. I realise that's your background, and possibly the way you've always sung this song, but something gets lost in the process.'

'Does it?'

She looked and sounded so disappointed that he felt guilty. 'It's not a huge problem. I just want you to think about the words. They're about unrequited love. The girl in the song is in love with a man who doesn't seem to be aware of it. She describes him as "cold", because he doesn't respond to her, but it makes no difference to the way she feels. She's still "bewitched, bothered and bewildered". Do you see what I mean?'

She nodded.

'You don't have to get it right the first time, so don't worry about that. You are worried, aren't you?'

'Yes.'

'Will it make you feel better if I tell you I like your singing and I want you to come on Sunday and sing with the band?'

'Oh, yes. Thanks, Craig. That's fantastic.'

'You're welcome. Now, let's try and perform this song as Rogers and Hart intended it. You're not only the three "B"s in the lyrics, you're also wistful and longing.' He played the introduction again and, before long, he came to the conclusion that he had a vocalist who could respond to constructive criticism. The need would no doubt occur from time to time.

At the end, she asked, 'Have you got anybody else to sing?'

'Yes, Matthew Greenwood sang for me this morning, and I've asked him to come along, too.'

'He's very good. He's a baritone, really, when he's not singing this kind of thing.'

'I know.' It reminded him of something else that had occurred to him when she was singing. 'When you're not singing popular idioms, you're actually a soprano, aren't you?'

'Yes.' She looked surprised. 'How did you know?'

He laughed. 'It's not difficult. You know that weekly half-hour we call "Aural Perception"?'

'Yes.'

'It's not just for passing exams, you know. Some of us use it all the time.'

'Of course.'

———◆◄———

Sylvia accepted a cup of tea from Leah and said, 'It was lovely, seeing Liz again.'

'Yes, Carla's on her half-term, so Liz is busy doing things with her, or she'd have been here today. I must say, you and she really started something.'

'Whatever do you mean?'

Liz and I had a chat about the need for a new band, now the Dalesmen have... retired, I suppose, and I told her that Gavin was too busy with various things. To be honest, I suspect Gavin couldn't see it as a viable project, but someone else does. He and Liz have started a band already.'

'You're going too quickly for me, darling.'

'Sorry, Mum. I'll start at the beginning. Liz asked me what had happened to the Dalesmen.'

'Oh, she must have been disappointed. She used to enjoy coming to gigs with us.'

'Yes, I remember that. Anyway, we wondered about the possibility of someone starting a new band.'

Sylvia put her cup and saucer on the coffee table and said definitely, 'It's a lot to ask of anyone, Leah. Gavin's far too busy, and I don't know who else could take it on.'

'That's what I was trying to tell you, Mum. Anyway, a new band was born last Sunday at Ickringill Building Trades Club.'

'Surely not.' Sylvia looked at her in amazement.

'Yes, it's called The New Collegians Dance Orchestra.'

'But, who have they got as bandleader?'

'Liz is sharing the job with a man called Craig. He's a lecturer at Airedale College of Music.'

Sylvia appeared to be assimilating the information with some difficulty. 'He can't be very old,' she said, 'or he'd be retired, like you.'

Leah forgave her for her clumsiness. 'I think he said he was thirty-one, a mere child, you might say.'

'In that case, Leah, how does he know the music?'

'He's grown up with it, Mum, although that's using the term "grown up" a little generously.' She recalled their conversation in the Sports Centre Cafeteria. 'He told Liz that his granddad had a cupboard full of seventy-eights that he inherited.'

'Full of what, darling?'

'Old records of the pre-war dance bands. Apparently he's more than an enthusiast, he's a devotee.'

'How wonderful. How did she meet him?'

'Oh, that's a story in itself.' She picked up the teapot and asked, 'More tea?'

'Not yet, thank you. I want to hear about Liz's new man.'

'It's not like that, Mum. At least, not yet.' Leah had her own ideas about that, but she knew from personal experience that her mum needed no encouragement with her matchmaking.

'Well, tell me how they met, anyway.'

'She fished him out of the swimming pool.'

'No.'

'Oh, yes. It made a change for her. I mean, you can kiss just so many frogs before it becomes downright tedious.'

'Be sensible, darling.'

'All right.' Leah got up from the chair she'd been occupying, and joined her mother on the sofa. 'Liz and I usually go swimming at about the same time. Well, we were standing on the side of the pool, talking, when I saw someone in difficulties. No one seemed to have noticed, so we dived in. Liz reached him first and towed him to the side. He had cramp in his calf muscle, so I dealt with that as soon as we'd got him out, and then I invited him to join us for coffee.'

'Well, I never.'

'Aren't you glad I popped in, now? It's been like story time.'

'Don't be silly, darling, I'm always glad when you come to see me.'

Leah felt a pang of guilt and resolved to visit her more often.

'Whereabouts does the band rehearse, Leah? You told me, but it's gone.'

'Ickringill Building Trades Club. Honestly, Mum, I think you'd struggle with the stairs. According to Liz, they're very steep.' She thought quickly and said, 'As soon as they get a gig somewhere more accessible, I'll take you to hear them.'

'Oh, that would be wonderful, Leah.'

'You know, you can't go on living here much longer. Those stairs are too much for you.'

'I can manage.'

'If you moved in with us, you'd have everything on the ground floor.'

'I know, darling, but let me enjoy my independence a little longer.'

Leah knew why her mum insisted on staying in the old house. It must be filled with memories. She looked across at the glass-fronted bookcase and saw their wedding photograph. Somehow, despite rationing, her mum had managed to find a new dress, and her dad looked immaculate in his petty officer's uniform. Apparently, and in spite of rationing, his tailor had found some special cloth for it. In another photo, they were joined by Auntie Joyce, her mum's bridesmaid, or matron of honour, as she hated being called, and Uncle Len, her dad's best man. He hadn't been able to contact Bailey at the time, or he would have been there.

'Bailey.' Leah spoke his name without thinking.

'What, love?'

'I was thinking about Bailey. He was the best godfather I could have had.'

'He was a lovely man,' agreed her mum.

'What else have you got in there, Mum?' Leah got up to peer into the bookcase.

'Just an old letter that I've kept.' She smiled self-deprecatingly and said, 'It's silly, but it means a lot to me.'

'Of course.' It was a prisoner-of-war letter form. 'Have you got all his letters somewhere?'

'What, darling?'

'I'm sorry, Mum.' She was on her deaf side. She joined her again on the sofa. 'Have you kept all his letters?'

'Of course.' Apologetically, she said, 'I'm afraid I can't always hear you. My right eardrum was perforated in Malta, you know.'

'I know. Don't worry.' She'd lost count of the number of times her mum had told her about the disability that had got her home from Malta, so that she and her dad could meet for the first time. Old people tended to repeat themselves. It was a fact of life that might catch up with her before very long. 'More tea, Mum?'

'No, thank you. It's not a good idea.' She laughed lightly. 'Each visit means a trip upstairs.'

'Just let Gavin and me know when it gets too much for you.'

'I will, darling.'

———◆◆———

Carla had just gone to bed when the phone rang. Liz picked it up. 'Hello, Leah.'

'It's not Leah, it's Craig.'

'In that case, hello, Craig.'

'Are you okay?'

'Never better. You?'

'Cock-a-hoop. We now have two vocalists, a pianist and a bass player.' He added, 'And they're all volunteers.'

'I should hope so. Conscription ended in nineteen… something, didn't it?'

'Give or take a month,' he confirmed. 'How's Carla?'

'She's fine, thank you. She's getting a hundred percent out of the book you bought her, and she's written an excellent essay about Captain Eyre Massey Shaw.'

'Who?'

'The man who revolutionised the London Fire Brigade and was immortalised by the Fairy Queen in *Iolanthe*.'

'Good. Everyone needs a testimonial at some time.'

'Tell me about the vocalists, first of all.' Suddenly, she had a mental image of Craig speaking into his candlestick phone, and the picture pleased her.

'There's Matthew, who's a baritone when everyone's correctly labelled, but so was Bing Crosby, so it's no detriment. He's sung with the big band, so he's not a beginner.'

'Is the other a girl?' It made sense.

'Yes, she's called Lauren. She's very good, as well as keen. I've given Matthew "April in Paris" and "The Very Thought of You" to learn for Sunday.'

'It's a tall order, following Al Bowlly.'

'You've got to aim high, Liz.'

She chuckled.

'What's funny?'

'I'm trying to cope with a mental image of you speaking to me on that two-piece telephone.'

'You've made me go all tongue-tied and embarrassed, now.'

'No, I haven't. What have you given the girl to learn?'

' "Dream a Little Dream of Me" and "Exactly Like You".'

'Good choices.'

'Yes, the girl's interesting.'

'In what sense?'

'Her experience of popular idioms has been as a Doris Day tribute singer. I gather she found it less lucrative than she'd hoped.'

Liz tried to imagine that. 'It's a shame,' she said, 'but is she suitable for our kind of music?'

'I've dealt with that. Much as I love Doris Day, she belongs firmly in the fifties and sixties, whereas Lauren has demonstrated her versatility.'

'Okay. I look forward to hearing them both.'

10

Liz's mother phoned early on Thursday morning with bad news. 'Grandma didn't make it through the night,' she said.

'Oh, Mum, I'm sorry.'

'It wasn't unexpected, and I never heard a sound, so the end must have come peacefully.'

Liz thought about the day ahead. 'I'm not all that busy,' she said. 'I'll have to bring Carla because she's on holiday this week, and there's no one I can leave her with.'

'The doctor's due anytime now, and the undertaker's men are coming shortly to take Grandma away. If you leave it until half-past ten, they should have been and gone.'

'Okay.'

'There's something I need to ask you about, to do with the undertaker.'

'Yes?'

'Yes, as the funeral is about music, flowers and that kind of thing, will you see to that? I'll be with you, but I'd like you to deal with it. I'll speak to the Reverend Crawshaw.'

'Okay.'

'I suppose we'll have to agree about a date for the funeral. I'm free anytime, so it's really up to you.'

'I'll be in London on the twenty-fourth and twenty-fifth of next month.'

'Oh, that's ages away. It'll have to be before then. When we know the date and time, I'll let Michael know.'

Liz's brother had never been particularly close to Grandma Wood, so there was no need to tell him immediately. 'All right, Mum,' she said, 'I'll see you at about ten-thirty.'

'Right, love. 'Bye.'

''Bye, Mum.'

Liz put the phone down and joined Carla at the breakfast table.

Carla lost no time in asking, 'Was that about Grandma Wood?'

'I'm afraid so,' said Liz, standing behind her and stroking her hair. 'It's all over. She was very poorly and unhappy, so it was the best thing for her to go peacefully and quietly.'

'Did she?'

'Yes, she died in her sleep.'

Carla absorbed that information without obvious distress before asking, 'Can I go to her funeral?'

'I don't see why not.' It wouldn't be her first. Liz had made a point of taking her to the funeral of a distant uncle she hardly knew. It seemed a good idea to give her the experience without the grief normally associated with it.

'Will it be in the church?'

'I don't know yet. I'll ask Grandma Frankland when I see her this morning.'

'When?'

'We'll go over for ten-thirty. They'll have taken Grandma Wood away by then, so it won't be too awful.'

———◆◆◆———

Fortunately, Mr Dawes, the funeral director, was able to see them that afternoon, so Liz picked up her mother and drove to his office.

After the usual condolences, he went through his check list. They elected to hold the funeral at Netherdale Crematorium. It made sense, because the church Liz's grandmother had attended for many years was temporarily without an organist, and church music had been an important part of her life. Mr Dawes booked a date and time at the crematorium and, having managed to contact the Reverend Crawshaw on his mobile, booked him for the funeral.

'I imagine you'd like a hymn, Mrs Frankland?'

Liz's mother deferred immediately to her daughter, who said, 'Yes, please. We'd like "Dear Lord and Father of Mankind" basically because it was her favourite.'

'Played by the crematorium organist or on a recording?'

'The organist, please. Let's have it done properly.'

'Quite, and music for the entry and exit?' Mr Dawes took a laminated sheet from his desk and offered it to Liz's mother, who deferred again to Liz. 'This is a list of the most popular music tracks played at the crematorium,' he explained. 'The digital library is very well stocked, and new tracks may be ordered.'

Liz put her glasses on and glanced down the list. 'Thank you,' she said, handing it back. 'No disrespect to Elvis Presley, Eric Idle, Frank Sinatra or anyone else, for that matter, but if the organist can play *Pastorale* by Cesar Franck as my grandma is being carried into the chapel, and *Marche Triomphale* by Siegfried Karg-Elert as we leave, we'd be very grateful. Don't worry, I'll write them both down for you.'

'Thank you, Miss Frankland. If you'll do that, I'll consult the crematorium about them.'

'They're not the easiest of pieces, so if the organist prefers it, we'd be happy with recordings instead. I've no wish to put anyone on the spot.'

'Thank you, Miss Frankland. I'm sure that will be appreciated. Would you mind telling me, though, why you chose those pieces particularly? Are they favourites of yours?'

'No, the organ's not one of my favourite instruments, but my grandma loved to hear both pieces played on the organ at St Mark's.'

———▶◀———

Liz met Leah, as usual, on Saturday morning at the swimming pool. She also had Carla with her, and all three stood at the deep end, waiting for Craig to complete his sixth length, Leah having taken charge of his fitness regime and imposed a strict limit on his swimming.

As he hauled himself out, he eyed them curiously, and then, dashing the water from his eyes, said, 'Liz, Carla and Leah. I wasn't sure it was you. You could rob a bank in those bathing caps.'

'In Craig's retro world,' explained Liz, 'swimming caps are "bathing caps", and swimsuits are "bathing costumes".'

'Oh, bless. We'll see you in the cafeteria, Craig.'

'I'll look forward to it, ladies.'

'Isn't it lovely,' said Leah, 'the way he calls us "ladies"? I don't know about you, but I'm not used to it.'

'Neither am I.'

They went to change, confident that Craig would be in the cafeteria before them, simply because men were always ready first.

In the event, they were right, and Craig, who had seen them coming, was already at the buffet. He greeted them with two Americanos and an orange juice. He asked, 'Were you two keeping tabs on me in case I needed rescuing again?'

'Of course not,' said Leah. 'You've learned your lesson. We just thought we'd meet you and invite you along. Thanks, Craig.' Taking the chair opposite Liz, she asked, 'What's new?'

'My grandma died on Wednesday night or Thursday morning. No one can be certain.'

'Oh, Liz, I'm sorry.'

Craig added his commiseration.

'She was very frail and miserable, and she obviously slipped away in the night, which was by far the best way to go.'

'I'm going to the funeral,' Carla told them.

'That's very brave of you, Carla,' said Craig.

Leah took her diary from her bag and asked, 'When is it?'

'Next Friday at four.'

'Bugger.' Leah looked apologetically at Carla and said, 'I'm sorry, Carla. You weren't meant to hear that.' Turning to Liz, she said, 'Gavin and I will be in London.'

'Don't worry. We'll be all right.'

'It's my easy afternoon,' said Craig, 'so, if anyone needs a soft landing, you know where to find me.'

'At the college?' It sounded to Liz like a strange offer.

'No, I'll take the last two hours off and go home.'

Liz said nothing, but squeezed his forearm in thanks.

'I told my mum about the band,' said Leah. 'She was delighted, but I had to tell her what you'd said about the stairs, Liz. I'm afraid she'll have to wait for the first "away" gig.'

Craig asked, 'Are the stairs a big problem?'

Leah nodded. 'They would be. She's very game for eighty-seven, but we have to be realistic.'

'It's obviously important to her that she gets to hear a band again,' said Craig. 'As soon as we can put a programme together, I'll scout around for possible gigs.'

'He doesn't let the grass grow under his rostrum,' said Liz.

'You're right about it being important to her, Craig,' said Leah. 'The band was a huge part of her life. Like so many features of her life that she associated with my dad, it left a....'

Liz stroked one arm whilst Craig squeezed the other.

'I'll be all right in a minute. Oh, bless you, Carla.' She took the tissue that Carla offered, and blew her nose. 'Look at us,' she said when she could speak. 'We're a picture of misery.'

'It's only to be expected,' said Craig.

Leah blew her nose again. 'Who have you lost, Craig, before we allow you into our club?'

'Just my mother, but she was all I had.'

'I'm sorry. If it's not too impertinent a question, what happened to your father?'

'He did a bunk some years earlier. I think it's fair to say he did us both a favour at the time.'

'I'm beginning to understand things a little better, Craig.'

To move the conversation on, Liz said, 'I told Craig how Bailey arranged for your mum and dad's song to be played on their first date.'

'Bailey was my godfather and one of their oldest friends,' explained Leah. 'You'd have got on well with him.'

'Would I?'

'Have you got another of those tissues, please, Carla?'

'Take the whole packet.' Carla passed it to her. 'I don't need them.'

'I'll just take the one. Thank you.' She blew hard before answering Craig's question. 'Bailey also lived in his own, gentle world, and was none the worse for it.'

'Just to fill you in, Craig,' said Liz, 'Leah's mum and dad got to know each other through letter-writing when her dad was a prisoner-of-war and her mum was serving in the Wrens. It was somewhere down south, wasn't it, Leah?'

'Dover,' confirmed Leah. 'They wrote to each other from nineteen forty-three, I believe, almost until the end of the war, when the Nazis marched the prisoners from Silesia to Germany. That was when they lost touch with each other for a while. Then, when my dad came home, my grandma and granddad took him in because my mum was still in Malta.'

'What a story.'

'That's not all. Through their letters, they came to know each other well, and one of my dad's things was writing songs. He wrote several for my mum because it was the only way he could repay her kindness, and in the last one, he told her he loved her.' She laughed shortly. 'He always joked that he was a son of Kingston-Upon-Hull, where the baring of souls was as rare as daffs in December, but he managed to tell her, all the same.'

'Many times after that as well, I imagine,' said Liz.

'Yes, they'd never met, but neither of them had the slightest doubt about how they felt.' She looked across the table at Carla and said, 'I'll take you up on your offer, Carla, if I may. I think I'm going to need another tissue.'

Craig squeezed her arm. 'Don't feel that you have to tell the whole story now, Leah,' he said. 'Not if it upsets you.'

'I'm not upset, Craig. Just let me tell you, though, that in those letters, they discussed music, and they agreed that "All the Things You Are" was the greatest song of all.'

'It takes some beating,' he agreed.

'It does, and they met for the first time in London, nervous and unsure, and my godfather organised their date. They had cocktails at the Savoy, dinner somewhere else, and then they went on to a night club to dance. That was where Bailey arranged for the band to play their number, and that's why it means so much to my mum.'

'We'll play it for her,' said Craig. 'It's just a question of when and where.'

—◆◆—

'If we do this too often,' said Liz, 'we'll all need to swim harder to keep our weight down.' She, Carla and Craig had gone back to the Shepherds' Rest for lunch.

'You and Carla haven't a problem, Liz. I'm the one with the expanding waistline.'

'We're not exempt, you know. We do have to take care not to go up a dress size, don't we, Carla?'

'Mm.' Carla was studying the haddock fillet on her plate.

Craig asked, 'Is something wrong, Carla?'

'No, I was just thinking how nice it is that the horrible-looking thing that swims in the sea can become something like the fish on my plate.'

'Similarly,' said Craig, 'a big, ugly potato can be transformed into something as desirable as a portion of chips.'

'I don't know,' said Liz, considering the argument from a different viewpoint. 'I wouldn't mind betting that haddock view each other with unqualified devotion, whereas potatoes have no life force of their own. That they can be made into chips is simply one of nature's blessings.'

'You always use difficult words, Mum. What does that mean?'

'It means,' said Liz, 'that haddock can't get enough of each other, and potatoes don't care either way.' She noticed that it was Craig's turn to be preoccupied. 'A penny for 'em, Craig. Old currency, of course.'

Craig ignored the gentle jibe. 'I was thinking about dress for the band,' he said.

'What thoughts have you had?

'Chaps in normal evening dress, I think, but the girls need to be different. Black orchestra dresses are out of the question.'

'Far too sombre,' agreed Liz. 'What's the alternative? Long evening dresses?'

'Not when the chaps are in short jackets. In any case, they're not all that easy to come by. I've noticed them recently in charity shops, but they're not plentiful.'

'Do you haunt charity shops, Craig?' It wasn't a habit she associated with him.

'Only when I'm looking for ideas for the band.'

'That's dedication for you. As it's a woman's thing, let me think about it, Craig.'

'Okay, but if the band's going to be on a platform at some time, and that's more than likely, the skirts mustn't be too short.'

Leaning across the table confidentially, she said, 'Girls can be prevailed upon to sit elegantly.' An enquiring look from Carla prompted her to explain, 'So that they don't show their knickers.'

Carla nodded discreetly and tried not to look at Craig.

'I was thinking, also, about the nineteen-thirties feel. Short skirts would be out of place.'

'Leave it with me, Craig.'

11

On Sunday morning, Craig surprised Liz by insisting on fixing Carla's seat temporarily into his Golf.

'It'll save you mileage and petrol,' he said as he closed the rear door, 'and it'll be a change for Carla.'

'That's very considerate of you, Craig, although the change Carla is looking forward to most is seeing the child seat up for sale.' A stray thought occurred to her as she went back into the house to collect Carla. 'Do you ever use your garage,' she asked, 'or is it full of junk, like mine?'

'It's full of junk,' he confirmed, 'but probably untidier than yours.'

'I wouldn't place a bet on it.'

They had been on the road ten minutes or so, when Craig said, 'Junk. That's it.'

'I'll have to take your word for it, Craig, as I've no idea what you're talking about.'

'We were talking about junk, and how yours is tidier than mine.'

'Wild guesswork on your part, I have to say.'

'No, listen. The college big band recently bought flashy new music desks, and I'm fairly sure they still have the old ones. If they have, and they're prepared to let them go, they'll only need painting and signwriting, and then we can use them.'

'Good thinking.' Liz was only a little surprised, as Craig's initiatives seemed to be endless.

'I'll speak to the bandleader tomorrow.' He was quiet for a while, and then he said, 'If we can only get the girls' dresses sorted out, we'll be almost there.'

'I've been working on that.'

'Have you?'

'Try not to sound so surprised, Craig. I did say I'd look into it.'

'So you did.' He nodded as he drove, possibly reminding himself of their conversation.

'I need to make a note of the girls' sizes before I'm sure. If my guess-work is wrong, I'll have a job lot of dresses on my hands. Keep your fingers crossed.'

Carla asked, 'Could you wear them, Mum?'

Liz laughed good-naturedly. 'Some of them are my size, but they're all the same colour and design. It wouldn't be ideal, Carla.'

Craig was still exploring the original problem. 'Okay, but what are the vocalists going to wear? I suggest Matthew wears his dress suit, like everyone else.'

'It makes sense,' she agreed. 'The girl vocalist.... What's her name again?'

'Lauren.'

'Right. The best thing will be if she can pick up a long evening dress at a charity shop or on one of the on-line auction sites.'

Craig thought again. 'She may just have a long dress left over from her Doris Day act.'

'True. I hadn't thought of that.'

'So that only leaves you.'

'I'll find something appropriate, Craig. Don't worry.'

'I shan't worry,' he told her confidently. 'I've told you before, you look exquisite in everything I've seen you wear.'

'Be realistic, Craig. No one looks exquisite in jeans and a T shirt.'

'Don't you believe it.'

There was the briefest of eye contact and then Liz looked away.

As they approached Ickringill, she asked, 'Were there many girl musicians in the thirties?'

'Yes, there were several girl bands, although they came to real prominence during the war, when so many male musicians were serving in the forces.'

'Mum, can I start piano again?'

'I've been giving that some thought, darling. We'll talk about it later.' Speaking to Craig, she said, 'I've heard of Ivy Benson and her All-Girl Band.'

'Ah well, Ivy Benson played with several dance bands before the war, both mixed and all-girl, but the famous All-Girl Band, which was actually a big band, flourished in the forties and early fifties.'

'O man of learning.'

'You asked me,' he said, turning into the club carpark, 'so I told you.'

———◆◄◆———

Liz surveyed the assembled company, gratified to see that, quite by chance, the two sexes were equally represented.

'Now,' she said, 'Lauren, where are you?' She saw a hand go up, and spoke to its owner. 'I'll speak to you in a minute, Lauren, but I'd like the rest of you girls to come and whisper your dress size and your height in my ear. It's so that we can fix you up with a band dress.'

The girls came forward, looking surprised, but also relieved that they weren't required to furnish the information publicly. Liz made a note of each before sending them back to their seats. 'Lauren,' she asked, 'have you a minute?'

Perhaps wondering what to expect, Lauren joined her.

'I believe you've performed as a tribute singer, Lauren. Have you, by any chance, got a long dress that you used to wear?'

'Yes. Can I just get my phone? I'll show you a picture of it.'

It was better than Liz had expected. She waited for Lauren to turn up the photo and treat her to a glimpse of her Doris Day persona.

'Here it is.' She held out her phone for Liz to see.

'Oh Lauren, you were a sight for sore eyes.' Her hair and complexion were naturally fair, as they needed to be for a Doris Day act, and the eau-de-nil dress was perfect for her.

'It's satin jacquard or something,' explained Lauren. 'I got it from a charity shop.'

'It's beautiful, and you say you still have it?'

'Mm. I haven't worn it for a while.'

'Well, you'll soon have another chance to wear it, Lauren. You're a pretty girl, and you're going to look stunning in that dress.'

'Thank you.' Lauren made her way self-consciously back to her place.

Craig waited for them to tune, and when they were ready, said, 'We're going to start with some vocal numbers, but we'll have a run-through before we ask our vocalists to sing. I think that's only right.'

Liz gave out the parts for 'April in Paris', more than ever convinced that, for all his other-worldliness, Craig had qualities that most men she'd known had been denied.

'Okay,' said Craig. 'Two bars' intro. It's a gentle two in a bar. A-one, a-two, a-one-and two-and....' They started the number, but Craig had to stop them after a few bars.

'Trumpets,' he said, 'it's my fault as much as yours. Have you both got a harmon mute?'

They nodded and took the mutes out of their cases.

'Pull them out halfway and then give me bars three and four again.'

Brandon and Zac obliged, and Craig announced that he was satisfied with the result. The adjustment had reduced the volume by half. He counted them in again and they played through the number.

'That was good. Matthew, are you ready?'

Matthew stood and nodded. Liz noticed that he wasn't holding a copy. He'd obviously learned the song by heart, and that told her something about his attitude.

He sang 'April in Paris' with great sensitivity, and his classical training was unintrusive. Liz was very impressed.

'That was excellent, Matthew,' said Craig. 'Thank you.'

Next, the band played through 'Dream a Little Dream' without having to be stopped, and Craig invited Lauren to sing her first solo.

It sounded unmistakeably like a tribute to Doris Day, who had actually recorded a cover of the song, but Craig let her sing to the end.

'Lovely, Lauren. Thank you. Liz, I hate to see you chafing at the bit. Would you like to take them through 'The Very Thought of You'?'

'Thanks, I will.'

She counted the band into the introduction and let them play one chorus before stopping them to ask, 'Have any of you heard the title "Try a Little Tenderness"?' Not surprisingly, no one had, so she said, 'I mentioned it because it's what I'd like you to do. It's coming over full of verve and enthusiasm, but this song doesn't call for that. Put your instruments down and I'll tell you a story.' She waited. 'Ready?' Their silence told her they were, so she began. 'The bandleader and songwriter Ray Noble was going out to the shops, and his wife asked him to call at the chemist's and pick up some nail polish remover.' She broke off momentarily to say, 'You can laugh, fellas, but those little things are important to us.' When they were settled, she went on. 'He did his shopping, but when he arrived home, he realised he'd forgotten to call at the chemist's, and Gladys, his wife, was furious with him. Well, the shops were closed by then, so Ray went to his studio and wrote this song. He must have poured his heart into it, and when he'd finished, he wrote the dedication to Gladys and took the manuscript to her as an apology and also as a token of his love for her. That's why I want you to play it very tenderly. Okay? Two bars' intro. A-one, a-two, a-one-and-two-and....'

The result was a significant improvement, and Liz was happy to invite Matthew to sing the number, which he did very sensitively.

'Thank you, Matthew. That was lovely.' She turned for a word with Craig and saw that he was talking with Lauren. She heard him say something about communicating the lyrics. As he left her, he was saying, 'I love Doris as much as you do, Lauren. If I'd been born fifty years earlier, I'd have wanted her to have my children, but try to put her aside and do as I ask. You're sounding terrific, anyway, so I'm only asking you to make a tiny adjustment.' He came to Liz and said, 'It might be a good idea for you to take this one, Liz. Lauren's a bit unsure, and I don't want her to be looking at me all the time to gauge my reaction.'

'Okay.' Liz took the band through 'Exactly Like You', a bright, cheerful quickstep that went remarkably well. 'Ready, Lauren?' The soloist stood up, looking far from confident, so she said gently, 'Just enjoy yourself. That's what it's all about, really. Nothing more than that.'

The band played the eight bars of introduction, and Liz winked at Lauren, mouthing the word, 'Enjoy.'

Lauren smiled in return, which was what Liz wanted. A relaxed expression always brightened the tone, and because Lauren enjoyed the sound that came out, she was encouraged to go on, inevitably singing the number much better than she'd expected.

Craig returned, ostensibly from downstairs, and said, 'Excellent, Lauren! Well done!' In a whispered aside to Liz, he said, 'I was hiding on the stairs.'

'Well,' whispered Liz, 'boys will be boys.'

On the way home, Carla treated Liz and Craig to 'Exactly Like You', getting quite a lot of the words right. As Craig said, after just one listening, it was an excellent effort. 'A lot of my Aural students would struggle to remember the melody,' he said, never mind the words.'

'It's an easy tune to remember,' said Carla.

'Yes, that was the idea.'

'Mum?'

'That's me.'

'You said, we'd talk about starting piano lessons again.'

'Yes, although I didn't mean that we'd discuss it on the way home.' For Craig's benefit, she explained, 'I had to stop Carla's lessons because her teacher was doing her no good at all. Her idea of technique came from a different planet.'

Craig asked, 'How far did you get, Carla?'

'I got Grade Two.'

'Good girl.'

'I had to help her with it. That woman was no help whatsoever.'

'I wonder,' said Craig, clearly turning something over in his mind.

'What do you wonder?'

'It's not usually recommended, I know, but....'

'Why don't I teach her myself? It could be the answer.'

'Yes, Mum,' said Carla. 'Will you teach me?'

'I'll let you know.' Something else was on her mind. 'What was that about with Lauren, Craig?'

'I'm just trying to get her to leave Doris Day at home and concentrate instead on the lyrics. I must say, you got her to sing that last song very well.'

'Thank you. I do my humble best.'

'There's nothing humble about it, and you've done another important job.' He was clearly dying to know. 'What's the latest about the dresses?'

'Ah, I have a number of work dresses that were made by a firm that's going to the wall, for a firm that's already folded. In other words, it was a cancelled order that had become an embarrassment. They're rather nice, too, plum red, and they include our girls' sizes. Some of them may need alteration to the length, but that's no problem. Lauren, on the other hand, showed me a photo of herself in her long dress, and she looks really lovely in it, rather like Doris Day, in fact.'

'Maidenly?'

'Very.'

'Bob Hope knew Doris Day before she was a… maiden.'

'He would. He'd been around a long time. What was that about Doris Day having your children?'

'It was an impossibility, but a pipe dream nevertheless. I used to dream at one time about Ginger Rogers, but I went off her.'

'Doris was much more the girl next door,' agreed Liz.

'She would certainly have kept me at home.'

They drove on in silence until Liz said, 'We need a tenor sax.'

'For "The Very Thought of You"?'

'Yes.'

'That's if we use the Ray Noble arrangement. Still, I suppose it takes some beating.'

'We're very lucky. We've got some excellent musicians and a pair of very promising singers.'

A warning came from the back seat. 'They shouldn't promise, Mum.'

'It's not the same as promising to do something, darling. When I say they're promising, I mean that they're likely to do well. In other words, they show *promise*. Are you with me?'

'Yes. Mum?'

'What?'

'Will you teach me?'

'As you're such a promising student, it'll be a pleasure.'

12

NOVEMBER

The Reverend Crawshaw read the words of the Committal and closed the curtains on the coffin. Carla looked up with tears in her eyes and whispered, 'Is it all right to cry?'

'Of course it is,' said Liz, handing her a tissue. 'I may join you in a minute.'

They listened to the words of the *Nunc Dimmittis*, words that Grandma Wood must have heard a thousand times at Evensong, and then the Reverend Crawshaw asked for God's blessing on everyone present. The *Marche Triomphale* cane as quite a jolt, but it ended the service in the right spirit.

Outside the chapel, Liz asked her mother, 'Are you and Michael going back together?'

'Yes, are you coming?'

'If you don't mind, we won't. Carla's a bit wobbly, so I think I'll take her somewhere where she can gather herself together.'

'That's a good idea.'

They took their leave of the few mourners who had attended, most of Grandma Wood's contemporaries having gone before her, after which they thanked the Reverend Crawshaw and left Liz's mother and Michael to return to the house and dispense hospitality to the few who might turn up.

Liz fastened Carla into her seat.

'Where are we going, Mum?'

'I'll tell you in a minute. I need to make a phone call.' She dialled Craig's number and heard it ring three times.

'Craig.'

'Craig, it's Liz. I'm just checking you're there.'

'Yes, I'm here. Are you coming?'

'If your offer still stands.'

'It's a standing invitation. What else can it do?'

'Right, we'll see you in about twenty minutes. 'Bye.'

''Bye.'

'Are we going to Craig's house, Mum?'

'Yes.'

'Yes!'

'It doesn't take much to raise your spirits, does it?' She put her phone away and started the car. 'Well done, darling,' she said. 'You were very good in there.'

'I was being prag... sensible.'

'And pragmatic, too, I suspect.' Liz drove up the wide driveway, thankful to leave the crematorium behind.

'What will Grandma Frankland and Uncle Michael do now?'

'They'll go back to Grandma Frankland's house to drink tea, eat sandwiches and cake, and talk about what a lovely old soul Grandma Wood was, and how it's a blessing that she's no longer suffering. After that, they'll bring each other up to date with their lives. Frankly, I don't think I could have borne that, and I didn't see why you should.'

After some consideration, Carla asked, 'Was that a pragmatic decision?'

'No, darling. It was born of maternal protectiveness and self-preservation.'

'I don't really mind. It'll be crowded at Grandma Frankland's because there's not much room, so it was probably the right thing to do, anyway.'

'Now, that was pragmatic thinking. Keep it up, darling.'

Whatever the style of her thinking, Carla was quiet for the rest of the journey, and Liz appreciated the silence. There was something about family funerals that engendered self-doubt. Could she have spent more time with Grandma Wood when she was alive and suffering? Could she have helped her mother more than she had? It seemed to Liz that some pragmatic thought was needed and that she was nowhere near as good at it as her ten-year-old daughter. It was a humbling thought that made her feel no better as she drove through the rain.

Eventually, they reached Craig's house. There was a light in the window, a sign of welcome in itself and, judging by the column of smoke rising from the chimney, the fire was well alight. Liz pulled in gratefully behind Craig's Volkswagen.

Immediately, the front door opened, and Craig came out to welcome them.

'Come inside, folks. It's turned nippy all of a sudden.'

They followed him into the house, which was as warm and convivial as Liz had imagined.

'Let me take your coats.' He helped Carla off with hers, by which time Liz had slipped out of her coat, scarf and gloves.

'We won't stay long,' said Liz. 'Don't go to a lot of trouble.'

'Trouble? I've never heard of it, and you're welcome to stay as long as you like. As a matter of fact, I did some shopping on the way home, so you must stay and eat.'

'But, Craig—'

'But me no buts.' He hesitated. 'I'm not sure what that means, but I read it once and it sounded reusable.' He hung their clothes in the porch. 'I'll put the kettle on for tea. 'Is tea acceptable, or would you prefer coffee, Liz?'

'Tea's perfect, thank you, Craig.'

'Right, but first....' He looked at Carla and made an instant assessment. 'I think you've been ever so brave, and now the whole thing has caught up with you,' he said. Turning to Liz, he asked, 'Are hugs in order?'

'Of course they are.'

He knelt on the hearth rug and held out his arms to Carla, who embraced him readily. 'Funerals are rotten things,' he said gently, 'and you've done well to get through this one.' He kissed her on the cheek and stood up to speak to Liz. 'You've done well, too, Liz. You've carried Carla and yourself through it, and that takes pluck.' Taking her smile as compliance, he gave her a gentle and discreet hug. 'Tea, I think,' he said, tactfully turning away while she plied a tissue. 'And what would Carla like? Ginger beer?'

'Ginger *beer*?'

'The non-alcoholic kind, I assure you.'

'I've never had ginger beer.'

'Plato said that you should try everything once, apart from bungee jumping and morris dancing. At least, if it wasn't Plato, it was some chap who was full of useful advice. Anyway, suffice it to say, the Famous Five regularly overdosed on ginger beer. It washed down the lashings of hard-boiled eggs and anchovy paste sandwiches they took everywhere. I'll get you some.' He left them to put the kettle on and prepare Carla's new treat.

Liz asked, 'Can I do anything?'

'Yes, sit by the fire and warm yourselves.'

She sat with Carla on the sofa, enjoying the crackle of the log and watching the sparks cling to the fireback before flying up the chimney. After a moment or so, she asked Carla, 'Are you all right, darling?' She seemed preoccupied.

'Mm. I thought I was going to cry, but it's because I'm happy again. Do you think I'm being silly?'

'No, darling, it's quite natural.' Blinking in the heat from the fire, she let her thoughts follow no particular pattern. Just for the time being, and for the first time in ages, her attention wasn't required elsewhere, and she could bask in warmth and comfort.

The kettle whistled in the kitchen, prompting the notion that, in the twenty-first century, only Craig would own such an item. As eccentricities went, however, it was as harmless as he was, and therefore immune to criticism.

Two minutes later, he emerged from the kitchen with a tray, which he placed on the coffee table. 'This is a deciding, and possibly defining, moment,' he announced, handing a glass of ginger beer to Carla. 'We'll find out in a second or three. Meanwhile, how do you like your tea, Liz?'

'With milk, but no sugar, please.'

'Quite right too. I'd have had to hunt for the sugar. I only ever use it when I'm baking.'

'Do you bake?'

Craig paused before answering, his attention having been taken by Carla's reaction to her first taste of ginger beer.

'It's lovely,' she said, sounding very surprised.

'Good. There's plenty more. The tanker came this morning.' Then, remembering that Liz had asked him a question, he said, 'Bake? Yes, but only when I'm entertaining.' That seemed to act as a reminder, because he handed Liz her tea and said, 'Excuse me for a second. I'd forgotten something.' He went to the kitchen and returned after a minute with a plate of biscuits. 'Oatmeal biscuits, baked on Wednesday,' he announced. 'That's why they slipped my mind.'

'You're the perfect host,' said Liz.

'That's very kind of you, but I'm not so sure, considering this afternoon's performance. Carla, you'll never guess what happened.'

Rather than try, she waited for him to go on.

'I got to the supermarket and realised I'd forgotten what we were having for dinner. I don't mind telling you, I held up quite a queue, just trying to remember. Anyway, I walked past the frozen foods, but nothing there jogged my memory. I went on to the fish counter, but nothing they had offered a clue, so I went to the meat counter. There was steak of various kinds, mince, lamb, pork, ham, bacon, burgers.... Then I remembered. We were having bangers and mash, so I bought the sausages and then rounded up the potatoes and vegetables.'

'Oh, good.' Carla's relief was tangible.

'I'm glad you approve, because, when you've finished that ginger beer, there's something I want you to do.'

'What's that?'

'In the normal way of things, I expect my guests to sing for their supper, but in your case, I have another idea. Will you play the piano for me?' He inclined his head unnecessarily towards the grand piano.

'I'm a bit out of practice.'

'I'm out of practice each morning, when I wake up. It's all relative.'

She hesitated again. 'I've never played a grand piano,' she said.

'It's just like playing an upright,' he told her, 'except that you can see over the top, or you will be able to when you're a bit taller.'

'Play one of your Grade Two exam pieces,' suggested Liz.

'All right.'

Craig adjusted the height of the stool for her and helped her up.

'It's called "Military March",' she told him. 'It's from a symphony by Haydn.'

Craig listened to her, and when she came to the end of the piece, he said, 'I'd say that was a pretty good performance for someone who's a bit out of practice. Touch is vitally important, and it begins with legato and staccato, which you do very well indeed.'

'Thank you.'

'Yes, that was very good,' said Liz. 'I'm trying to get her to use her wrists. I stopped her lessons because her teacher had her relying too much on her fingers.'

'Quite right. Injury is something we can do without.'

'What's this?' Carla was pointing to the book of pieces on the desk.

'Those are Rachmaninov's *Etudes Tableaux*. It means "Picture Studies". I played one of them recently at a recital.'

'I remember being blown away by that one,' said Liz.

Carla asked, 'Will you play something, Craig?'

'All right. I won't play that piece, because I don't think it's very suitable. I've even been told that it's scary. Instead, I'll play you an *un*scary piece.' He sat at the piano. 'If you ever need to be unscared, think of this one.'

'What's it called?'

' "The Bumble Bee." ' He played the Rachmaninov transcription for her, to her evident delight.

'That was… incredible,' she said.

'Rimsky-Korsakov originally called it "The Flight of the Bumble Bee",' he told her. 'When it's played backwards, it's called "The Bum of the Flightle Bee", but I shan't do that, because I'd be showing off.'

Carla appeared distracted. She whispered in Liz's ear.

Liz asked, 'Where's your loo, Craig?'

'Upstairs, turn left, and it's straight ahead.' He pointed towards the stairs for Carla's benefit.

When Carla was out of earshot, Liz said, 'This is the best distraction she could have had. It's doing me a power of good, too.'

'That's the idea. These things can be bad enough for us, but we can only try to imagine the effect they can have on children.' He lifted the teapot and asked, 'More tea?'

'Yes, please.' She couldn't help smiling.

'What's the matter?'

'Nothing at all. I was only thinking that most people would put a teabag into a mug, but you brew it in a teapot and serve in cups and saucers. It's a civilised touch.'

'I started doing that when I was a student. Too many people I knew were doing the bohemian thing, living in chaos and disarray simply because they were students, and I wanted to avoid that. Having lived with a father who had no standards at all, I was keen to maintain mine.'

'You know, there's a lot about your early life that I find terribly sad.'

'I rose above it, Liz. You must do the same.'

She laughed. 'I'll try.' She poured milk into her tea and asked, 'Are you swimming tomorrow?'

'I must, if I'm going to get fit.'

'It'll just be Carla and me. Leah and her husband are in London.'

He considered the information and said, 'She mentioned something about him doing a similar job to mine.'

'Yes, but he concentrates on piano nowadays, and he does a lot of accompaniment and ensemble playing. He's very good. That's why they're in London this weekend, for one of his recitals.'

'Good for him. I may have come across him. What's he called?'

'Gavin Lowe.'

His face registered recognition. 'I was right. I have met him, and I agree, he's very good.'

'Who's very good?' The question came from Carla as she arrived downstairs.

'Gavin.'

'Mm. He likes bangers and mash, too.'

'So did Rachmaninov and Liszt, I believe. There must be something in it for it to keep fuelling pianists the way it does.' He looked up at the clock and said, 'Very soon, you'll hear heartrending sobs coming from the kitchen. It'll be me peeling onions.'

'I think I'd better give you a hand,' said Liz.

———— ▶◀ ————

Two hours later, Liz and Carla took their leave of Craig and drove home, both tired and relaxed.

'We are going swimming tomorrow, aren't we, Mum?'

'Oh, yes.'

'Good. Is my dad coming for me on Sunday?'

'He hasn't mentioned it.' Liz left her thoughts unspoken.

'Good, because then I can go with you and Craig to the band rehearsal.'

13

On Saturday afternoon, Liz phoned Craig to ask for a lift to Ickringill the next morning.

'My car died on the way home, she explained. 'It was shortly after we'd left you, and it wasn't the first time.'

'Electrics?'

'Yes.'

'The usual suspect. Yes, I'll come over for you.'

'Thank you. Carla was going to spend the whole day with Simon, but as usual, he's found something else to do. Fortunately, he made his feeble excuse in good time.'

'How did Carla take it?'

'In her stride. She's used to it, and she was quite relieved that she didn't have to rub shoulders with Hannah and her boys. It also means she can come to Ickringill with us.'

'Oh, good.'

Liz laughed. 'She told Simon that, and it didn't go down very well.'

'Oh well, he can't have it both ways. What's the problem, that he has to keep making excuses?'

'Hannah's two boys are into football, formula one racing and all the things that appeal to Simon. Carla struggles to compete with that.'

'Poor girl. So, is Simon very much a bloke?'

'A hundred percent, yes, but there was room for me in his life.'

'That's something, at least.'

'Not really. He needed me to feed his mates when they came round to watch football on our wide screen television.'

In a puzzled tone, he asked, 'Have you got a wide screen television?'

'No, it went with him, along with Sky Sports and Sky everything else, really. He left the satellite dish behind. At least, Sky did. Carla and I don't watch much television.'

'It's none of my business—'

'Don't worry. I've complained about him so often to anyone who'll listen, that most aspects of my previous life are public property by this time.'

'I was only going to ask you what he does for a living.'

'He's an electrical engineer.'

'Ah.'

It was a response that could be taken several ways, so she asked, 'Why did you say, "Ah" like that?'

'It's my standard reply when I hear about something that's beyond my mental compass. If you were to mention nuclear physics, I'd say, "Ah". Likewise, chemistry and maths. Electrical engineers deal in numbery things, such as amps, volts, watts and ohms, don't they?'

'So I understand.'

'That's just it, you see. I *don't* understand.'

'If it's of even the smallest consolation, Craig, I can't imagine Faraday or Eddison getting much beyond the first bar of Rachmaninov's *Etudes Tableaux*.'

'You're a great comfort to me, Liz. I'll be over at about nine-thirty.'

'Thank you again, Craig. 'Bye.'

''Bye.'

Carla was waiting to ask, 'Is Craig going to take us to the band rehearsal, Mum?'

'Yes. When did you get in?' Carla had been up the street at her friend Madison's house.

'About five minutes ago. Madison's mum called her in for din... lunch.'

'She sounds like an organised mum. I suppose I should do something about lunch.'

'What are we having?'

Liz put her thinking face on and said, 'Stewed bugs and onions.'

'Ugh.'

'Sorry – my mistake. That's for dinner tonight. How about game pie with coleslaw and potato salad?'

'Yum!'

'You see, I haven't lost my touch.'

Carla looked thoughtful, a signal that told Liz to expect a change of subject.

'Mum?'

'I'm still here, darling.'

'What are you going to do about the car?'

'In what sense? The AA man got it going for us, didn't he?'

'But he won't always be around.' It was typical of Carla to take the common-sense view.

'He, or one of his colleagues, will be at the end of a telephone. That's their pledge.'

'What's a pledge?'

'A promise.' It was an unfortunate concept, given recent events, but there was no avoiding it.

'And they keep their promises, don't they?'

'Yes, they do. They're lovely people.'

Carla was thoughtful again. 'Mum?'

'I'm at your side.'

'I've been thinking prag....'

'Pragmatically?'

'Yes.'

'I was afraid so. Are you going to give me the benefit of your wisdom?'

'Yes.' She seemed to be preparing her next contribution to the debate.

'Or shall we discuss it over lunch, like the civilised people we are?'

'Yes, let's.'

Liz went to the kitchen and took a piece of game pie from the fridge, along with two polystyrene pots containing coleslaw and potato salad respectively. She divided everything by two and set it out on to two plates, which she carried to the dining table. 'Knives and forks, please, Carla.'

'Right.' Carla picked up the cutlery and brought it through.

'Right.' Liz took her seat opposite Carla. 'You were about to tell me what you had in mind,' she said.

'Mm.'

'The floor is yours.'

'What?'

'That's just a way of saying it's your turn to speak.'

'Right. I'm worried, Mum.'

'Are you?'

'Yes, because that car keeps letting you down, and I'm worried that if we have a lot of snow, we could be stuck in it, or you could be, all on your own.'

'It's always on the cards, darling. It's the price we have to pay for living in this blessed plot.'

'Isn't it time we had a car that doesn't let us down?'

Liz nodded sagely. 'That would be one solution,' she said.

'Is there another?'

'We could keep calling out the AA, or....'

'What?'

'Stay at home and not worry about a car.'

'That's just silly.' Her expression lent force to her remark.

'I agree. I was just throwing ideas across the table, brainstorming the problem, as they say. On balance, I suppose your idea is the only sensible one. We'll look for a car that's more reliable, and one that regards a snow-covered landscape as its natural habitat.' It went against the grain, but she would have to consult Simon on the subject. Being of a technical frame of mind as well as a regular contributor to bar room conversations of the automotive kind, he would be able to give her some ideas. She would grit her teeth and phone him later.

———◆◗◀———

On the way to Ickringill, Craig asked, 'What's the story with your car, Liz?'

'It's under sentence. I had thought of asking my ex-husband to accompany me to a dealership so that I can trade it in against a more reliable one, and hopefully one that can cope with a Dales winter. It's his kind of thing. He loves car hunting and he thinks it makes him look clever.' Seeing that Carla's attention was elsewhere, she said, 'It's a pity I couldn't trade him in for something more reliable.'

'But you thought again, presumably.'

'Yes, I have to be sensitive to his domestic situation. I don't think it would have gone down at all well with Hannah.'

Craig appeared to be lost in thought.

'A penny for them, Craig.'

'I was just thinking about all the cars I considered before I got this. One possibility is an SUV.'

'What is an SUV?'

'A sport utility vehicle. It's techspeak for one that has high ground clearance and, more often than not, four-wheel drive. They're worth considering. I hate the idea of you sitting at the roadside, waiting to be rescued, especially in bad weather.'

'You and Carla should get together, Craig. As a partnership, you could take pragmatism to new heights as well as being two of the most thoughtful people I know.'

His smile told her that the thought pleased him.

'Speaking of weather,' he said, 'I keep my insurance against snow in the garage.'

'Oh?'

'I have an elderly but faithful Land Rover. It was bored mindless in London, but coming up here put a huge smile on its face.'

'Oh, bless. I can almost see it.'

———— ▸◂ ————

When everyone was settled and the amplifier was plugged in, Craig addressed the band. 'The good news,' he told them, 'is that we can have the old music desks.' There was a gratifying murmur from the students, and then a signal from Liz reminded him to say, 'There's more good news for the girls. Your dresses have arrived, and you can have a try-on after the rehearsal.'

Having registered their appreciation, they gave the appearance that they were waiting for more.

'It's all right,' said Craig. 'There's no bad news. We've come here to enjoy ourselves.' He saw them relax. 'Let's start with "Begin the Beguine".'

Jessica raised her hand to ask, 'What kind of dance is it, Craig?'

'Strictly speaking, it's a beguine. There really is such a dance, and it originated, I believe, in either Guadeloupe or Martinique. but not many people are familiar with it, so they usually treat it as a slow rhumba. At all events, it's a very sensuous dance, so let's hear that from the first beat.'

They played through it once, and then again after a few small adjustments, after which Craig signalled his approval.

The remainder of the rehearsal was as successful, and it was a cheerful group that took their dresses downstairs to try them on.

Surprisingly, only one required alteration. Jessica was of only modest height, and her dress was ten centimetres too long for her.

Liz asked her, 'Will you be able to shorten it yourself?'

'No,' said Jessica, 'I'll get my mum to do it.'

Liz said to Carla, 'Mums have to be clever people, don't they?'

It came as no surprise that Carla agreed with her.

Craig gathered everyone together to ask, 'Does anyone know of a tame signwriter?'

'Yes,' said Andrew the alto sax player, 'my uncle.'

'Does he live locally?'

'In Shipley, yes.'

'Do you think he'd be willing to help us out?'

Andrew looked thoughtful. 'I'll get my mum to work on him,' he said.

———◆◄———

'All of which,' said Liz on the way home, 'bears out what I said about mums being clever people.'

'I've never doubted it,' said Craig.

'And speaking of cleverness, you sounded erudite, talking about the beguine.'

'In my line of work, it pays to do your homework.'

'Can you dance? It's a rare skill nowadays.'

'Yes, I took lessons. It was part of my cosy world, you know, and it was also a useful ploy for getting to meet fellow pupils of the opposite sex. Of course, some came ready-paired, but others were obligingly single.'

It was an aspect of Craig's life that Liz had never considered, but she reminded herself that, like everyone else, he was only human. 'Sylvia, Leah's mum, taught me,' she said. 'Just the waltz and the foxtrot. I used to go to some of Leah's dad's gigs, and it was fun to be able to join in.'

'I'll teach you the quickstep, if you like, and then you'll know three dances.'

'Are they the only three you know?'

'Madam, you've cut me to the quick.' He feigned hurt.

'Go on, tell me you know them all if it'll make you feel better.'

'No, I can do the rhumba, and that makes four.'

That seemed to jog Carla's memory, because she sang, 'When they begin to begin....'

' "When they begin *the beguine*", darling. It's the dance we were talking about earlier.'

'Are you going to dance with Craig?'

'Craig's going to teach me the quickstep.'

'When?'

'I don't know. I expect he'll let me know when he's ready.'

Craig's thoughts had evidently moved on, because he said, 'I have a decent suggestion to make.'

'That's very reassuring, Craig.'

'I said that so that you'd know it wasn't going to be an *in*decent suggestion.'

'I'd never expect a suggestion from you to be less than proper.'

'Good. My suggestion is that we have lunch, as before, and then we go car hunting. The main dealers will all be open.'

Liz hesitated. 'I feel guilty, taking up your time.'

'It's freely given, so there's no need for guilt. I'm thinking about that winter scene, Liz, a broken-down car and two of my dearest friends huddled together for warmth. It's more than I can bear.'

'All right. Thank you, Craig, It's very kind of you.'

14

Liz returned from London after a recording session followed by a meeting with a music editor, that resulted in more work. This time, it was to be a score for a documentary about nineteenth-century female novelists.

She had left the train at Leeds and retrieved her car from the carpark. It was a four-year-old Suzuki Vitara, and she was delighted with it.

Leah and Gavin were on their travels again, so Liz had left Carla with her mother and was now on her way to collect her. It seemed a good idea to call at the supermarket in Thanestalls on her way there, where she could find something quick and easy for dinner and buy some flowers for her mother as well.

She was walking down the frozen food aisle when a voice that sounded disturbingly familiar claimed her attention.

'Hello, Liz.'

She turned and had no difficulty in recognising the owner of the voice, even after eleven years. 'Jimbo Watkinson,' she said. 'But maybe it's not such a surprise. I imagine you're visiting your dad. Anyway, how are you?'

He shrugged modestly. 'Muddling through, as always. How about you? Chic and desirable as ever, of course. Naturally, I've seen your name among the credits. Richly deserved, in my opinion.'

'I've been lucky, Jimbo,' she said. 'By "muddling through", I take it you're referring to your current success as resident growler with Opera Enlivened. I saw you in Rigoletto and I thought at the time what a shame it was that Sparafucile only gets a cameo part.'

'Hired assassins do tend to lurk in the shadows rather than hog the limelight.' Changing the subject, he said, 'Listen, Liz, we must meet.'

'I thought we just did.'

'Unfortunately, I have to go back to London tomorrow. Have you any plans for this evening?'

Some people never changed. Jimbo was still a self-propelled penis with a camouflage of charm. 'Yes, I'm looking forward to spending some time with my daughter. I've just returned from London, and she's been staying with my mother.'

'Of course, there's a man in your life.'

'No, just a ten-year-old girl.'

'Lovely. Well, we could always arrange something when I'm in Thanestalls again. I believe your email address is on your website.'

'I'll give you full marks for persistence, Jimbo.' She sighed. 'Everything that happened between you and me is in the past, and that's where it must stay.'

'I had in mind a social get-together for old time's sake, that's all.'

'I know exactly what you had in mind, Jimbo, and the answer's still "no".'

'I'll be in touch in case you change your mind. You never know.'

———◆◄———

It was Liz's habit to bring Carla a small gift when she returned from London, the most recent being a tin of pencil crayons. The irony of a present from London that had been made in Cumbria was lost on Carla, who was simply enjoying the picture on the tin and looking forward to using them.

'These will be very useful in Geography, Mum,' she said in her serious way.

'Don't restrict them to that, darling. Life is for living, so just enjoy them.'

Before Carla could say anything, the phone rang, so Liz picked it up. 'Hello.'

'Liz, it's me.'

'Not Simon Tyersal, the man of a thousand excuses? How unexpected. What is it this time?'

'There's no need to be like that, Liz. The thing is, there's something I, like, can't get out of.'

'Let me guess. Is it your irritating use of the meaningless "like"?'

'No, it's—'

'A mantrap? A dungeon cell? Malham Tarn? Oh, my beating heart! Tell me it's one of those three, and my life will be complete.'

'You really are impossible. It's to do with work, actually.'

'And that's far too technical for me to understand, as you know, so your excuse is conveniently obscure. Would you like to speak to Carla, as it's the next best thing to actually spending time with her?'

'Yes, all right. Put her on.'

'Carla, your dad's on the phone. He'd like to talk to you.' She handed the phone to Carla and went into her studio to remind herself of some of the decent things in life.

After a couple of minutes, Carla came to say, 'He rang off. He's not very pleased.'

'Oh, was I too hard on him? I must confess, a battle of wits with him is rather like a duel with an unarmed man.' She put her arms round Carla and kissed her. 'Forget I said that, darling. It was naughty of me.'

'It's true, though, but that wasn't what he was cross about. At least, I don't think it was.'

'What do you think upset him?'

'It was when I said it was all right that he couldn't come, because it meant I could go to Ickringill with you and Craig. He wanted to know who Craig was, but I just said he was someone you work with.'

'That's all he needs to know, so you've nothing to worry about. Think instead about the good things in life. The weekend beckons. Tomorrow we'll go swimming, and then on Sunday....'

'The band.'

'I'm glad you enjoy it.'

'I like everything about it.'

'Good. Kiss goodnight and off to bed.'

''Night-night, Mum.'

''Night-night, darling.'

Habit was a comfortable master or mistress – Liz suspected it embodied the qualities of both – so, as soon as Carla had gone upstairs, she phoned Leah, being fairly sure they'd be back.

'Hello, Liz. How was your session?'

'Quite straightforward, thanks. Did Gavin's recital go well?'

'Very well. Tell me, Liz, have you played much music by Granados?'

'When I used to practise, yes, I played the odd thing. Why do you ask?'

Leah adopted a confiding tone, as if she couldn't get close enough to the phone. 'He played the "Love Duet" as part of the recital, and, you know, it's never lost its ability to… well, to *excite* me.'

'I think I know where you're going with this, Leah. It's like the Rachmaninov effect, isn't it?'

'Phew! You can say that again.'

'I take it you enjoyed your night away.'

'Didn't we just. I tell you, Liz, whatever they say about me, there's life in the old dog yet.'

'You're nothing of the kind. You're an attractive and desirable woman.' 'Desirable' seemed an odd word to use, and Liz could only think she'd heard it recently, for it to be so conveniently on her tongue. She dismissed the thought.

'With a flat chest.'

'Your modest bust notwithstanding.'

'And a muscular physique.'

'All the better to wow them with, my dear. I'm sure you can achieve things that other women can only dream about.'

'Okay, I feel better about my ageing body.'

'I'm glad I can do that for you. I did the opposite to Simon this evening.'

'Oh, don't say the bugger let Carla down again.'

'Okay, I shan't, but I told him what I thought about him, and then Carla upset him.'

Leah snorted. 'It serves him bloody right. How did she do that?'

'She said she didn't mind being stood up, because it meant she could go to Ickringill with Craig and me instead.'

'Ouch. Well played, Carla!'

'I have to agree.' Liz enjoyed the thought, and then, for no apparent reason, remembered when she'd heard the word 'desirable'. 'Leah,' she said, 'Would you describe me as "chic"?'

'When you're dressed for an occasion, yes. No one looks chic in jeans and a T shirt.'

'Apparently, opinions vary on that score,' she said, recalling something that Craig had once said. 'Anyway, what about "desirable"? Would you call me "desirable"?'

'Oh well, that's very much a man's-eye-view description, isn't it? It's unfair to ask me. Has Craig been calling you "desirable"?'

'No, someone else has. I had a blast from the past this afternoon. I bumped into an old flame in the supermarket, although now I think of it, he was really more of a flicker than a grown-up flame. Did you ever meet Jimbo Watkinson?'

'No, I didn't, but I've heard you mention him. That's the opera singer you're talking about, isn't it?'

'The very same. I knew Jimbo at the Guildhall.'

'In the biblical sense?' Leah had a way of asking very direct and personal questions.

'Yes.'

'And he finds you chic and desirable?'

'So he said.'

'Go on. Describe him to me.'

'Is it a good idea, considering your current excitable and susceptible state?'

'Indulge me, Liz.'

'All right. He's tall, dark and good-looking in a mail-order catalogue kind of way. Even when he's speaking, his voice reminds you that its foundation is bottom "D", and he has a beguiling charm that, if he catches you off-guard, makes you forget that his life is ordered solely by his man-parts.'

'Oh,' said Leah with a shiver in her voice, 'temptation. Does he really live to serve his penis?'

'Yes, and he does that quite faithfully.'

'Hm. Penile servitude for life.' Recovering slightly, she asked, 'Are you going to see him again?'

'No.'

'That sounded categorical.'

'It was meant to. He wanted me to go somewhere with him this evening, no doubt with a view to coming back here later, but I disabused him of that notion.'

'How long has it been since you lingered at Aphrodite's shrine, Liz? It must be a while, now.'

'I can't remember. Even when it was happening, it wasn't exactly memorable.'

'My poor friend, you've missed out on so much.'

'I don't feel that I have, Leah. I may change my mind at some time, but I don't feel at this stage that anything is missing from my life.'

'And on that surprising and positive note, I must leave you. See you in the morning?'

'We'll be there. 'Bye.'

''Bye.'

Liz put the phone down, amused by Leah's revelation and pleased for her friend that her marriage was so complete, although she'd known that for some time,

---

Unusually, Craig was the last to arrive at the cafeteria. Leah had already got the coffee and Carla's orange juice when he came through the door.

'Hey, Craig,' she said, 'the whole idea of saving you from drowning was so that, being a fella, you'd get here first and get the coffee in.'

'I'm sorry,' he said, 'I had a phone call from one of my students just as I was changing.'

'A likely story. Come and meet my other half.'

'We've already met,' said Gavin. 'Hello, Craig. How are you?'

The two shook hands and exchanged greetings.

'I brought Gavin,' said Leah, 'to get him fit. So you see, you two have something else in common.'

'Hard, cruel woman,' said Gavin.

'That's why you've stayed with me all this time, isn't it, darling?'

Liz asked, 'Do your students often phone you at the weekend, Craig?'

'No, it was Andrew, the alto sax player. His uncle's designed a logo for the band, and he wanted us to see it.' He took out his phone and brought up the picture, handing the phone to Liz.

'Look at that, Carla,' she said. 'Isn't it lovely?'

'Yes, it's old-fashioned, but it's nice.'

'The style's Art Deco.' Liz handed it to Leah, who showed it to Gavin.

' "DO" is obvious enough,' he said, 'but what does "NC" stand for?'

'New Collegians,' Craig told him. The musicians are all students, you see.'

'The New Collegians Dance Orchestra,' said Gavin, almost weighing the words on his tongue.' Turning to Leah, he said, 'Hutch would have loved all this.'

'Hutch was Gavin's clarinet and sax teacher,' explained Leah.

'He also helped Frank set up the New Albion Dance Orchestra back in nineteen… something, I think.'

'Gavin and Frank were at school together,' said Leah.

'And the College.'

'I think,' said Liz, 'that you and I should pay Frank a visit some time, Craig. I'd like to hear the band again, and I think you'd get something out of it as well.'

'That's an excellent idea,' said Gavin. 'I could be tempted to do that myself.'

'Do you mean,' said Leah with theatrical astonishment, 'that you could drag yourself away from your piano for a whole evening?'

'For something like that, yes, and I'd like to see Frank again.'

'And speaking of reunions,' said Leah, 'you haven't heard the latest. Liz's romantic past has caught up with her in the shape of the opera singer James Watkinson. They were at the Guildhall together.'

'There's nothing romantic about it,' protested Liz. 'Anyway, it was a long time ago.'

'Oh, but glowing embers can be fanned into life.'

'Take no notice, Liz,' said Gavin. 'Leah learned matchmaking at her mother's knee, and she couldn't have had a finer example, let me tell you.'

Craig stood up and asked, 'Can I get you people another coffee before I go?'

'Relax,' Leah told him. 'I was only joking about the coffee. You mustn't take me too seriously.'

'I did,' said Gavin, 'and look what happened to me.'

'All right, then. It's been good to see you again, Gavin. Whose car are we using tomorrow, Liz?'

'We'll call for you, if you like.'

'Good. I'll see you both then. 'Bye, everyone.'

Liz watched him go and said, 'I think it's time we weren't here, Carla.'

Gavin looked at his watch and then at Leah.

'I know,' she said. 'You can't wait to go back to your piano.'

'We'll see you two soon, I hope,' said Gavin, giving Carla a farewell kiss.

'Keep coming,' said Liz. 'It's good for you. 'Bye.'

Gavin waited until they were out of earshot and said, 'You know, Leah, for a graceful ballerina, you really excel at clumsiness.'

'Clumsiness?'

'The verbal kind,' he explained.

'What have I said?'

'Didn't you see Craig's face when you were laying it on about Liz seeing her old flame from the Guildhall?'

'Oh, heck.' Realisation came to her. 'Maybe I did get rather carried away. Mind you, if it encourages Craig to get his act together, it won't have done any harm.'

15

As they got into Liz's car, Craig placed a mysterious case between his feet and asked, 'Have you heard from Jimbo yet?'

'No, he's back in London, and when he's not presiding over the Temple of Isis, he'll be assassinating, despoiling, forbidding, and all the other things basses are called upon to do, in addition to the various activities that call for a bass-baritone. He'll be far too busy to be a nuisance.'

Craig made no reply, but gave her an odd look.

'You know,' said Liz, innocently changing the subject, 'we musicians are far too hard-headed, and the more experience we accumulate, the harder our heads become.'

Craig waited for an explanation.

It seemed to Liz that one of his great virtues was that he never dominated a conversation. After centuries of inequality, women had earned the right, after all, to do most of the talking, and he, being the honourable soul he was, usually allowed it to happen. 'You and I,' she went on, 'listen to beautiful music critically and analytically, whilst the non-cognoscenti enjoy it for what it is. They just wallow in it and get much more out of the process than we do.'

'But don't you think that when we're teaching and directing we have to be analytical and critical?'

'Oh, yes. I'm just saying that we need to take time out, now and then, to rediscover the tingle factor.'

'Oh yes, that.'

'The one that runs down your spine,' she prompted.

'I remember it.'

Liz gave him a quick, sideways look to see if he was serious, but as usual, his expression gave nothing away, so she asked him, 'When did your spine last tingle? She added hurriedly, 'In response to music, that is.'

'Let me think. It wasn't classical music.'

'It doesn't have to be.'

'Okay, it was when I discovered my granddad's hoard of seventy-eights, and I put one on the turntable for the first time. It was Al Bowlly singing "Love is the Sweetest Thing" with Ray Noble and the New Mayfair Dance Orchestra.' He looked at her and said, 'Your turn.'

'My very first was Marian Henderson singing "Deep River". That was when I was very young, but I'll always remember it, because it brought forth not just a tingle, but the feeling of tragedy and longing had me in tears as well.'

'A real bonus. I can imagine it with Marian Henderson.'

'But my re-awakening came, by a glorious coincidence, with Al Bowlly. too. It was "The Very Thought of You". I thought about it when I was taking the band through it at the second rehearsal. I had to concentrate like mad, although it helped that Matthew, good though he is, didn't sound like Al Bowlly.'

A voice from the back seat said, 'I think it's exciting.'

'What's exciting, darling?'

'Aren't you talking about the music the band plays?'

'Yes, we are, and you find it exciting? That's wonderful.' She turned to Craig and asked, 'What did I tell you?'

'We may soon be able to include "Love is the Sweetest Thing" in our repertoire,' said Craig.

'Oh?'

'Two violinists are hoping to join us. That would give us all the strings we need.'

'It'll bring the band up to fourteen-strong,' she reminded him.

'It doesn't matter. Some of the pre-war bands grew bigger than that, and however big our band becomes numerically, it'll never be a "big band" as such, because it won't play big-band repertoire.'

'True.' Liz pulled into the club's carpark. Craig picked up the case that had travelled in the footwell, and Liz was no longer able to contain her curiosity. She asked, 'What have you got in there?'

'A digital sound recorder. I thought Leah's mum might like to hear a band in the making.'

'What a lovely idea,' she said, following him into the club.

They were treated to the usual welcome by the members at the bar, and continued upstairs to what they now thought of as the band room.

Presently, the musicians arrived and set up their music stands and equipment. When they were ready, Craig stood in front of them.

'Two new members have come to join us,' he told them. 'They're Tori and Alex.' He held out his hand to welcome the two violinists. 'I'm sure you'll make them feel at home. We have some more numbers for you to add to your repertoire, and when we have enough and we're feeling confident, we'll arrange our first gig.' His announcement seemed to go down well. 'Will someone please give out the parts for "Embraceable You"?' He waited until the task was complete and counted them in. 'A-one, a-two, a-one and two and….' The music began, quite dryly at first, but Liz, who was listening carefully in spite of what she'd said earlier, reminded herself that the music was new to the students, and that they'd never heard the expression the pre-war bands had put into it.

They played to the end, when Megan on alto sax said cheekily, 'You're leading us with the wrong part of your body, Craig.'

'What?'

'When Liz stands in front, she conducts with her… behind… and it gives us the feel of the music.' She looked quickly at Liz and said, 'You don't mind me saying that, do you, Liz?'

'Not really. I'll just be aware that whenever I stand in front, everyone will be watching my bum.'

'That's right,' said Tyler.

'Let's get on,' suggested Craig. 'You'll just have to make do with my bum for now.' He counted them in and let them play the first chorus, before stopping them. 'That was much better,' he said. 'Lauren and Matthew, 'this is a "he and she" number, so I'd like you to learn it for next week.'

The two vocalists consulted briefly, and Lauren said, 'We'll sing it now, if you like, Craig. We can read it easily enough.'

'Excellent. Ready, folks? A-one, a-two, a-one and two and….'

By the end, Craig was so pleased that he asked Liz to stand in front, while he recorded another playing.

'Okay,' she said, counting them in.

Craig concentrated on recording the number. At the end, he said, 'That was very good indeed, folks. Thank you, Liz and everyone. Someone, please give out "Love Walked In." We'll treat it as an instrumental for now.'

When they were ready, he said, 'Very simply and gently this time, folks.' He counted them in and let them play through the number. At the end, he said, 'Harmon mutes, I think, trumpets, halfway out.'

Tyler looked at him inquiringly.

'No, Tyler, you're okay. Folks, I'm going to start you off and then leave you to it. You know what you're doing.' As he counted them in, he pushed the 'Record' button and spoke softly to Liz. 'May I have the pleasure?'

She was surprised, but she said, 'Of course.' She accompanied him to the dance floor section, and let him take her in hold. On the next down-beat, she felt him lead her into the slow foxtrot. Dancing in jeans and trainers wasn't ideal, but she put that from her mind and went with the glorious, gentle pulse of the music. It was luxury to have the whole floor to themselves, and they used it liberally. The whole thing had been unexpected, but the greatest surprise was that Craig was an excellent dancer. His lead was positive, but he was sensitive throughout.

All too soon, the music reached its end, and Craig thanked her before returning to the recorder to switch it off. Before he could do that, however, the band put down their instruments and applauded enthusiastically.

'That was brilliant,' said Nicole, the guitarist, 'just like *Strictly*.'

'Except,' said Tyler, 'without an audience clapping just off the beat. I don't know why they do that.'

'It's because they're enjoying themselves,' said Nicole, 'and they can't join in any other way. Anyway, rhythmic accuracy's not given to everyone.'

'At the end of a dance number,' said Craig, 'it's customary for the dancers to applaud the band, but you didn't allow that, so let me say that you played that number superbly well. You're really getting the feel of the music, with or without Liz's unique direction.' That also received a round of applause. When it was over, he said, 'It's time now for you to be led the way you prefer it, and Liz is going to take you through a waltz. Will someone please give out "I Can Give You the Starlight"?'

———◆│◆———

At the end of the rehearsal, they went down to the bar, as usual, and Liz, Craig and Carla had just sat down when Zac, the trumpet player, came to them.

'Craig,' he said, 'you were talking this morning about us getting a gig.'

'That's right.'

'It just sounded funny. Like, rock 'n roll language coming from, like, a music lecturer.'

'That's because the word's been around ninety-odd years, Zac.'

'Yeah?'

'Yes, dance band and jazz musicians were using it thirty years before rock 'n roll came to these shores. It's one of those words that have come to the stars of today via session musicians, and I can tell you that with some authority. It's like *segue* and *a cappella*. Today's shining stars use *a cappella* to mean simply "unaccompanied", whereas you and I both know that it describes a form of, admittedly unaccompanied, seventeenth-century sacred music. I've been there, Zac. I know how it works. Chances are, if someone said, "*Colla voce*" to a recording star, you'd hear it trotted out as accepted rock 'n roll terminology next week on *The One Show*. Likewise, members of a rock band bellowing expletives at each other across a platform in Glastonbury might, given a mischievous session musician, introduce the concept to their followers as "antiphonal music", and if you don't know what that really is, you weren't listening last Tuesday morning.'

Zac patted Craig reassuringly on the shoulder. 'I was listening, Craig,' he said. 'Thanks, mate.'

Craig asked Liz, 'Do I sound bitter?'

'Not really, and you had a wretched time doing sessions.

It seemed that it was a morning for enlightenment, because Carla, who had been extremely quiet, asked, 'Why are most of the numbers called foxtrots?'

'It's because the foxtrot was the most popular dance in the thirties, right up to the Americans introducing the jive, the lindy-hop and so on.'

'Is it a sensuous dance?'

Craig caught Liz's eye momentarily. 'That's not how I'd describe it,' he said.

Liz asked her, 'Where did you hear that word?'

'Craig told the musicians that the rhumba was a sensuous dance.'

'The rhumba's rather like this,' said Liz, twisting and swaying her upper body, 'and you don't get that in the foxtrot.'

'I just wondered.'

———◆│◆———

'It just shows that we have to be careful in what we say,' said Liz. 'Little pitchers have big ears.'

'Who's got big ears, Mum?'

'No one. I was talking about Roman vases. They have large handles that look like ears.' To change the subject, she asked, 'Did you speak to Andrew about the music desks, Craig?'

'Yes, I'll take them to his uncle next week. Fortunately, they fold almost flat, so I can get them all in the Land Rover.'

'Oh, good.'

'I've been wondering....'

'Yes?'

'I know you have other commitments, but while Jimbo's in London, I wondered if we could pay the New Albion Dance Orchestra a visit, as you suggested.'

'What...? Why is everyone talking about Jimbo?' It made no sense to her, unless Craig was referring to Leah's nonsense at the pool.

'I just thought things might have changed for you.'

'So did Leah, and you were both wrong.' Speaking warily because of Carla, she said, 'Look, Craig, the situation is this. Jimbo thinks we have unfinished business, whereas I told him we have not. Being a tenacious soul, he may well contact me again, but the answer will still be "no".'

'I'm sorry. I misunderstood.'

'Evidently, but to return to the subject of the New Albion Dance Orchestra, I will phone Frank. Leah and Gavin are members of the Wool Exchange Club, but we'd have to go as guests. Also, I'll need to arrange things with my mum.'

Carla asked, 'Where are you going, Mum?'

'To visit one of Gavin's old friends. We'll be out very late at night, so you'll have to stay with Grandma Frankland.' She mentioned her mother's name out of habit, forgetting for the moment that she was Carla's only surviving grandparent. Then, as one thought led to another, she remembered that she had something to put to Craig. 'Craig,' she asked, 'what are you doing for Christmas?'

'Oh, this and that.'

'In other words, nothing. Would you like to join Carla and me on Christmas Day?'

'Well, if you're sure I won't be in the way.'

She gave the possibility some consideration and said, 'No, we'll find a corner where you can sit out of sight, and you won't be a nuisance. Of course you won't be in the way. I wouldn't have asked you otherwise.'

'In that case, thank you. I'd like that very much.'

'Did you hear that, Carla. Santa fancies a day off this year, so Craig's coming instead.'

'Yes!'

'It seems you've got the popular vote, Craig.' As if explanation were needed, she said, 'We usually had my mum and grandma for Christmas lunch, and before you say it, I know a turkey is more sustaining, but parents' and grandparents' feelings have to be considered. This Christmas, however, my mum, who is now living alone, has taken up my brother's invitation to join him, his wife and their brood instead.'

'Well, I'm very grateful for your invitation. Should I wear a red overcoat and white whiskers and wellies?'

'Black or green wellies will do just as well, won't they, Carla?'

'Yes, and holly and mistletoe.'

Liz opened her eyes in surprise. 'Mistletoe? It sounds as if she has plans for you, Craig.'

'That's all right. I'm looking forward to a warm welcome.'

It seemed only right to issue the invitation, but Liz had seen Craig's fleeting look of concern when Leah brought up the subject of Jimbo at the pool, and his more recent reference served as warning for her to tread very carefully.

16

DECEMBER

A phone call to Gavin elicited the information that Cullington Wool Exchange Club's annual Christmas Ball was to be held on Saturday the seventeenth of December. After a hurried conference with Leah and a call on his mobile phone, he confirmed that four tickets were on their way to him, and that Liz and Craig would be his guests.

That evening, Liz phoned Craig to tell him she had another invitation for him.

'We're invited to the Christmas Ball in Cullington,' she said. 'It's formal, evening dress. The Exchange Club always does things properly. I realise it's just like overalls for you, but the hardest work you'll have to do will be to listen to the band.'

'That'll be no hardship, Liz.'

'No, I'm the one with the problem. The only thing I've got that resembles a ballgown is ages old.'

'I'm sure you'll look magnificent in it.'

She wondered, not for the first time, why men were so unimaginative about such things. 'It's *five years old*, Craig. That's how long it's been since I went anywhere special.'

'Is five years considered old for a dress?'

She summoned her patience and said, 'I'll have to find a new one, and just before Christmas, too.'

'Will that be a problem?'

She smiled at his innocence. 'No,' she said, 'I'll just drop in on Amanda Wakeley and ask if she's got something off-the-peg and totally stunning in a size twelve hanging around in her bargain basement.'

'Oh, good. I must confess, it's all a mystery to me.'

'I get that impression. Don't worry, I'll find something.'

Liz's next call was to Leah.

'What's new, Liz?'

'I'm off to the big city, well, Leeds. I need to find a ballgown.'

'When are you going?'

'Today.'

'Well, it *is* urgent. Can I come?'

'Of course you can.'

'Good. We can have lunch again at that brilliant Italian restaurant.'

———▶◀———

'Which exclusive fashion outlets have you considered, Liz?'

'The usual ones: Oxfam, Mind, The British Heart Foundation.... They all have the same thing going for them.'

'Don't they just? There's a BHF in Boar Lane we could try.'

They did, but it bore no result, so they tried the next one they came to, which was home to Relate. It looked promising at first, but an intensive search yielded nothing, as did the next three outlets. They concluded that Christmas was most likely the culprit.

'By this time,' said Leah, 'Gavin would be tearing his hair out with boredom and frustration.'

'I see now why you didn't bring him.'

'Oh, what do I see?' Leah was staring into the window of the British Red Cross.

'What? Oh, yes. Let's take a closer look.' It was a sleeveless, chartreuse ballgown with a scoop neck. Put simply, it was extreme temptation on a dressmaker's dummy 'I don't believe it.'

'This is excitement on a grand scale for you, Liz.'

'I don't get out as often as you. I still have to work for my living.'

'That's true, Cinders. I shouldn't mock.'

They made their way towards the object of their interest, briefly appraising various articles on their way.

'Oh, rats.'

'Where?'

'I've just seen this.' Liz was holding the tab that revealed the dress to be a size ten.

'Try it,' suggested Leah. 'Maybe it's a flattering sizing, or just an idle threat. You never know.'

'They do vary,' said an assistant.

Leah and Liz nodded hopefully. One manufacturer's size ten was often another's twelve and could be someone else's eight.

'Which of you ladies is interested in the gown?'

'I am,' said Liz, still clinging to the possibility. 'The genuine size ten is my friend. She has the job of persuading me not to jump under a bus if the gown's too small for me.'

'The lady who brought it in had a similar figure to yours. She was about your height, too, I seem to remember. Take it and try it on.'

Liz took the dress to a changing cubicle, now hardly daring to hope. Then, having divested herself of her everyday garb, she took the gown off its hanger and pulled it over her head. Just the feel of it was luxurious, and so far... Dare she believe it? There seemed to be no problem. She stepped out of the cubicle and asked, 'Will somebody do me up, please?'

The assistant completed the fastening and said, 'It looks lovely on you.'

Leah was inclined to be less restrained. 'Oh, Cinderella,' she breathed, 'you *shall* go to the ball.'

———◆◗◆———

Carla waited until Liz was off the phone, to ask, 'Why am I staying with Grandma Frankland again?' The question came out as one of casual enquiry rather than protest.

'Craig and I are going with Leah and Gavin to a ball in Cullington.'

'A ball?' Not surprisingly, the concept, with its fairy-tale association, appealed to her. Her next question, however, was infinitely more grown-up. 'Are you going out with Craig now?'

'No, Craig's coming because he wants to hear the band.'

'Do you think you will go out with him, Mum?'

'I've no idea. Honestly, Carla, you could make a marble statue blush with embarrassment.'

'I only wondered because you bought that beautiful dress, and I thought it was to go somewhere with Craig.'

Clearly, it was time for maternal guidance. 'Come and sit down, Carla.' She waited until Carla had joined her, and said, 'The ball is going to be very formal. That means that all the ladies will be wearing long gowns and the men will be in evening dress.'

Inclining her head towards the shelf of DVD's, Carla asked, 'Like the man who dances in the films?'

She smiled. 'Yes, like Fred Astaire. Well, sort of.'

Carla was thoughtful for a moment. 'I wish I could go,' she said.

'I'm sorry, darling. It's for grown-ups only.' She drew her close, half-remembering some of the frustrations of childhood. 'There's something else,' she said, and it's about the question you asked me earlier, about Craig. The thing is, you mustn't say anything like that when he's around, because he'd be more embarrassed than I was.'

'Why would he be more embarrassed?'

'When you asked me about it, there was only you and me here, so it wasn't really awful.' It was ridiculous that she was struggling to explain something as simple as everyday diplomacy to her ten-year-old daughter.

'Do you mean it would be worse for him if you were there?'

With a feeling of awkward relief, Liz said, 'Yes, it would, so please don't.'

After a period of silence that Liz found disturbing, Carla said, 'My life is full of things I'm not allowed to do.'

'Don't think about it like that. Remember the things you *are* allowed to do.'

'That doesn't help.'

'What's on your mind, darling?' Liz kissed her. 'Tell your mum all about it.'

'I'm not allowed to go to the ball because I'm not old enough.'

'That's true, but you won't always be too young. Anyway, as soon as our band gets a gig that doesn't finish too late, you can go to that.'

'Will everyone be wearing evening dress?'

'If it's an evening performance, Craig and I will, Lauren will, and all the young men in the band will be in black tie and short jacket evening dress. The girls will be wearing the dresses I got for them. Does that help?'

'Yes.' It was as if the sun had signalled a reappearance.

'Was that all?'

'No, there's something else.'

'Well, don't keep me in suspense.'

It was clear that Carla was struggling to express her problem. So much was evident from her facial expression.

'Let the words tumble out, darling. We'll rearrange them later.'

Carla opened her mouth and then closed it. Eventually, she said, 'I don't want to embarrass you again.'

'Ah.'

'If I tell you, you'll be embarrassed.'

'I don't think so. I think I know what you want to talk about, and I'm sure I can handle it.'

'In that case, there's something I want to happen.'

'Okay so far. Would you like to tell me what it is?'

Almost shyly, Carla looked down as she spoke. 'I want you to find somebody really nice to go out with, like that Frenchman you went out with when you were a student, and he taught you to speak French properly.'

'He was nice, I have to admit, but why do you want that?'

'Because now that you and my dad are divorced, he's got horrible Hannah, but you've got no one, and I don't want you to be lonely.' Suddenly, her eyes filled with tears.

'Oh, sweetheart, I'm not lonely as long as I've got you, and my work keeps me so busy, I never have time to notice that there's no man in my life. It's not compulsory, you know. Some of the greatest women in history have been known to live without a man.' She reached for a tissue and handed it to her. 'So, you see, there's nothing to cry about.' She held her close until she was sure the tears had stopped, and they sat together like that for some time. Eventually, Carla said, 'When Leah was talking about that man, when we were at the pool….'

'Which man was that?'

'The man you knew when you were a student, the opera singer.'

'Ah, Jimbo.' Clearly, Carla had missed nothing during that conversation.

'I wondered if you were going to start going out with him, and then you told Craig you weren't.'

'Yes, I did. I went out with Jimbo for a short time when we were at the Guildhall, but that was all over a long time ago.' It was surprising how much Carla had overheard in the car as well as in the cafeteria.

'I was glad, really, because I'd rather you went out with Craig. I don't know that Jumbo man, but I know Craig.'

'I know. He's kind, thoughtful, reliable and clever, and if anything like that were to happen, you'd be among the first to hear about it, but don't hold your breath. I have no plans as yet, and I don't think Craig has, either.' Largely out of habit, she looked up at the clock.

'Is it bedtime?'

'Ordinarily, it would be, but you're not going to bed in that state of mind, darling. When you go upstairs, you need to be happy and content. Leaving out the obvious, which, as you know, is not negotiable, what shall we do to make you happy and content?'

'I don't know.'

'When you were little, I used to read to you, but you can read for yourself now.'

Carla looked wistful as she said, 'I liked it when you read to me and did all the voices.'

'It's the only way to do it. That settles it, then. Get ready for bed and then come down and I'll read to you by the fireside.'

'What will you read?'

'Anything you like.'

Carla put on her thinking face. 'Am I too old for *The Big Friendly Giant*?'

It was a difficult age. She was too young for some things and too old for others, but there was no age restriction on bedtime reading. 'No one is too old for *The Big Friendly Giant*,' Liz assured her.

'Good, because it makes me feel happy.'

'There's no better reason. Away and get your jim-jams on.'

17

Craig stood in the open doorway, staring. 'Liz,' he said, 'you look....'

'Come inside, Craig.'

He stepped inside, closing the outer door behind him. 'I'm trying to think of a word that's not a cliché,' he said. 'I think I'll take a risk and say that you look *exquisite*.'

'If that's a cliché, it's one that's never been used to describe me until now. Thank you, Craig.'

'That's not the gown you told me about, is it?'

'No, I bought this one last week.'

'I'm glad you did. It might have been made for you.'

'As it happens, it wasn't, but I like to think it was waiting for me.' She accepted a kiss on her cheek. 'I'm ready now.'

'Let me help you with your coat.' He picked it up and held it for her, inhaling deeply as he did so.

'You're going to say something extravagant about my perfume, now, aren't you?'

'Not extravagant, but admiring. It's... compelling.'

'It's Euphoria by Calvin Klein.'

'It's still compelling.'

'Oh, Craig, what can I say? Thank you.'

They walked out to Craig's car and he unlocked it, holding the passenger door for her and waiting for her to gather her skirts. 'I must say, it's a nice touch on the part of the Exchange Club.'

'Insisting on formal dress? Yes, they're old-fashioned, but there's nothing wrong with that when they're hosting a band that's more than twenty years old and playing music that's been around for... almost ninety years, I suppose.'

' "Old-fashioned" means "in the best of taste" in my personal dictionary,' he told her.

'That's no surprise.'

A little later, he asked, 'Will you fill me in about Frank Morrison and the band we're going to hear?'

'With pleasure. I'll begin with Frank, who does what I do, although it's more accurate the other way round, because he started first. It was hearing some of Frank's scores that got me into film and TV work. He's a lovely man, and you're bound to like him.'

As Craig turned into the main road, he said, 'I've heard the band on CD and I've never forgotten the score they recorded for that film. What was it called, the one set in the Depression?'

'*Hey, Young Fella.* It had some of Frank's original songs in it as well as a few golden oldies.'

'I know. They were brilliant.'

'I gather the band had only been formed a few months earlier, but they knew what they were doing. Some of the players were veterans of the golden age.'

Craig dabbed his footbrake to discourage the driver of an Audi from following too closely. 'How did it all begin?'

'I heard it all second-hand, via Gavin, because Frank was too modest to tell me the story himself, but I'll tell you what I know. As I understand it, the local orchestra, which is now defunct, formed a breakaway orchestra, that excluded the older members. Naturally enough, they were hurt and resentful at losing the weekly get-together they'd all enjoyed. Enter Frank, then, who looked at the line-up and hit on the idea of forming a retro dance band. I think Gavin said that the average age of the musicians was around seventy, but they included people like Gavin's clarinet teacher, who'd played with some of the top bands, and there was a trombonist who'd played on an ocean liner as well.'

'Another age,' said Craig. 'We'll never know them, because they're all dead and gone.' He raised his middle finger in response to an angry horn blast from the driver of the Audi, who now had room to overtake.

'They created a special sound,' said Liz, 'and it's been troubling me that we're not quite there yet with our band.'

'It's early days yet, Liz, and I'm expecting to pick up a few ideas tonight. In any case,' he said, 'I'm confident that our youngsters will deliver the goods. They just need time and guidance.'

'The enthusiasm's there,' she agreed.

They reached Cullington, and Liz directed Craig to Albion Street and the carpark behind the Wool Exchange.

Liz showed the tickets to the official at the door as they entered. For his part, Craig appeared to be fascinated by the marble floor and pillars, and Liz whispered encouragingly, 'It's all very grand, isn't it? Wait 'til we get to the ballroom. You'll love it.'

They left their coats at the cloakroom and took the marble staircase lined with the portraits of past wool magnates, arriving at a scene of warmth, welcome and gaiety as they entered the ballroom.

'It's like coming home,' said Craig, looking at the Art Deco bandstand, curtains and colour scheme.

'Isn't it wonderful?'

'I thought you'd like it, Craig,' said a voice he recognised.

He turned to greet Leah and Gavin. 'Hello,' he said, kissing Leah on the cheek, admiring her Burgundy gown as he did so, and shaking hands with Gavin, 'it's very kind of you both to invite us.'

'We're glad you could join us,' said Gavin. 'Come and meet Frank and Sarah.'

'As usual,' said Frank, when the introductions were complete, 'there's only bar service, but I don't see why that should apply to us. What would you all like to drink?'

It seemed that dry white wine was the favourite, so Frank went to place his order. He returned briefly to say, 'It'll be along in a minute. Meanwhile, I'll have to ask you to excuse me while I get things started.'

'This is the moment I like best,' said Sarah. She was wearing a pearl-grey satin gown that seemed to accentuate her tall, slender figure. 'Ever since the old boys adopted this as their signature tune, it's never failed to thrill me.'

The band were making their way on to the stand. They took their seats, and a moment later Frank walked on to start 'The Sun Has Got his Hat On'. Liz could see the effect it had on Sarah, whose face was like a child's on Christmas morning.

The short signature number reached its end, and Frank turned to address the members and their guests.

'Good evening, ladies and gentlemen. Welcome to the Exchange Club's Christmas Ball. Let's begin with a waltz by that master tunesmith Eric Coates, "By a Sleepy Lagoon".'

'Off you all go,' said Sarah. 'Frank will be down in a minute.'

First, Leah and Gavin, and then Liz and Craig took to the floor. Liz had only danced once with Craig, at the club in Ickringill, but it had felt very natural, as it did now, and she relaxed to the gentle pulse and the rise and fall of the dance. 'Just remember,' she said, 'I can manage the waltz and the foxtrot, but nothing else.'

'I shan't embarrass you,' he promised.

'I know you won't. I'm just conscious of my limitations.'

'We'll take care of it. In any case, you're doing fine.'

'Thanks, but look at Leah. She just flows.'

Craig glanced in Leah's direction and nodded. 'She's good,' he agreed, 'but, as in the words of the song, "I only have eyes for you," and I'd be a poor sort of dance partner if I spent my time admiring someone else. In any case, who could possibly compete for my attention tonight?'

Reluctant to say anything he might regard as encouragement, she simply smiled, and they danced without speaking.

They returned to the table to find two bottles of white Bordeaux and six glasses. Frank was introducing the pianist, who would continue as host for much of the evening.

'You two look very good together,' said Sarah.

'Thank you.' Liz felt reluctant to take any of the credit. 'Craig is the dancer. I only know two dances.'

'I remember my mum teaching you,' said Leah.

'And I remember you teaching me,' said Gavin. 'I still have the bruises.'

'He tells a pathetic story very convincingly,' said Leah. 'Who would believe he idolises me?'

'I daren't do otherwise.'

She laughed and squeezed his hand.

Frank arrived at the table, surprised to find the wine untouched.

'We've been waiting for you,' Sarah told him.

'You know better than that.' He began pouring. 'Liz,' he said, 'it's lovely to see you again, and you've brought another devotee tonight. It's good to meet you, Craig. I gather you're both involved in a new project.'

'The band, yes. I'm hoping to pick up some ideas tonight.'

'Be patient,' advised Sarah. 'It's taken Frank a long time to get the band as far as this.'

'Craig and Liz have youthful energy on their side, darling,' said Frank. 'They'll be there in no time.' On hearing his assistant announce 'Embraceable You', he asked Sarah, 'Are you going to let me embrace you?'

'Go on, then.' She got up and let him lead her on to the floor, followed by the others.

'This one follows us around,' said Liz.

'The best numbers always do.'

'This is heaven. I could do it for evermore.'

'There may be a lyric in there,' said Craig. Then, after a few seconds, he said, 'I've just had an idea.'

'Your first idea, and you're only thirty.'

'Thirty-one, actually. I've been thinking about a signature number. How about 'Dancing Cheek to Cheek'?'

'I'm thinking.'

They danced without speaking, and then he asked, 'Have you thought?'

'Yes, I like it, but what about a last number?'

'After the last waltz, there's only one contender.'

' "Goodnight, Sweetheart"?'

'Two minds in perfect tandem.'

They danced to the end.

When the pianist announced a rhumba, Liz said, 'That lets me out, I'm afraid.'

'Either you or my mum has work to do, Craig,' said Leah. 'You can't let Liz go through life sitting out "Begin the Beguine" and "April in Portugal".'

'Leave it with me, Leah.'

Sarah asked, 'Do you mind if I get Craig up to dance, Liz?'

'Not in the least. I'll watch, learn and inwardly digest.'

When they were alone, Frank asked, 'How are things going, Liz?'

'Work wise? Quite steady. Are you as busy as ever?'

'No, I'm not accepting as much work nowadays. I'm leaving it for you youngsters.'

'It's greatly appreciated, Frank.'

He nodded towards the dance floor and said, 'Craig seems a nice bloke.'

'He is, but I wish Leah would put the brakes on her matchmaking.'

'Are you not sure about him?'

'No, I'm not. I think he's only hesitating because I'm not exactly showing him the green light, but I'm still not convinced about him. Once bitten, you know.'

'There's no sense in rushing into anything. Of course, it was easier with Sarah and me.'

'Was it?'

He grinned. 'We disliked each other passionately at first. It was all down to a misunderstanding, of course. Once that was cleared up, there was no stopping us.'

'I'm glad.'

He opened his mouth to speak, and then hesitated. 'It's not for me or anyone else to tell you how to live your life, Liz, but I would advise you against making one man pay for the sins of another.'

'Thanks, Frank. I'll remember that.'

'Mind you, I can't help being nosey. How did you meet him?'

'We were at the Guildhall together, and then, back in September, he was swimming in the Netherdale pool and he had an attack of cramp.' She shrugged modestly. 'I dived in and, with a bit of help from Leah, pulled him out. That was when I recognised....' She stopped. Frank's head was on one side, and his eyes were closed. 'Frank, are you all right?'

'Yes.' He opened his eyes again. 'I was enjoying a fantasy about being on the point of drowning and being rescued by a bathing belle.'

'Oh Frank,' she laughed, 'you're hopeless.'

'He is,' agreed Sarah. 'What's he being hopeless about now?'

Without Liz realising it, the number had ended and Sarah and Craig had returned.

'He told me a lovely, romantic story about meeting you, Sarah, and how it all developed, and then he said something silly.'

'Well done, Frank,' said Sarah. 'You managed puberty. Have another go at maturity while you're still young enough.'

As the evening continued, there were spot prizes and, inevitably, the band played 'Winter Wonderland' before tempting providence to its limit with 'I'm Dreaming of a White Christmas'.

Eventually, the ball ended, and Liz and Craig thanked Leah and Gavin for inviting them, and Sarah and Frank for making the occasion what it was.

On the way out, Craig offered his arm to Liz, who accepted it, still wondering when he would exhibit some anti-social tendency that would justify her reservation.

On the way home, they shared their impressions of the band, which were naturally favourable.

'There's something about the reed and brass sections,' said Craig. 'I think I put my finger on it tonight, but I need to think more about it before I approach the band with it.'

'What is it?'

'If you don't mind, Liz, I'd like to go on thinking about it at this stage. If I discuss it, it might easily distract me from the idea I've formed so far.'

'Okay.' She was happy to go along with his objection.

He pulled up outside Liz's cottage.

'If you don't mind,' she said, 'I won't invite you in. It's very late, but thank you for a lovely evening.'

'Not at all. I should be thanking you. Anyway, I'll see you to your door.'

'There's no need, Craig.'

'Yes, there is. I'll see you to your door, and when you're safe inside, I'll be on my way.'

'All right.'

He let her out of the car and walked her to the door of her cottage.

'Thank you,' she said. 'Christmas Day, then? Token presents only, remember.'

'Christmas Day.' He bent to kiss her cheek. 'Thank you for a wonderful evening.'

18

CHRISTMAS DAY

There was one unpleasant job that could not be avoided, so Liz decided to deal with it as soon as she could. She dialled Simon's number, forcing herself to radiate peace and goodwill.

'Hello?'

'Happy Christmas, Hannah.'

'Oh, yeah. Merry Christmas.' The greeting was devoid of enthusiasm.

'Carla would like to speak to Simon if that's at all possible.'

As usual, Hannah made no attempt to cover the mouthpiece. 'Simon,' she said, 'Little Miss Perfect wants to talk to you.'

Before Liz could put her hand over the earpiece, she heard her ex-husband say, 'Fucking hell! What a time to choose.' It was even more unfortunate that Carla had heard them both. Liz waited until Simon came on the line and handed the phone to Carla, whose dismay was evident.

Less than a minute later, she joined Liz with tears in her eyes. Hardly trusting herself to speak, Liz knelt down and hugged her.

'They were having a row,' said Carla eventually, 'and the Christmas lights on the tree had stopped working.'

'We caught them at a bad time,' said Liz.

'He didn't give me a present this Christmas.'

'He gave me some money towards your things.' It was a lie, but somehow, the innocent had to defend the guilty. 'Put it behind you, darling, and let's enjoy the rest of the day.' She hoped she wasn't asking too much from a hurt and disappointed child.

◆◈◆

An hour later, Craig sat on the sofa with Liz at the other end and with Carla between them.

Carla asked, 'What did you get for Christmas, Craig?'

'Lots of things, but there's one thing missing. Do you know what would be the best present of all?'

'No.'

'It would be to see a smile on your face. Go on, give it a try. See if you can squeeze out a smile.'

She tried, and the effort was evident, even if the smile lacked substance.

Craig asked, 'Is a hug in order, Mum?'

'I think so.'

He held out his arms and wrapped them around Carla. 'You poor child,' he said, kissing her cheek, 'I don't know what's happened, but it had no business happening to you today.' After a moment, he said, 'Let's see if we can do a magic trick. Let's think about something really nice. Think hard and really enjoy it, and then, when I let go of you, let's see the big smile it's put on your face. Are you ready?'

She nodded, so he began releasing her slowly. 'I need to be ready for this,' he said. 'I'm going to give you ten seconds before I look. Ten, nine, eight....' He completed the count down and sat back to look at her. She was tearful but smiling. 'That's my girl,' he said, 'and because of that, Christmas is now complete.'

Liz got up. 'I have things to do in the kitchen,' she said.

'Let me help.'

'There's no need.'

'Call it a bonus.' He followed her into the kitchen.

'Craig,' she said, turning to face him and blinking tears away, 'thank you for coming today.'

'What is it? Everywhere I look, I see tears.' He held out his arms to her, drawing her towards him, and she buried her face against his shoulder. Carla appeared in the doorway, looking up at them both in surprise. 'It's Christmas Day, Carla,' he said. 'Everyone gets a hug.' He held out one hand and beckoned to her to complete the threesome.

After a minute or so, Liz turned to say, 'Tidy your things up before we have lunch, Carla. You can play afterwards.' When Carla was gone, she said, 'We phoned Carla's dad this morning. He was in the middle

126

of a row with his horrible partner and he could hardly spare the time to speak to Carla. It was awful.'

'Well,' he said, 'Christmas is what you make of it, so let's make it a good one from now on. What needs to be done in here?'

'Nothing yet. I didn't want you to see that I was upset.'

'If you don't let people know you're upset, you can't expect them to help you, can you?'

'I suppose you're right,' she said, smiling.

'There, you're both smiling now. No problem.'

———— ◆◀ ————

'More Christmas pudding, anyone?'

Craig gave a theatrical groan. 'I couldn't eat another crumb,' he said, 'wonderful though it was.'

'It was from the supermarket.'

'But it was served with lashings of goodwill, wasn't it, Carla?'

'Mm.' Whether or not Carla understood him, she was happy to agree with him.

'I have to say,' he announced, 'that this is the best Christmas I've ever known.'

'Me too,' said Carla.

'As Christmases go,' said Liz, 'this one will take some beating.'

'It's done me a power of good. If you hadn't invited me, I'd have spent the day practising, and with just a bacon sandwich to keep my strength up.'

Liz asked, 'What are you practising for now?'

'A recital in London, at St Barnabas, Whitechapel.'

'When?'

He had to think about it. 'The twentieth of January.'

'I'm in London on the nineteenth and twentieth.'

'Copycat.' He looked at Carla for agreement, but she just giggled.

'Will you sell me a ticket?'

'No, but I'll give you one.'

'You're too kind. What are you playing?'

'Scarlatti, Beethoven, Chopin, Liszt and Granados.'

'Oh.' Liz made no attempt to disguise her excitement. 'What are you playing by Granados?'

'One of the *Goyescas*, "The Maiden and the Nightingale".'

'Leah likes "Love Duet" for personal reasons, but "The Maiden and the Nightingale" is my favourite.'

'In that case, you shall certainly have a complimentary ticket.'

Carla said, 'I wish I could hear you play.'

'Seeing as it's you,' said Craig, taking her small hand between his, 'as soon as we've finished the washing-up I'll play the Granados for you. How's that?'

'Yes!'

'We have a machine to do the dishes,' said Liz.

'Ah, but the pots and pans won't scour themselves.'

'Nobody *scours* pots and pans nowadays. I just wash them.'

'So let's wash them, and then I'll play the piano for Carla. You too, if you want to listen.'

Liz sighed happily. 'What a topsy-turvy Christmas Day this turned out to be.'

Ten minutes later, they gathered in Liz's studio.

'This is about a conversation between a girl and a nightingale, Craig explained. The girl doesn't understand dicky-bird, and the nightingale only knows a few words of Spanish and is absolutely hopeless at verbs, nouns and cases, so it gets a bit hectic at times.' He sat at the piano. Liz closed her eyes and, after the dramas of the day, let the music drift over her. It began its story tentatively, introducing the theme that would return repeatedly in various guises, ecstatic and then plaintive until it became a towering sequence of rich, romantic harmonies and crashing chords. Eventually, it returned to the opening theme, which gave way in turn to an evocation of nightingale song, bringing the piece to its soft and peaceful end.

Liz dabbed at her eyes with a tissue and blew her nose. 'Thank you, Craig. That was beautiful, but I still want to hear it again in London.'

Carla also wanted more. She asked, 'Will you play the bee-thing again, Craig?'

'How can I refuse?' Once again, for Carla's entertainment and to her undiminished delight, he played the Rachmaninov transcription.

'That was wonderful.'

'I'm glad you enjoyed it, Carla. That's what it's for.' As she stood beside him, he put his arm around her because it seemed perfectly natural.

'Thank you, Craig,' said Liz.

'The pleasure was mine, and speaking of which....'

'Yes?'

'I've made a CD for Leah's mother from the recordings I made of the band, and I'd like to meet her if possible. She sounds like a lovely old girl.'

'She is, and I think that's an excellent idea.'

Carla asked, 'Can I come?'

'Yes, darling, I think you should.' The poor child had been left out of too many things lately.

When Craig had gone, Liz and Carla sat together on the sofa.

'Mum,' asked Carla, 'what are we going to do when we go to see Leah's mum?'

'That's a good question. Craig will give her the CD he's burned, and she'll want to know all about the band.' She thought a timely word of warning was in order. 'Don't be surprised if she's a bit emotional. Her husband died only a short while ago.'

'What did he die of?'

'He was ninety-two, darling. Nature didn't need an excuse.'

Carla nodded in her old-fashioned way and asked, 'What was he like?'

'He was a lovely man, full of fun and very clever. He had a band, and he used to write musicals and pantomimes.'

'Leah's mum must miss him.'

'She does. He was, as I said, rather special.'

Carla remained thoughtful for a spell, and then she said, 'Mum?'

'I'm still here, darling.'

'When Craig was playing the piece about the bird singing to the lady, why were you crying?'

'Because the music was so beautiful.'

'Was that all?'

'No, there was something else as well.' She got up to put another log on the fire.

'Is it a secret?'

'No, it's not a secret. You see, before Craig arrived, you and I were feeling sad, weren't we?'

'Mm.'

'And then he made us both happy.'

'It's the best Christmas ever,' said Carla.

'It is,' agreed Liz. 'We must see if we can bring a touch of it to Sylvia when we visit her.'

19

Liz kissed Sylvia on the cheek. 'Happy Christmas, Sylvia. This is Craig Townsend.'

'How kind of you to come, Mr Townsend.'

' "Craig", please, Mrs Hinchcliffe.'

'In that case, I'm Sylvia.'

'I don't think you know my daughter Carla, Sylvia. She's very keen to meet you.'

'Carla, what a lovely name, and it's quite right for a lovely girl like you. You know, you're the image of your mum.'

Carla smiled self-consciously, prompting Liz to say, 'She's rather sensitive about being blonde. She comes in for a lot of leg-pulling at school.'

'Oh, what a shame.' Suddenly conscious of her duty as a hostess, she said, 'Come in, all of you, and I'll put the kettle on. I don't know what I've got for you, Carla. Do you like orange juice?'

'Mm. Yes, please.'

'I'll get you some of that, then.'

Liz asked, 'Can I do anything?'

'No, thank you, dear. I can manage.'

Carla was fascinated by the photographs that lined the room. Some were of wildlife, others of horses and pets of various kinds, but the theme that dominated the collection was clearly the Aberdeen terrier. She asked, 'Are all these pictures of the same Scottie?'

'I don't think so,' Liz told her. 'As far as I know, Sylvia and Freddy had several of them at various times.'

'This one's playing with plant pots.'

'So she is. I remember Leah telling me about her.'

'They took a lot of photos.'

'Freddy did. He was a photographer, and he specialised in animal pictures.'

Carla's attention had wandered to the wedding photograph in the bookcase. She asked, 'What was he doing in that uniform?'

'He was in the Navy during the Second World War. He was a naval airman, and he was taken prisoner by the Germans and held in a prison camp in Poland. Sylvia and he wrote letters to each other and she sent him parcels.'

'What was in them?'

'I don't know. Clothes, I suppose, and maybe food of some kind.'

'No, not food. It wasn't allowed.' The voice came from the doorway.

'Carla was looking at your wedding photo, Sylvia.'

'In that case, let me get it out for you.' Sylvia knelt and opened the bookcase. 'He was a petty officer airman,' she told Carla, 'a telegraphist-air-gunner, and he used it as an excuse for everything. If he did something silly or odd, he used to say, "It comes of being an air-gunner, stuck in the after cockpit with no one to talk to, and always facing aft." That's backwards,' she translated. 'He knew that I knew it was a load of nonsense, but he used to tease me with it.' She handed a tumbler of orange juice to Carla just as the kettle began whistling in the kitchen.

'Thank you.'

'You're very welcome, darling. Just let me scald the tea.'

'I'll come and carry it in for you,' said Craig.

Carla was still studying the photograph. 'He looked very happy,' she said.

'It was their wedding day, so he would.'

Carla looked closer and said, 'That's the church in Leyburn.'

'Well spotted, darling. I wouldn't have noticed that.' Carla's remark about Freddy looking happy had set her thinking. 'Just imagine, Carla. He'd come home from Poland, free again, and he knew Sylvia was waiting for him. No wonder he was happy.'

'But I wasn't waiting for him in Leyburn,' said Sylvia as she followed Craig into the sitting room. 'I was still serving in Malta with the Wrens.'

'What wrens?'

'Not the little birds, darling. The Wrens were the Women's Royal Naval Service. I served from nineteen forty-one until nineteen forty-five.' She took another picture from the bookcase to show her. 'I was seventeen when that was taken.'

'You were very pretty.'

'And you're very kind.'

Still fascinated, Carla asked, 'What did you do?'

'I was a telegraphist. I suppose nowadays I'd be called a radio operator, if they still have such people in this technical age.' A memory made her smile for a moment. 'If I was cross or being strict about something, Freddy used to call me "Leading Wren Charlesworth" and tell me I terrified him. He was just being silly, of course.' She shook her head at her own folly and said, 'Don't let me go on and on about Freddy. It must be very boring for you.'

Surprisingly, Carla was the first to disagree. 'No, it isn't,' she said. 'He sounds lovely.'

'He was, darling.'

As much as a distraction than anything else, Liz asked, 'Shall I pour the tea?'

'Yes, please, dear. That's very kind of you.'

Taking advantage of the lull in the conversation, Craig said, 'I've brought you a CD I recorded of the new band. They're very new and very young, but I think you'll find that they show promise.'

'How very kind. Thank you, Craig.'

'Perhaps we should test it to make sure it works in your CD player.'

'Yes, it's on the shelf behind you. I'll leave you to do it.'

'Of course.' He switched the player on and inserted the disc. Suddenly, the room was filled with Matthew singing 'The Very Thought of You', and Sylvia turned to listen. When it ended, Craig stopped the CD. 'I think that's all right,' he said.'

'And was that one of your students?'

'The singer, yes. He's called Matthew.'

'How old is he?'

'Let me see.' Craig thought. 'He's in the third year, so he's twenty or twenty-one.'

'And he's singing the music of....' She struggled to make the necessary calculation.

'Ninety years ago,' prompted Craig. 'That's the best part about it. The music lives on through yet another generation.'

'How wonderful. I'll enjoy listening to that, Craig.'

'Craig's going to teach me the quickstep and the rhumba,' said Liz.

'Oh, good. You'll find she's a rewarding pupil, Craig.'

'I imagine so. She dances the foxtrot and the waltz very well.'

'I had a good teacher,' said Liz patting Sylvia's hand.

Suddenly remembering, Sylvia said, 'You must be the young man Liz rescued from drowning, Craig.'

'I have that distinction.'

'I'm glad she rescued you.'

'So am I, and I was particularly glad at the time, as you can imagine.'

'It could have happened to anyone,' said Liz, conscious of his thinly-concealed discomfiture. 'Cramp chooses its victims completely at random.'

'My mum's a brilliant swimmer,' said Carla.

'I'm sorry, darling.' Sylvia turned her head. 'I'm afraid you're on my deaf side.'

'I said that my mum's a brilliant swimmer.'

'It's just as well, dear.' Turning to the others, she said, 'Swimming caused my deafness, you know.'

Liz had heard the story several times, but Craig said, 'Really?'

'Yes, I was swimming in St Paul's Bay in Malta. It was on VE Day, and a tiny creature swam into my ear and infected it. The infection perforated the eardrum.'

Carla was instantly sympathetic. 'It must have been awful,' she said.

'It was certainly painful, but it got me discharged from the service, and I was able to go home and meet Freddy for the first time. He called it my "Blighty wound".'

'The *first* time?' Once again, Sylvia had Carla's rapt attention.

'Yes, we'd exchanged letters for two years, but we had yet to meet.'

Liz sat back while Sylvia told Carla the story she'd told so many times, but Carla wasn't the only spellbound listener. Craig leaned forward in his chair, careful not to miss one word.

As they drove home, Craig said, 'You'd described Sylvia to me, but I had no idea just what a lovely person she is.'

Liz nodded. 'I love her to bits. I was very fond of Freddy as well.'

'Mum,' asked Carla, 'will you measure me when we get home?'

'I think that might be arranged. Do you think you've grown much since September?'

'Yes.' She was almost indignant. 'My jeans don't reach my trainers now.'

'A sure sign,' said Liz.

Presently, they entered Eskgarth, and Liz turned into Hardacre Lane.

Liz asked, 'Are you going to come in and watch the measuring ritual, Craig?'

'I wouldn't miss it for anything. It could turn out to be a defining moment.'

Liz parked the car in the drive. 'Okay, to the measuring wall, we go.' She locked the car and led the way into the cottage. 'We approach this ceremony with due reverence,' she said, taking Carla to the graduated line on the wall. 'Now, we're hoping for a hundred and thirty-five centimetres.' She placed her hand on Carla's head and asked, 'What do you think, Craig? Could I get away with letting her ride like a grown-up?'

'No one's going to stop you to quibble about a fraction of a centimetre.'

'No, they're not. Carla, you're so close to the mark, I'm going to stretch a point and put your child seat on eBay, Gumtree, or some such thing. I'll need the money from the sale to pay for your new clothes now you've grown out of your old things.'

'Yes!'

'I'll get the child seat out for you,' said Craig.

'Thanks, Craig, but I've done it so many times, it's second nature. You can come and watch the grand taking-out ceremony, if you like.'

'Oh, I like.'

Once again, Liz led the way and unlocked the car. 'It's quite a relief, getting rid of the thing,' she said. 'It's not easy to fiddle with when you've only got three doors.' She opened the passenger door and leaned into the car to unfasten the anchors that held the seat in place. She'd just released one, when she felt a kind of rippling in her lower back and then she was seized with pain. 'Oh, hell!'

'What is it, Liz?'

'I've done myself a mischief.'

'Come out and let me do it.'

'That was my fault for being clever about it.' She eased her way out of the car and leaned against it as she made the last few painful degrees to became upright.

'What's the matter, Mum?'

'I've pulled a muscle in my back. Don't worry, darling, it's not catching.' She stood, helpless, while Craig unhitched the child seat and lifted it out.

'Come inside, Liz,' said Craig. 'You can walk, can't you?'

'Painfully, but yes.'

He carried the seat into the house and put it down, clearly anxious about Liz's back. 'Where does it hurt?'

'A few... inches below my... waistband.' She reached slowly and touched the place with her fingers.

'That's your *gluteus maximus*,' he told her. 'No wonder it hurts. It's a big muscle, but I can relieve it for you.'

'Can you?'

'My student past, remember? Manual massage at the sports club?'

'Of course. If you think you can make it less painful, you're welcome to try.'

'Okay. Have you any massage medium? Baby oil or anything like that?'

'I've no baby oil, but there's some suntan oil.'

'That'll do the job. All you need to do is go upstairs, find the suntan oil, loosen your jeans, lift your shirt out of the way, and lie on a towel on your bed. I'll come up when you're ready.' Turning to Carla, he said, 'As for you, Lofty, stay down here and take it easy. Your mum's going to be fine.'

They waited until they heard Liz shout, 'Ready,' and Craig went upstairs. 'Where are you?'

'In the big bedroom. I've put out a hand towel for you.'

'Thank you. Are your jeans undone at the waist?'

'Yes.'

'Well done. You'll probably have to wash them after this.'

'That's a small price to pay.'

'I'll have to move your clothes out of the way so that I can work on the place that's painful.'

'Go ahead. When I hurt like this, coyness is a luxury.'

She felt him ease her jeans and pants down past the affected area, and then she felt the heel of one hand and then the other press down on the contracted muscle. His touch was warm and positive, and she was conscious at once that she was in strong and capable hands.

He continued to work on her in the same way until, after a while, the worst of the pain seemed to have dispersed, and she had to admit to herself that she was actually enjoying the massage. The warmth of his hands was soothing and comforting as well as going to the core of the problem. Using mainly the heels of his hands, he was applying pressure to the contraction without causing pain or discomfort; in fact, she was gradually becoming conscious of a different kind of sensation. Deep in her lower abdomen, she felt an insistent ache that she'd not known for a long time. She tried to breathe naturally, as if she were unaffected by his attentions, but the movement of his hands was triggering responses that mocked self-restraint. She hoped it wasn't obvious to him, because she could do without that kind of embarrassment. The sensation was exquisite, but she wanted him to stop before…. She just wanted him to *stop*.

Then, he withdrew his hands and said, 'I think you'll find that easier now. I'm going to wash my hands. I'll see you downstairs.'

Downstairs. Carla was downstairs. Thank goodness… but nothing had happened…. Nothing could happen. She eased herself off the bed, fastened her jeans and turned down the hem of her top, still waiting for her startled senses to return to their previous, dormant state.

—————

Leah phoned after Carla had gone to bed.

'Thanks for going to see my mum,' she said. 'She loves to see you, and she thought Craig was wonderful.'

'It's never any trouble, but you'll never guess what happened after we arrived home.'

'Probably not. Throw me a clue.'

'Okay. To cut a long story short, Carla's tall enough not to need the child seat any longer.'

'Oh, good.'

'Well, I was unfastening it to take it out, when I realised I'd pulled a muscle in my back.'

'Oh, no.'

'In my *gluteus maximus*, a very big muscle, apparently. I owe that information to Craig, who was there at the time, quite conveniently, as it turned out.'

'Did he put his strong arm round you and help you indoors, or just go on talking dirty in Latin ?' There was growing excitement in her tone.

'You should write for Mills and Boon, Leah.'

'Only the naughty series. There would have to be some action in it for me.'

Liz sighed. 'Anyway, he asked me where it hurt – it was a few inches below my waistband – and he said he could ease the pain for me. I remembered him saying he'd worked as a masseur when he was at the Guildhall.'

'What?'

'A genuine one, Leah. Now, do have a stab at grown-up listening. It's not so hard.'

'I'll try.'

'Okay, I had to loosen my jeans and lie on a towel.'

'What then?'

'He put sun tan oil on his hands and started working on me.'

'Below your waistband?'

'Naturally. That's where the pain was, although there was nothing untoward about what he was doing. He pulled my jeans and pants down four ot five inches – at least, it seemed no more than that – and worked on the bit that hurt. That was fine, but after a while....'

'Go on.' Leah sounded breathless.

'I was well and truly aroused. What I was feeling and thinking at the time was.... I hadn't felt like that for a long time. His hands were kneading my behind and ironing out the seized muscle, but the effect was going straight to my naughty bits, and I was gritting my teeth to keep myself from making the noises men find so encouraging.'

'And you kept your hands off him?'

'Be realistic, Leah. Carla was downstairs.'

'Yes, children can be an effective contraceptive. So, was that as far as it went?'

'Absolutely. When he'd finished, he went to wash his hands while I fastened my jeans.'

'After all that, how's your back?'

'A hell of a lot better. He knew what he was doing.'

Leah was quiet, a sure sign that she was thinking. 'Do you think he knew how it was affecting you?'

'He must have known. There are some things you can't hide.'

'Has he ever given you the impression he was interested in you in that way?'

'Yes, he has, now I think about it, but the trouble is, I've been trying not to encourage him.'

'Until this afternoon.'

'Yes, it has rather changed my attitude, that and... other things.'

'What other things?'

Liz gave the sigh of a woman whose resistance was exhausted. 'He's just a lovely fella.' There was no need to go into detail.

'When will you see him again?'

'On the eighth, at band rehearsal, the same on the fifteenth, and then we'll be in London at the same time on the twentieth, when he has a piano recital. I said I'd go to that, and it made sense to book accommodation at the same hotel. Incidentally, could you and Gavin have Carla?'

'While you're in London? Of course we will.' Leah seemed to

be having another of her thinks, because she said, 'You mustn't let yourself be caught out.'

'It's not likely.'

'I'm talking about....'

'I know.' There were times when Leah treated her as if she were naïve.

With that matter dealt with, Leah asked, 'What's he going to play?'

'Scarlatti, Beethoven, Chopin, Liszt and Granados.'

'What's he playing by Granados? One of the *Goyescas*?'

'Not the one that starts your motor. He's going to play "The Maiden and the Nightingale".'

'Ah.' She sounded disappointed.

'I love it.'

'Maybe it'll do for you what "Love Duet" does for me. You never know.'

20

LONDON

The two sonatas by Scarlatti were an excellent way to start a recital. Originally written for harpsichord, they were lively and entertaining. By contrast, the Beethoven sonata was a full-length work with many facets. Beethoven had dedicated it to Count Ferdinand von Waldstein, and Craig hoped that Waldstein appreciated the gesture, because it was a fine sonata. It was also popular, it seemed, with the audience at St Barnabas in Whitechapel, who applauded enthusiastically.

Craig returned to the piano to begin Chopin's *Ballade in F minor*. He'd seen Liz in the audience and caught her eye. He had a surprise for her later in the programme, but for the present, he was enjoying the *Ballade*, which had long been one of his favourites, with its wistful, yearning phrases, its colossal build-up and towering climax.

Liszt's *Rigoletto Paraphrase* was equally popular with the audience. It was little more than a transcription of the celebrated quartet from Verdi's opera of the same name, but the effect was always dramatic, which was why Craig had kept it in his repertoire for so long.

He knew that his final piece would find favour with Liz, at least. It was 'The Maiden and the Nightingale' by Granados, and he approached it with his usual, intense concentration; in fact, he was so detached from his surroundings that the applause at the end took him quite by surprise, and he realised that there had been a moment's silence between the final note and the start of the applause, a sure sign that the audience had enjoyed an unusually intense experience.

He waited for the clapping to die down, finally consulting his pocket watch. 'Ladies and gentlemen,' he said, 'you're very kind. Thank you all very much. There's time for one more piece. It's a short, seamless set of variations on a sometime popular song. Modesty prevents me from saying too much about the composer, except to offer the excuse that I was very young when I wrote it. What I will say, however, is that this is for Liz, who is here tonight.'

He played his variations on 'The Man on the Flying Trapeze', hoping the audience, as well as Liz, were enjoying it. He had no way of knowing until their applause told its own story, continuing until he agreed to another encore, which was Liszt's *Valse Oubliée Number One*. He'd chosen it deliberately to induce calm after the excitement.

Eventually, he was free to return to his dressing room, satisfied that he'd done a good job in entertaining his audience.

He was drying his face with a towel when he heard a knock on the door. Somewhat preoccupied with his drenched state, he called, 'Come in if you can swim.'

The door opened, and Liz said, 'You, of all people, should know I can swim.'

'Hello, Liz. Thank you for coming. You'll have to excuse me if I don't get too close.'

'I just wanted to tell you how much I enjoyed the recital, and to thank you for "The Man on the Flying Trapeze". I was the Liz you mentioned, wasn't I?'

'I don't know any others, and I'm glad you enjoyed it.'

'It was wonderful. Rachmaninov himself would have been envious.'

'He might just have been flattered that I wrote it in his style.' Politeness, as well as modesty, prompted him to change the subject and ask, 'How was the session?'

'Uneventful, so okay.'

'Look, instead of chatting here, shall we share a taxi to the hotel, and then I'll have a quick shower and change, and I'll see you in the bar.'

———◆◆———

Twenty-five minutes later, Craig stood beneath the shower, rediscovering the meaning of bliss, after which he dried himself hurriedly and changed into something infinitely less formal. Eventually, he made his way down to the cocktail bar, where he found Liz.

'Before you collapse, Craig, tell me what you want to drink.'

'That's kind of you,' he said. 'I'd like a gin and slimline tonic with ice and lime, please.'

He took a seat gratefully in the armchair adjacent to hers while she went to the bar. At that distance, he was able to admire her dress, which was a deeper blue than the one he'd seen her in at his lunch-hour recital. Maybe it was her going-to-evening-recitals number.

She returned with their drinks.

'Thank you, Liz. I was just admiring your dress.'

'Thank you. It's my going-to-fairly-formal-functions number.'

'I was close, then.'

'What?'

'Nothing. Tell me about the session.'

'It was very straightforward. It was for a TV series about lust and betrayal in the Cotswolds.'

He sighed. 'Some people get it all, don't they?'

'It should be worth seeing. They're screening it this autumn.'

'I don't know,' he said, shaking his head. 'It doesn't pay to get too excited.'

'You played some very exciting music tonight.'

'Yes, and look at what it's done to me.'

She laughed. 'The *Ballade*'s a real tour de force, isn't it? I remember practising it as a student, but it never sounded like it did tonight.'

'It's kind of you to say so.' A moment later, he asked, 'How's Carla?'

'She's happy enough, staying with Leah and Gavin. She'll get sausages and mash, because Gavin's as keen on it as she is.'

He smiled. 'It'll go some way to making up for her disappointment at Christmas.'

'Oh, you needn't worry about that, Craig. It's now gone down in Carla's memory as the best Christmas ever.'

'Did he get his act together?'

'No, and I don't suppose he ever will.'

'What happened, then?'

She laughed again. 'You've really no idea, have you?'

'Have I missed something?'

'No, you were there all the time.' She reached across the arm of her chair to pat his hand. 'Having you there made all the difference. You turned misery into happiness.'

'I'm glad I was able to cheer her up.'

'You cheered me up as well.'

'Did I really? Well, that was a good day's work.' He turned his hand palm-up to accept hers. 'It doesn't take a lot of effort to make people happy as long as they're prepared to go along with it,' he said, stroking the back of her hand with his thumb. 'Some people are determined to be miserable, and there's no helping them.' As if realising it for the first time, he said, 'All of a sudden, we're holding hands. You don't mind, do you?'

'Not in the least.'

'Good, because I'm rather fond of yours. Very fond, in fact. This must be the hand I felt under my chin when I was drowning.'

'It was the other hand, actually. The one you have there was doing the hard work, the sidestroke.'

'I'm indebted to both of them, but most of all, to you.'

She produced her other hand to sandwich his. 'Cast your mind back to Boxing Day at Sylvia's, when she asked if you were the man I rescued in the pool.'

'I remember her asking that.'

'She said she was glad I'd rescued you, and so am I. You're a lovely fella, Craig, and I'm glad you're still with us and not a tragic story in the *Netherdale Reporter*.'

'It's good of you to say so, Liz.'

''Tis but the truth. Are we going to have another drink?'

'I think we should. It seems to have an emboldening effect on me.'

'Is that what's doing it? Well, I shan't argue.'

'Same again?'

'Yes, please. Gin and slimline tonic.'

Craig went to the bar for the drinks, scarcely able to believe his good fortune. When he returned, he poured some tonic into each glass and took her hand again. 'I'm really glad you came tonight,' he said. 'They were an excellent audience, but you made all the difference.'

She smiled. 'It's all tumbling out now, isn't it? You've been very buttoned up until this evening.'

He lifted her hand and kissed it lightly. 'I wasn't sure where I stood,' he said.

'You were unsure of me, and that was my fault.'

He took a generous sip of his gin-and-tonic and said, 'Let's not talk about fault.'

'Good thinking. We shouldn't cloud the atmosphere with negativity.'

'Negative thoughts or not,' he said, looking round the bar, 'we seem to have cleared the place.'

'They can hardly blame us for that. Shall we leave them and ease their embarrassment?'

'We probably should.' They took their drinks and the lift to the first floor. Liz said conversationally, 'I'm in room one-oh-five.'

'I'm in one-oh-nine.'

The lift stopped at the first floor and they got out.

'As you're a gentleman, I'm sure you'll escort me to my room,' said Liz.

'Only a cad would leave you to make the journey alone.'

When they reached one-oh-five, Liz unlocked the door and beckoned him inside. 'Come into my parlour,' she murmured, dimming the lights.

Placing his glass on the nearest available surface, he drew her towards him and kissed her softly, conscious of her perfume and the reaction of her lips against his. Closing the door with his free hand, he said, 'I've wanted to do this for a long time.'

'You can do it for as long as you like, now.'

They kissed at some length before he said awkwardly, 'There's a machine in the gents'….'

'It's all taken care of,' she assured him. 'Will you unfasten me?' She turned for him to undo the hook and eye and the zip fastener of her dress, and then pulled it over her head so that she stood before him in nothing but a bra, seamless knickers and, as far as he could make out without staring, hold-up stockings.

'Oh, Liz,' he breathed, still trying not to stare.

'Were you expecting tights? They're practical all right, but not what you'd call inspiring.'

'Passion killers,' he agreed, kissing her again, partly to cover his embarrassment at being found out.

'Your turn to disrobe,' she prompted.

145

He undressed quickly. Fully-dressed or naked, he was happy, but he felt ridiculous half-clothed. Meanwhile, Liz peeled off her stockings, hanging them over a chair. Then, unbidden, she put her arms round him and kissed him eagerly.

When he'd recovered from the surprise, he took the opportunity to fumble with the fastening of her bra, finally unhooking it to reveal her fine breasts. He draped her bra over the chair with her stockings, and they stood together in nothing but their nether garments.

'Ready,' she said with her thumbs poised inside the elastic, 'steady... go!'

They performed the release simultaneously.

'Oh, Liz.' His surprise came out in an ecstatic whisper.

'Swimming as much as I do,' she explained, 'I find it easier to remove it all. It's much more convenient than topiary.'

He held out his arms, and she joined him in a prolonged and searching kiss. When they finally broke apart, she said, 'I don't know why we're still upright.'

He looked down self-consciously.

'Oh, I know why that's upright. Anyway, let's get horizontal.' She added, 'All three of us.'

They sank into the king-size bed, where Craig experienced again the joy of holding her soft, naked body against his, kissing her blissfully and repeatedly on the lips. After a while, he moved downward to extend the same favour to her breasts.

'Okay?' She sounded breathless.

'Oh, much more than okay.' His hand stroked her smooth, soft body.

Meanwhile, she was carrying out her own exploration, an operation that, given frequent distractions, demanded persistence and concentration. Finally, she capitulated, kissing him ardently and whispering an urgent request in his ear.

Obliging as always, he made room for her and was subsequently rewarded with a welcoming gasp.

———◆◆———

They lay together, he in uneasy reflection and only able to guess at her thoughts. 'I'm sorry it turned out to be a quickie,' he said.

'I'm not complaining. As first times go, it was very respectable,' she assured him, kissing him as if to confirm her assessment, 'and you'd already given a colossal performance of another kind when you were fully clothed. It was a lot to ask of yourself.'

'You're very kind.'

'If you think that's being kind, you must have had quite a past.' After some thought, she said, 'I can't believe that we were aware of each other at the Guildhall, but never got acquainted.' She raised herself on one elbow to ask, 'Why do you think that was?'

'When I saw you with Jimbo, I reckoned you were out of my league.'

She gave him a weary look. 'I showed Jimbo to the exit after less than three weeks,' she told him. 'Anyway, if you thought he was impressive, it was only because that was the image he'd created. He was full of himself in those days, but he had a lot of growing up to do, and if our last meeting was any indication, he still has some way to go.'

'I'm glad, even though I've always liked him.' He rolled on to his side to look at her and to remind himself that he hadn't imagined the past hour.

'No one can help liking Jimbo. It's just a mistake to take him too seriously.' She was thoughtful for a spell, and then she said, 'I'm sorry I kept you at arm's length. I mean over the past few months. Being married to a total bastard made me ultra-wary of men, but it was wrong of me to tar everyone with the same brush.'

'That wasn't your fault,' he protested.

'It was my fault that I was daft enough to marry him in the first place, and that I let it become an obsession.'

'As I see it, you're hurting for two, and no one can blame you for that.' He leaned forward to kiss her.

When she was able to speak, she asked, 'Do I detect the stirrings of re-awakening below?'

'I think that's what he's trying to tell you.'

'And he's doing it rather well,' she said, manoeuvring herself until she knelt above him. 'You're both very persuasive, each in your own way.'

21

Liz found Carla happy as ever after her stay with Leah and Gavin.
'How did it go, Mum?'

'All straightforward, no hitches and in the can within the time allowed, and thank you for asking, darling.' It was unusual for Carla to take so much interest in a recording session.

'I meant Craig's recital.'

'Of course. We must get our priorities right. It was excellent....' She hesitated. 'No,' she corrected herself, 'it was more than excellent, if that's possible.'

'The last time I heard Craig play,' said Gavin generously, 'he was brilliant.'

'Yes, "brilliant" just about describes it.' Liz was trying to avoid meeting Leah's eye. 'Yes, it was a brilliant performance. I really don't know why he's not doing it full-time.'

'I can tell you why,' said Gavin. 'It's because there are too many of us for the work available.'

Carla was impatient to know more. She asked, 'Did he play the bee piece?'

'No, he played something he'd written, that you haven't heard, and another piece, a waltz, by Liszt.'

Gavin asked, 'What was the piece he'd written?'

'A set of variations in the style of Rachmaninov on "The Man on the Flying Trapeze".'

'I'd like to hear that,' he said. 'You said your session went well?'

'Oh, I'm glad I haven't been completely forgotten. It went very smoothly, thank you, Gavin.' In an effort to turn the conversation away from the events in London, she asked, 'And what have you been up to, Carla?'

'We went shopping in Ilkley. We went to Betty's, and then Leah bought me some pyjamas and slippers and a new dressing gown.'

'Oh, Leah,' protested Liz, 'I didn't want you to spend money on her.'

'They were an unmissable bargain.'

'I'll believe you. Anyway, thank you. It was lovely of you to do that.'

Leah made no response, but said, 'Let's get Carla's things together, shall we? No, Carla, you needn't come.' She led the way upstairs, ignoring Gavin, who was shaking his head at his wife's fixation.

When they'd reached the landing and were safely out of earshot, Leah asked, 'Well?'

A little embarrassed, Liz nodded her head.

'You actually…?'

'Yes, we actually,' confirmed Liz.

'Good?'

She wondered how best to answer her friend's prurient cross-examination. Finally, she said, 'It would have been a shame to follow a brilliant recital with anything less… and we certainly didn't.'

'Fantastic!'

Liz could only smile at the pleasure her weekend development had given to Leah.

When they took Carla's bag downstairs, Leah gave the double thumbs-up to Gavin, who shook his head again at the ways of women and those of his wife in particular.

After thanking Gavin and Leah for their hospitality, Liz and Carla went out to the car.

'Snow's threatening again,' remarked Liz.

'But now we've got a car that'll go through it.'

'It should cope, as long as we don't get a huge fall.'

'Mum,' said Carla after a while, 'why did Leah hold her thumbs up when you both came downstairs?'

'Ah, well, there's something I have to tell you. Do you remember asking me if I was going out with Craig?'

'Yes.'

'Well, now I am.'

'Yes!' Then, for good measure, Carla followed her exclamation with, 'Re-*sult*! That's fantastic, Mum!'

'I'm glad you approve.'

'Did he ask you out when you were in London?'

'Sort of.'

'I expect he took advantage of you both being there at the same time.'

'You could say that, but it's true to say that I rather took advantage as well.'

'So you fancied him all along?' It was almost an accusation.

'Not until quite recently.' It was almost as bad as being grilled by Leah.

'When did you first know you wanted to go out with him?'

She had to be careful. 'I think it was on Christmas Day, when he was so kind to us and he made such a difference.'

'As long ago as that?'

'Grown-ups don't rush into these things, darling. We tend to weigh up the situation and look at it from various angles before we do anything.'

'So that you can make a pragmatic decision?'

'No.' In the dark interior of the car, Liz allowed herself to smile. 'In those circumstances, I'm afraid pragmatism doesn't get a look-in.'

———◆�=———

When Liz parked outside Craig's house, she saw the Land Rover, first out and ready to give service. It might yet be needed, but she had another, more immediate, concern.

'Remember, Carla, don't say anything that might embarrass Craig.'

'Yes, Mum, that's the third time you've told me.'

'That's how important it is,' she said, opening the car door.

'I suppose you have to keep reminding me,' said Carla in her grown-up way, as they walked up to the door. 'I don't like to be embarrassed, either.'

It was a little unfortunate that Craig heard her last sentence as he opened the door. 'Who's going to embarrass you, Carla?' He bent and kissed her cheek. 'He'll have to get past me.'

'I was just saying, I can understand people not wanting to be embarrassed.' As an afterthought, she said, 'Hello, Craig.'

Liz leaned against the door, burying her face against her arm and laughing because there was no other course open to her.

'From all this,' said Craig, greeting Liz with a chaste kiss, 'I get the impression that the secret is out.'

'I told Carla last night,' confirmed Liz. 'It was very important to her to know that we were going out together.'

'And does the match meet with your approval?' He directed the question at Carla.

'What does that mean?'

'It means, do you think it's a good idea?'

'It's the best idea since... since we invited you on Christmas Day,' she said confidently.

'Right,' said Craig, 'the next question is, do we take your car or my Land Rover?'

Liz considered the question only briefly and said, 'Much as I'd like to put a smile on your Land Rover's face, my car must be more economical.'

'In that case,' he said, picking up a bundle of band parts, 'let's go and find out how many New Collegians have braved the blizzard.'

———◦◦———

They were pleased to find that only Emilia, the clarinettist was missing, having made her apology via Megan. She lived near Oakenshaw, where the roads were still dicey, so she had a good excuse.

'Would you like to start things off today, Liz? I've done a new arrangement of "The Way You Look Tonight".' He handed her the score.

'With pleasure, but I hope you're going to let me do some arranging. When you're at your most industrious, I feel rather like a spare part.'

'You'll never be a spare part, Liz. Anyway, I want to see you conduct this with your bum.'

She shook her head sadly. 'You were doing so well until the moment you mentioned that,' she told him. 'It's not the kind of thing a woman likes to hear.'

He shrugged. 'It was a compliment.' He handed the band parts to Nicole, the guitarist. 'You can be monitor today,' he said.

'Oh, Craig, what an honour. I can't wait to go home and tell my mum.' She gave him a cheeky smile and set about distributing the parts.

'Matthew,' said Liz, 'You might like to learn this one.'

'I can read it, Liz, and I've heard it a few times. It's from *Swing Time*, when Ginger Rogers is washing her hair, and Fred sings to her from outside her room.'

'We have a believer, Craig,' said Liz.

'I've always been that,' Matthew assured her. 'since I saw my first Fred and Ginger film.'

'Bless you, Matthew. Right, folks, it's a gentle two in a bar. Ready? A-one, a-two, a-one-and-two-and....' They played the four bars of introduction, and Matthew came in at the fifth bar. The students needed no preparation or explanation. From the first note, they played with a degree of sensitivity that more experienced musicians might have envied, and the number exerted its charm to the last note, as it always did.

'Excellent,' said Liz. 'Well done, everyone, and that top "G" was a gem, Matthew.'

'Thanks, Liz.'

Craig was taking a set of parts from his folder. 'This is one of Frank's old arrangements,' he said, 'but it should be okay.'

'They're really getting the feel of the music, now, Craig.'

'With or without your bum to inspire them,' he agreed. 'I just need to speak to the reeds and brass about something that occurred to me when we heard Frank's band.'

'Do you think their playing is too precise?'

'Too meticulous, yes. It's the way they've been brought up.'

She thought quickly. 'I suppose, if they heard an example, it might give them an idea.'

'Great minds,' he confirmed, taking out his digital recorder, 'but first, let's hear our band play "Paper Moon".' He handed the parts to Nicole. 'We'll have a play through and then a listen.' When the parts were distributed, he spoke to the band. 'We're going to play through this one, and then we're going to examine our interpretation of it. Lauren, this will be a solo for you, but don't sing yet. I'll explain later. Right, everyone? A steady two in a bar.' He counted them in, and they gave a creditable performance of the song.

'That was pretty good,' he said, 'but now I want you to listen to the Paul Whiteman Orchestra playing it. They recorded it in nineteen thirty-three, and you have to remember they were an American band. The American sound was brighter and more in-your-face than the British equivalent. Ours tended to be smoother and more under-stated, but it's actually the articulation I want you to hear, and that was universal.' He switched the recorder on and treated them to Paul Whiteman's recording, during which they listened intently, some with their eyes closed, and others simply staring at nothing, but soaking up the music. As it reached its end, he switched off the recorder and asked, 'What did you think of that?'

For a moment, there was no reaction, and then Andrew on alto sax said, 'Julia Haynes would have had something to say about the sax and clarinet playing.' Julia Haynes, Liz knew, was the single-reed *suprema* at Airedale, known for her aversion to sloppy articulation.

The others laughed, but Craig said seriously, 'Be as honest as you like. Paul Whiteman is no longer around to be upset.'

Zac had been toying with his trumpet, obviously framing his response, and now he said, 'I agree with Andrew. The articulation wasn't what you'd call meticulous, but I don't think that took anything away from the number.'

There was a mutter of general agreement, prompting Craig to say, 'That's what I wanted you to notice. Over a period of time during the last century, performance became more streamlined than ever before. It began to owe more to the head than the heart. Now, there's moderation in all things, and I don't want your playing to become undisciplined. I want you to play as the thinking musicians you are, but I also want you to think about the meaning, the *message,* of the song. That, after all, was what the lyricist wanted, and kind of musical dialect you've just heard was his route to the listener's ear.' He tapped his score and said, 'Okay, everyone? Let's go again, and this time, Lauren, would you like to join us? You can leave it for later, if you'd rather.'

'No, that's okay, Craig. I can read it.'

Craig counted them in, and a different performance began to emerge. Lauren had also taken Craig's advice to heart, because her first rendering owed something to the example set by Peggy Healy, the vocalist in the Paul Whiteman recording.

'That was much better,' said Craig. 'We have a lot of work to do yet, but you've got the general idea.' He couldn't help adding, 'You clarinettists and sax players, just be careful that you don't play like that when Julia Haynes is within earshot.'

The students were still laughing when Craig spoke to Liz. 'It's unforgiveable,' he said. 'I actually said, "in your face".'

'We shan't tell a soul,' she assured him, 'and particularly after you taught that lesson so well.'

———◆◄———

Some habits are quickly acquired, and lunch at the Shepherds' Rest was an example.

'We wouldn't normally have a roast at home,' said Liz. 'It would be difficult with only two of us.'

'If Craig came,' said Carla, 'could you do it then?'

'Very likely.' Heading off what threatened to become an embarrassing line of enquiry, Liz said, 'I liked the way you handled the question of articulation, Craig.'

'Thank you, but it's what I do for a living.'

'That's true.'

The dissenting voice at the table said, 'I was disappointed.'

'Were you?' Liz was unsure where this was leading.

'I was waiting for you to dance with Craig.'

'But that's not what we go there to do.'

'No,' said Carla, 'but the students enjoyed it as well.'

'You evidently did,' said Craig.

'Yes, I like it when you dance together.'

Liz sighed wearily. 'Two nights with Leah,' she said, 'and Carla's already adept at matchmaking.'

22

O n Monday morning, Craig drove his Land Rover through the snow to the college, where he was delighted to find that a large number of students had made the effort to attend. It seemed that only those who lived locally but outside the city had been unable to make the journey. For those in student or rented accommodation there was no problem.

He was walking past the library when he saw Jessica, the diminutive drummer, with a male student almost twice her size, or so he seemed, and he wondered if they were romantically involved. The mental picture amused him until he realised that Jessica was trying to introduce her companion to him.

'This is Ryan,' she told him, 'clarinet and tenor sax. He's interested in joining the band.'

'How d' you do, Ryan.' He shook his hand. 'Is clarinet and sax your first study?'

'Yes.' His dark hair hung uncombed and in disarray.

'He plays first clarinet in First Orchestra,' said Jessica, evidently determined to bring her *protégé*'s credentials to Craig's notice. 'He was in the Big Band,' she went on, 'but he's not now.'

'I think Ryan might like to speak for himself, Jessica.'

'No,' she told him confidently, 'he's very shy.'

'Do you get nervous when you play in public, Ryan?' Craig held up his hand to pre-empt another intervention from Jessica.

'A little bit,' admitted Ryan, looking as if he might be about to retreat behind his unruly locks, 'but not much. Not when I get started.'

'Why did you leave the Big Band?'

'Too noisy. It isn't subtle.'

'I think we're agreed on that.' Then to avoid any misunderstanding, he said, 'I mean big bands generally. What do you know about the music we play in the New Collegians?'

Ryan seemed momentarily at a loss, but Jessica said, 'I've told him about it, Craig. He'll be all right.'

'We have an opening for a tenor sax. Are you free on Sunday mornings, Ryan?'

'Yes.'

'Do you know the place where we rehearse?'

'I'll bring him,' said Jessica.

'Thank you, Jessica. I'll look forward to seeing you next Sunday, Ryan.'

Ryan nodded.

'He'll be there,' promised Jessica.

It seemed to Craig that, with Jessica holding the reins, Ryan would have little choice.

———◆◆———

Six hours later, Liz parked beside the school gates and waited. Shortly after three-thirty, the first children came out of the building, and she caught sight of Carla through the thickening snow. She was talking with her friend Emily. In fact, she seemed so involved in conversation that she'd not yet fastened her anorak, and her hood was still on her shoulders. Liz left the car and hurried over to her, mindful to avoid the snowball crossfire created by two groups of boys.

'Carla,' she said, 'you're going to freeze if you leave your anorak open.' Quickly, she fastened it and pulled the hood over Carla's head, stopping to say, 'Hello, Emily. How are you?'

'All right, thanks, Mrs Frankland.' It was hardly surprising that most children assumed that Liz was a 'Mrs.'

'Where's your mum, Emily?'

'She's just coming.'

Liz looked around and saw her coming towards them. 'Hello, Laura,' she said.

'Hello, Liz.'

'Do you need a lift?'

'Oh, would you mind? This stuff's coming down harder than ever.'

A teacher hurried out to remonstrate with some boys who were trying to create a slide just outside the entrance.

'It's no trouble.' She led the way to the Suzuki, unlocking it and opening the passenger door to let the children into the back.

When everyone was inside, Liz started the engine. 'Barleycorn Street, isn't it?'

'That's right. Number nineteen, but anywhere on the street's fine.'

'No, I'll take you to the door.'

From the back, Emily asked, 'Mum, can I have a sleepover?'

'When?'

'Next Friday.'

'Who do you want to invite?'

'Just Carla.'

'I'll have to ask Carla's mum. What do you say, Liz? Do you fancy a night's peace and quiet next Friday to Saturday?'

Liz laughed. 'If that's what they want, and you're happy with it, I think you can go ahead.'

'Why not?' Laura looked around her and said, 'This is a lovely car.'

'Thanks. My old one died, or it was about to, so I had no choice.' She was awkwardly aware that Laura and her family, like many others, had suffered financially from the foot-and-mouth epidemic, and even ten years on, they had little to spare. She would have to think of how she could make some innocent-looking contribution to the sleepover.

———— ►◄ ————

Craig had almost finished marking essays on the Mannheim School of symphonists, so he didn't mind too much when his phone rang.

'Craig.'

'Craig, it's Liz.'

'So you do exist. It wasn't just an exquisite dream, after all.'

'Flatterer. You saw me only yesterday. Am I interrupting anything?'

'Only marking, and I've almost finished, so don't worry.'

'Good, because I have welcome news.'

'So have I. I bet your news is more welcome than mine, so go ahead.'

'I wouldn't dream of it, although…. On second thoughts, mine is probably better than yours, so you go first.'

'All right.' He wondered, now, if he might have set up an anti-climax, but he continued all the same. 'I've found a tenor sax player, so we can do "The Very Thought of You" properly, with Ray Noble's arrangement. He's very shy, but he comes highly recommended.'

'By whom?'

'Our petite percussionist, our dinky drummer, our Jessica, in fact. She does all his talking for him. At least, she does if she's allowed.'

'I always thought she could talk for two. It's just as well she's got a kind heart and she's a good percussionist.'

'Okay, dearest one, that's my news dealt with. What have you got to tell me?' He was excited already.

'Am I really your dearest one?'

'You're the only one I've got, so the title's automatically yours.'

'You have a way with clumsy compliments. Anyway,' she said, delivering the news like a banner headline, 'Carla's going to a *sleepover* next Friday.'

'A what? It sounds as if it might be advantageous, but I'm not counting chickens until I know what a sleepover is.'

'You can be obtuse, Craig. A sleepover is a hectic and noisy girlie session followed by an overnight stay. Carla's going to stay all night at her friend Emily's house, which means that we have the whole of Friday night to ourselves. To put it in a nutshell, we can have a sleepover, too.'

'Wow! The things we can get up to.' He thought quickly. 'There's salacious Scrabble, strip snap, libidinous Ludo, promiscuous patience….'

'I think we can arrange something better than any of them. One thing we mustn't do, however, is to let Carla know you're coming over. She's been asking me when I'm going to see you again. According to her rule book, we should be inseparable, now that we're "going out" together. That's what she calls it. You have to remember that she's only ten, at least until August.'

'When in August?'

'The fifth.'

He took a sheet of paper from his printer and wrote, 'Carla 5th Aug'. 'Noted.' While he still had his pen in his hand, he asked, 'When's yours? I'd hate to miss it. That kind of thing can have repercussions.'

'And how. The tenth of May. When's yours?'

'The fourteenth of July. In France, they mark it with parades and firework displays, but I'm not so vulgar as to encourage that here.'

'I should think not. You're a gentleman, as I believe I've already told you. Do you like pork?'

'Yes, I do, but I fail to see the connection.'

'I'm sure that liking pork and being a gentleman are two distinct qualities. I confused you by introducing the subject of pork without adequate introduction. The reason I ask is that I'm going to cook dinner for us on Friday.'

He was genuinely surprised. 'You're going to cook dinner?'

'Yes, it doesn't happen by accident.'

'I realise that, but no one has cooked for me since…. It was so long ago, I've forgotten who, what, when, where, how or why.'

'There's something endearingly tragic about you, Craig. You just keep on bringing out the nurturer in me.'

'Is that what did it on Friday night? I must work on it, because it was wonderful.'

'There's something else we need to talk about.' Suddenly, she sounded business-like.

'Will I like it?' He felt a shade uneasy.

'I don't see why not.'

'Okay, I'm listening.'

'It's about Sylvia, actually. More particularly, about the song that means so much to her.'

' "All the Things You Are"?' He could relax again.

'Yes, that one. Do you mind if I arrange it? It's one of those that Frank gave me, but his line-up was already changing by then, and it's not usable in its present state.'

'I don't mind in the least. Anyway, we're equal partners, so it's not up to me.'

'You've done the lion's share of the work.'

'I tend to take a lot on,' he agreed. 'You must let me know if you think I'm hogging the work, rather like last Friday night, in fact.'

There was a moment's hesitation, and Liz asked, 'What's the connection with last Friday night?'

'I'm just inviting you to climb on top whenever you feel like it.'

'I see. It was a clumsy analogy. I'm sure I'll get used to your style of metaphor. At least, I hope I will.'

'What time do you want me to arrive on Friday? I don't want to give the game away to Carla.'

'I'll pick them up from school and take them to Emily's house, and then I'll be back here by about four, so come as soon after that as you like. Anyway, look, I've interrupted your marking and monopolised you for far too long.'

'Don't give it a moment's thought.'

'I'm going, Craig. Have a good week, and I'll see you on Friday. 'Bye.'

''Bye.'

———◆◆———

The following morning, Craig was requested to report to Harley Stewart at his earliest convenience, which he did, an hour later.

Rosalyn caught him as he waited for the green light, and said, 'I still play your recording, Craig. It was a lovely thought on your part to record the recital.'

'It was no trouble at all, Rosalyn. I'm glad you enjoyed it.' The green light glowed, preventing further discussion, so he pushed open the door and entered the hallowed place.

'Ah, Craig, come in and take a seat.'

'Good morning, Harley.'

'I'll come straight to the point.'

'I appreciate that, Harley.'

'Yes.' Harley hesitated, giving the impression that coming straight to the point was less easy than he'd anticipated. Eventually, he said, 'I believe you've created a band of some description.'

'I would describe it as a dance band, Harley,' said Craig helpfully.

'Hm. There is, as you know, such a band within this college.'

'Is there, Harley? You surprise me. I know of the Big Band, but I wasn't aware of a dance band.'

Harley assumed the look he reserved for fools when declining to suffer them gladly or even at all. 'It is to the Big Band that I refer,' he said coldly.

'I see. I was beginning to scent competition, but now I can relax. The band with which I am associated is, as I said earlier, a dance band, and therefore not to be confused with a big band.'

'Do you mean there is a difference?'

'A significant difference, Harley. You're obviously acquainted with the essence of the big band, so let me just say that a dance band plays music of an earlier period as well as producing a more restrained and mellow sound. Does that help?'

'Not to any great extent.'

'In that case, we have some way to go. How can I help you, Harley?'

The principal switched to the look he reserved for students who failed to grasp the basic rules of Baroque harmony. 'The point is, that you have engaged in competition with your own college. In forming this... this *dance band* as an independent entity, you are in direct competition with the Airedale College of Music Big Band, whether you see it or not. I believe you have named it The New Collegians Dance Orchestra, although how you can call it an orchestra defeats me. At all events, you are claiming a relationship with the college whilst competing with it for students.'

By this time, Craig was beginning to bridle. 'I stand wrongly accused, Harley,' he said. 'I claim no relationship with the college. They are called "Collegians" because they are students by day, and because the name has an historic association. The Astoria Ballroom Collegians, among others with similar names, was celebrated in its day, which was forty years before the formation of Airedale College of Music was minuted under Any Other Business at a meeting of the City Council. Furthermore, the New Collegians rehearse on Sunday mornings at a venue in Ickringill, which means that any student who wants to play with the Big Band whenever and wherever they rehearse, is completely at liberty to do so. There is no competition, and I resent the accusation.'

'Do calm down, Craig.' Harley was clearly rattled at the way his confrontation had left its rails and apparently careered into uncharted territory. 'I may have been under something of a misapprehension regarding the exact nature of your venture, but I'm still concerned about the name you've chosen for it.'

Craig mustered his patience. 'The Astoria Ballroom Collegians were so called because they were all graduates of the same Oxbridge college. Is there anything about their name that tells you which college of which of those two universities it was?'

'Of course not—'

'Is there anything in the name New Collegians Dance Orchestra that tells you which college they attend?'

'Not exactly.'

'Not at all, Harley, but before I go and enlighten the first year BA students about the Viennese School, which is my reason for being here, let me deal with this question of band or orchestra. Most professional musicians refer to their orchestra familiarly as a "band" – it's only like calling a violin a "fiddle", which most violinists do, incidentally – and when an orchestra accompanies an opera, their copies are known familiarly as "band parts". If it comes to that, in the world of rock 'n roll, a small group of participants is called a "band". I'm telling you this because these things are alien to your specialised world of organ and church music, and you weren't expected to know what I've just told you. Now, however, you have no excuse.' He stood up. 'May I go now and do what I'm paid to do?'

'Of course, but there is one more thing, and it shouldn't take a minute.'

'Go on, Harley.'

'It's about First Orchestra's BBC broadcast in April. Jason Hunter is putting together his programme for the concert, and he wants to include....' Harley searched through the pile of documents that obscured his desk and found what he was looking for. 'Schumann's *Piano Concerto in A minor*,' he concluded. 'We've invited Philip Henderson as guest pianist, but Jason is going to need someone to play the piano part in rehearsals.'

'So he wants a sparring partner.'

'I must say, Craig, you use the oddest terms, but yes, he'd like you to do that.'

Craig looked thoughtful. Eventually, he said, 'It's a lot to ask, Harley. It'll be time-consuming, and what will I have to show for it? A guest pianist will perform on the night and receive the bouquet.'

'Jason says it's very necessary.'

'So necessary that he left it to you to ask me.'

'He knew I was going to speak to you, Craig. It simply made sense.' He hesitated. 'Will you do it?'

'I don't know. The task could be shared by a number of students.'

'But Jason wants you. He believes he can rely on you.'

'Foolish man.'

'It's very important, Craig. I wish you'd take it seriously.'

'If it's so important, I could see myself doing it, but I'd have to insist on one important condition.'

'What's that?'

'That, as far as the dance band is concerned, you get off my back and stay off it.'

'All right. Now that you've explained the minutiae, I can agree to that.'

'Good. I'll go and teach. It'll be a pleasant change.'

As he left, he called in on Rosalyn. 'I'm to help with orchestra rehearsals by playing the Schumann Concerto,' he told her.

'The Schumann? Lovely.'

'Philip Henderson will be guest pianist. I've heard him, and I don't rate him very highly, so I'll record the dress rehearsal for you, Rosalyn. I wouldn't want you to be short-changed.'

'That is good of you, Craig.'

'I just like to be appreciated.' He inclined his head towards the Principal's door and adopted a long-suffering look. It was as well that he had Friday to look forward to.

23

Craig closed the door behind him to ensure privacy, and drew Liz closer. 'You look wonderful,' he said, kissing her.

'Thank you, but I wore this dress for your lunch-hour recital.'

'I know. I recognised it immediately.'

'How not like a man.' She kissed him in honour of the fact.

'I'm not like most men,' he agreed, 'and my fellow-Martians agree with me.'

'Come and talk to me while I prepare the meal.'

'Can I do anything?'

'There are lots of things you can do, but I don't want you to do any of them yet. Just come and talk to me.' She led him to the kitchen, kissed him and donned an apron. 'Have you started rehearsals on the Schumann yet?'

'No, they need to do some work on it before I get involved.'

'It was good, the way you agreed to do it as long as he left you alone. I can't believe he was arguing about bands and orchestras. Where has he been all this time?'

'In one organ loft or another, I suppose.'

Liz squinted at the recipe and then reached resignedly for her glasses.

'You look sexier than ever in those specs,' he told her.

'Don't be silly. "Men seldom make passes at girls who wear glasses". Dorothy Parker said so.'

'She must have been wearing the wrong glasses, because it's not true.' He put his arms round her from behind and kissed the side of her neck. 'With or without glasses, you are downright desirable. Not only that, you're clever.'

'What makes you say that?'

'You can conduct with your bum, and not every woman can do that.'

She sighed. 'You were doing so well until you mentioned my bum.'

'But I admire you for it.' He kissed her again to demonstrate the fact.

'I never thought I was anything special,' she said quite seriously. 'I suppose it was because of the blonde thing. When you spend your life having to prove you're not stupid, vanity doesn't get a look-in.' After a moment's thought, she said, 'And to think I passed the baton to Carla, the poor little scrap. Mothers are supposed to nurture and protect, not bestow genetic hardship on their offspring. That's why mine is darker now.'

'Is that how it works?'

'Yes, some of the melanin is passed to the child, and the blonde parent's hair darkens as a result.'

'You couldn't help that,' he said, kissing her neck again, 'and you give Carla something a great many mothers don't. Whatever her dad gets up to, she's going to grow up confident and secure because of her relationship with you.'

'I hope so,' she said, wriggling free, 'but you must let me do this. The vegetables won't prepare themselves.'

'What vegetables are we having?'

'Roast parsnips, beetroot and sweet potato.'

'In that case, let me help you.'

'All right.' She took out a peeler and pointed to the sweet potatoes. 'I had to carry out a subterfuge today,' she said. 'I'm a hopeless liar, so I hope it worked.'

'With Carla?'

'No, Carla's happy enough. It was Laura, Emily's mum. That's where Carla's staying. The thing is, Laura's partner is a farmworker, and they're still living hand-to-mouth ten years after the epidemic. It's had an awful knock-on effect on a good many people.'

'I can only imagine.' He surprised Liz by peeling a sweet potato very quickly and skilfully.

'Well done. Anyway, I wanted to help in some way that wasn't obvious.'

'What did you do?'

She paused, partway through preparing beetroot, to tell him. 'I bought some frozen food today. I got meat, sausages, fish and some vegetables, and I told Laura my freezer had broken down. I asked her to take those things rather than let them go to waste.'

'Do you think she believed you?'

'As far as I could tell. She was so grateful, it rather got to me, and she thought I was upset because of the freezer.'

'Put that peeler down, Liz.'

'What's the matter?'

'Put it down and come here.'

She laid the peeler on the worktop and allowed him to put his arms round her.

'Liz,' he said, 'you're not just gorgeous with or without glasses, inspirational in bed, capable of writing truly memorable scores, and brilliant at posterior conducting. You have a kind heart, and that's the most wonderful thing of all.' He kissed her in celebration.

'You say the loveliest things, even when you include my bum.'

'Why not? As bums go, it's a real goer.'

She laughed. 'I'm not sure what that means, and I suspect neither do you, but let's finish preparing these vegetables.'

———◆◄———

'I do like roast loin of pork,' said Craig.

'Have you only just realised it?'

'It's the first time I've tried it. Living alone, I don't do things like that, and my previous home life didn't lend itself to epicurean experiences.'

She pretended to study him intently, and asked, 'Has your unfortunate past always enabled you to pull?'

'Something has, but I've always lacked staying power.'

'You could have fooled me last Friday.'

'I don't mean that. I mean that I've been able to pull, but they've somehow never hung around for long.'

She nodded thoughtfully. 'I suppose clumsy compliments might have been an occasional problem.'

'Liz,' he said earnestly, 'when I mention your bum, I do so with unbounded respect, nay, I have to say, *affection*.'

'I don't think it's experienced that before. It's incurred wolf-whistling and coarse remarks, but nothing at all noble until now.'

'I told you I was different from the rest of the species.' Looking around the table, he asked, 'Should we tackle the washing-up, do you think?'

'I told you the first time you came, I have a machine to do that.'

'Well, the pots and pans.'

'I remember, you offered to *scour* them. Do you scour pans at home?'

'No, they're the easy-maintenance kind.'

'Will it make you happy if we wash them now?'

'As long as we do it together.'

'How romantic can you get?' She began gathering the plates and cutlery, and he joined in.

Presently, the pans were clean and dried. Liz asked, 'Was that romantic enough for you?'

'It sort of got me started,' he confirmed.

They kissed until Liz broke away and said, 'I don't know why we're doing this in the kitchen. Let's go upstairs.' She added, 'That's unless you have some more housework in mind.'

'No, I think we've seen to everything.' He followed her upstairs, where she left him for the bathroom. He undressed quickly, and she returned to lift her dress over her head, placing it on a hanger.

His eyes opened wide in surprise as he saw her completely naked.

'It made sense,' she explained. 'I mean, it all had to come off again, so why create work?'

'I can't argue with that,' he said, joining her in bed.

They kissed deeply and unhurriedly until, like a loutish intruder, the bedside phone shrilled, and Liz groaned as the recorded voice invited the caller to leave a message. The tone sounded, and the caller spoke.

'Liz, it's me. Are you there?'

'It would be bloody Simon,' she said through gritted teeth.

'Liz,' he insisted, 'if you're there, will you pick up the phone? We need to talk.' He waited maybe half a minute and said, 'I'll come over in the morning.'

That was enough for Liz, who picked up the phone and said, 'Don't you dare. I have someone with me, and I don't need you to swell the ranks.'

'You would,' he said, 'just when I need to talk to you.'

'Yes, I did it quite deliberately. Listen, Simon, if it's about Carla, and I can't think why, when you've ignored her for three weeks, phone me tomorrow evening. If it's not, don't bother to phone me at all. Right?'

'Liz, you don't understand. It's not about Carla… well, not directly, anyway.'

'In that case, hang up and leave me in peace.'

'Why are you being like this?'

Rather than explain the obvious, Liz lowered the phone on to its dock and heard a satisfying click as the line closed. 'I'm sorry, Craig,' she said hopelessly.

'It wasn't your fault. Actually, it confirmed what you've told me about him, not that I doubted your description.'

'He's a hopeless case,' she agreed, 'and as long as he has access to Carla, he'll go on being a nuisance.'

'On a practical level,' he suggested, 'shall we have a drink?'

She nodded. 'We could finish the wine.' She got out of bed and took a garment from the hook on the back of the door. 'That should help retain your modesty,' she suggested, handing it to him.

'I've never worn a negligée,' he said.

'It's actually a dressing gown. It's just a bit… feminine, I suppose.'

'I love it. What are you going to wear?'

'This.' She picked up another gown and slipped it on. 'I'm so sorry, Craig. It was going to be a special evening.'

'It has been, and it still is. Let's have that drink. Who knows what it might inspire?'

'You're a lovely fella.' She kissed him before leading the way downstairs.

She took fresh glasses and poured the last of the wine into them, handing one to Craig. 'Here's to a life free from interruptions. If only that were possible.'

'It could have been worse,' he remarked, laughing at the mental picture it created.

'Yes it could.' She laughed too and joined him on the sofa, where they let the peacefulness of the moment distance them from the recent interruption.

'When we go back upstairs….'

'I'll take the phone out of its socket,' she said, reading his mind and clearly relishing the idea. 'If only I could lose him the same way, just by pulling him out of his socket and leaving him trailing on the floor or, better still, getting BT to disconnect him permanently.'

'Think of rosier things,' he suggested, slipping his arm round her and enjoying the sensation. 'You feel wonderful in silk,' he said.

'Silk and cashmere mixture,' she corrected him.

'It still feels good, although it makes for poor poetry. "She walks in beauty like the night of cloudless climes and starry skies;" in silk and cashmere mixture....' He shook his head. 'No,' he confirmed, 'it doesn't work.'

'Maybe not, but quoting Byron does with me. Shall we resume our tryst?'

'I don't see why we shouldn't. You will unplug the phone, won't you?'

'I'll do that,' she promised, 'if you'll recite Byron.'

'I'll do my best.' He followed her upstairs once more.

'You have an uncanny way,' she said, taking the phone plug from its socket, 'of turning dross into pure gold.'

'I try.' He slipped in beside her and asked, 'Are you ready?'

'I'm always ready for Byron.'

He waited until her head was settled against his shoulder, and began:

' "She walks in beauty like the night
Of cloudless climes and starry skies;
And all that's best of dark and bright
Meet in her aspect and her eyes;
Thus mellowed to that tender light
Which Heaven to gaudy day denies.

One shade the more, one ray the less
Had half impaired the nameless grace
Which waves in every raven tress,
Or softly lightens o'er her face;
Where thoughts serenely sweet express,
How pure, how dear their dwelling place.

Daffs in December

And on that cheek and o'er that brow,
So soft, so calm, yet eloquent,
The smiles that win, the tints that glow,
But tell of days in goodness spent,
A mind at peace with all below,
A heart whose love is innocent!" '

'Craig.' She sounded breathless.
'Mm?'
'That's the best foreplay ever devised.'
'I'm told Byron swore by it, and he knew his craft.'
'You're no novice yourself,' she said, taking a quick intake of breath
as she accepted him.

24

Craig made a discreet departure before Liz went to pick up Carla, whose excited chatter on the way home was proof enough that the sleepover had been a success.

'Mum,' she said as they turned into Hardacre Lane, 'are we going to the band in the morning?'

'As far as I know. Your dad phoned last night, but he didn't say anything about coming for you.'

'Good.'

Liz let that pass without comment.

'What did he phone about?'

'I don't know, darling. I was busy at the time, so I asked him to phone again later.' She pulled up outside the cottage. 'Bring your bag in and I'll unpack your stuff.'

'Mum?'

'I'm still here,' she said, closing the front door behind them.

'Will we have to get a new freezer?'

'No. What gave you that idea?' Then Liz remembered her white lie, which would doubtless give rise to more. 'Oh, the freezer went off yesterday, and I thought I'd have to get someone in to see to it, but then I checked the plug, and the fuse had gone, so I replaced it. Everything's fine now.'

'Good. Emily's mum and her mum's boyfriend were really pleased with all that stuff you gave them.'

'I'm glad it went to a good home. Now, take these things up to your room and bring me your jim-jams from last week so I can put them in the wash.'

'Okay.' Carla went upstairs, leaving Liz relieved at having survived her deception. She hoped it would no longer be necessary.

When Carla came down again, she dropped her pyjamas in the washing basket and pushed it back beneath the worktop. 'You didn't make your bed this morning,' she said.

It was role reversal of the worst kind. 'I know,' said Liz. 'I had a lot to do before I came for you. I'll make the bed next time I go up there.'

'What are you making?'

'Coffee. Would you like something to drink?'

'No, thanks.' Clearly, another question was on its way. 'What were you doing when my dad phoned?'

'What?'

'You said you were too busy to talk to him, so you asked him to phone you later.'

'Oh, yes. I was arranging a song, the special one that Sylvia likes so much. It wasn't straightforward, because I'm arranging it as a duet, the way it was first performed.'

'Are Matthew and Lauren going to sing it?'

'Yes, and on the subject of music, now would be a good time for you to put in some piano practice.'

'All right.'

'Good girl.'

Carla had been in the studio only a few minutes when the phone rang. Liz heard her answer it, and then she came to the kitchen to say a little wistfully, 'It's my dad. He wants to talk to you.'

'Thank you, darling.' Liz took the phone from her. 'Hello, Simon. What do you want?'

'Charming. Are you alone yet, or still, like, *entertaining*?' He emphasised the last word, and it sounded ridiculous. He'd never been adept at sarcasm.

'One of those two, but it doesn't concern you either way.'

'You and I once had something special, Liz.'

'Yes, I wonder what it was.' She was also wondering what his phone call was about.

'We meant something to each other.'

'Incredibly, but for a very short time. Where is this leading, Simon?'

'Are you, like, actually alone?'

'That's an oxymoron, and before you reveal your ignorance, "like" and "actually" are at odds with each other, wouldn't you say?'

'I meant,' he said with heavy patience, 'have you still got a bloke there?'

'Not that it's any of your business, but no, I haven't. Why do you want to know?'

'For goodness' sake, Liz, we used to be able to talk and share our feelings.'

'I still can. You're the one who always struggled to communicate, just as you're struggling now. Put me out of my misery and tell me what you want to discuss.'

'The thing is, things are not, like, as easy as they might be between Hannah and myself.'

'And what does yourself think is the reason for this state of affairs, or is yourself still searching for a conclusion?'

'I don't know. All I know is… I need to spend a night or two away from her to get things, like, straight in my mind.'

'I don't see a problem there, Simon. You live in a national park, a centre of tourism, where hotels and guest houses are plentiful. Okay, it's off-season, but you'll find a hotel easily enough.'

'Liz!' It was clearly a cry from the heart, even if it failed to arouse her sympathy. 'All I want is to spend a night with you, so that we can talk and sort something out.'

'Why with me?'

'Because you understand me. Hannah doesn't.' It was almost a wail.

'I've got news, Simon. I know you only too well, which is why I live here and you don't. It wouldn't surprise me, either, if Hannah's also got your measure.'

'What happened to you and me was a misunderstanding, Liz, a temporary hiccup.'

'I'd hate to experience a long-term one.'

'You know what I mean. We could have cleared things up quite easily.'

'And that doesn't even qualify as an understatement. It's a flagrant misrepresentation of the truth. We have a Decree Absolute. What is it about the word "absolute" that you haven't yet grasped? There is no way you're going to spend a night on my sofa, bewailing your misfortunes and upsetting Carla, so forget it.' Thankfully, she could hear Carla practising in the studio. She couldn't have heard any of the conversation.

'Just like that? You're, like turning me away out of hand?'

'No, not just like that, Simon. First, if you remember, we consulted our respective solicitors, then there was the time we spent apart, and then more business with our solicitors, followed by the Decree Nisi. The grand finale was the Decree Absolute. We are finished, Simon, *finito, kaput, n'y a plus*. Get it?'

'You really know how to lay the boot in.'

'It took me a long time to learn, but your behaviour provided the motivation. You have a responsibility to Hannah now that she's carrying your child, and no one can deny that you and she deserve each other. You've made your bed, so lie on it!' She was alarmed as well as surprised to find her hand shaking as she touched the red button to end the call, and she sat for a while, collecting herself. Simon had lost none of his ability to infuriate her. The anger she felt against him was usually on Carla's behalf, but this was different. Thinking of Carla, though, brought to mind her truncated conversation with Simon the previous night, when she'd asked him if it was about Carla, and he'd said, 'Not directly.' That could only mean that he was considering re-entering both their lives. The thought horrified her until she reminded herself of the impossibility of such a disaster.

After a while, she felt calm enough to go into the studio to listen to Carla. She was practising a study by Loeschhorn, and it was sounding quite good. She resisted the urge to suggest improvements, knowing that the child had already had a brush with disappointment. Instead, she said, 'That's really coming on, Carla. Well done.'

'Have I done enough yet?'

'You can never really do enough, but I think you've done plenty for one day. Take a break.'

They sat together in the sitting room, and Carla said, 'He didn't want to talk to me.'

'No, he had something on his mind.' Although it grieved her to make excuses on his behalf, she had to project an image of normality.

'You sometimes have things on your mind.'

'That's true, darling.' It was as well Carla didn't know the extent of it.

'But you still talk to me and listen to me.'

'Well, you see, that's a skill that mums have, In fact, most women can do more than one thing at a time. Men give it a posh name. They call it "multi-tasking", because they think it's mysterious, but we just think of it as normal behaviour.'

Carla seemed to digest that fact, and then she asked, 'Will I be able to do that when I'm older?'

'I'm sure you will.'

'I'll be eleven in March.' It was as if she'd just remembered the fact.

'Maybe that's a bit soon, but your multi-tasking skills should have developed by the time you're about fourteen.'

Carla was quiet for a spell, and Liz, who knew the signs, expected a question at any moment. When she spoke, it was in a somewhat pensive tone. 'Some mums have men living with them, even when they're not married to them. Emily's mum and her boyfriend aren't married, and neither are Horrible Hannah and my dad.'

'Yes, many people do nowadays. It's a personal choice that people make.'

'Mums and boyfriends sleep in the same room. I sort of know what they do, but it's very grown-up.'

'Yes, it is, really.'

'You must have to know someone really well.'

'That's true. It works best of all when two people love each other.' Sensing unease on Carla's part, she said, 'Of course, you won't be involved in anything like that for a very long time, but when you are, it will all fall into place.' She brushed a lock of hair away and kissed her. 'Do you feel happier about it now?'

'Yes.' It was a confident response.

'You'll hear things in the schoolyard, from time to time, that'll make no sense at all, but you mustn't worry about them. If you have a question, come and ask me.' As she spoke, she remembered that she'd left her contraceptive pills on the bedside table. Carla had noticed the unmade bed, but hopefully not the pills, although Liz reminded herself, a child of ten wouldn't know them from normal medication, or even be aware of the nature of the pill. Even so, the web was becoming increasingly tangled.

———◄►———

Craig greeted them at the door. He kissed Liz and drew Carla into a hug, asking her, 'How was the sleepover?'

'It was good.' Then, almost without a break, she went on to say, 'My dad phoned up after I got home, but he didn't want to talk to me.'

'That's too bad. Let's have another hug to take away the taste. Mmm.'

When he released her, she said, 'I don't really mind, because you always make us feel better, anyway.'

Liz screwed up her eyes with embarrassment, but Craig said, 'It's a big responsibility, Carla, but I'll try to live up to your expectations.'

They got into Liz's car and headed for Ickringill.

Craig asked, 'Have you anything booked for Saturday, the third of March, Liz?'

'Straight off the top of my head, Craig,' said Liz, 'I can't think of anything.'

'Good, because we've got a gig at the Old Town Hall in Ickringill. It's where the Darby and Joan Club meet. One of the Building Trades Club members put them on to us.'

'I've heard of the Darby and Joan Club, but I didn't know it still existed.'

'Apparently, it doesn't in most places, but no one's told them in Ickringill, so it lives on as the club that time forgot.'

Carla asked, 'Is it one I can go to?'

'Yes,' said Craig, swivelling in his seat to speak to her, 'it's a tea dance.'

'It'll be a good first gig for the band,' said Liz.

'What's a tea dance?'

'One where they have sandwiches, cakes and tea, Carla, and they get up and dance when they feel like it.'

'Great!'

'It will be.'

'What will the students wear at a daytime gig, Craig?' The question had just occurred to Liz.

'Normal wear for a daytime gig.'

'Of course. It's so long since I was a student, I'd forgotten. That's good.'

Carla was quick to notice the change in her mum's mood. She said, 'See, Mum? Craig's made us both happy again.'

‘Did you think I was unhappy?’

‘Yes, because when I was practising, I heard you getting really cross with my dad.’

‘How did you hear that when you were supposed be practising?’

‘I was multitracking. I’ve found out how to do it already.’ She added with no little satisfaction, ‘I don’t have to wait until I’m fourteen.’

The students were naturally delighted at the news, Matthew and Lauren sang Liz’s arrangement of ‘All the Things You Are’ for the first time, and the rehearsal was very successful. Carla naturally concluded that Craig had made everyone feel happier, even though he insisted that her mum deserved some of the credit for that.

25

Liz and Laura arrived at the school gates at the same time.
'Emily's still talking about the sleepover,' said Laura.
'Carla's the same. I'll have to let her have one, and then Emily can come.'

'That would be lovely. By the way, I really appreciate the food you brought, Liz. I must give you something for it.'

'I wouldn't hear of it. You did me a favour by taking it. It would have been a sin to throw it away.'

'Oh, it would.'

Through the falling snow, Liz saw the door open. 'Here they come,' she said. 'Can I give you and Emily a lift?'

'Only if you're going our way.'

'It's the only way we'll get there, Laura.' She bent to greet Carla and Emily, and to fasten Carla's anorak, and then led the way to the car. When they were all inside, she opened her mouth to speak to Carla, but Carla got in first. 'Mum, can I have a sleepover and can Emily come?'

'I was just going to ask you if you'd like to do that. We can't do it this weekend, because you'll be staying with Leah and Gavin.'

'Will I?'

'Yes, I phoned Leah this afternoon and arranged it. You could have a sleepover the next Friday, the seventeenth. That's if it's all right with Emily's mum. It'll be the last day before half-term.'

'That's fine by me,' said Laura.

'Lovely.' There were also sounds of excited agreement from the back of the car.

Having dropped off Laura and Emily, Liz headed for home.

Carla asked, 'Why am I staying with Leah and Gavin again?'

'Because I have to be at another session in London. I only heard about it today.'

'Oh, good. Will Craig be there as well?'

'I doubt it. He does have his own life to lead, you know, and he was only there last time because of his recital.'

'I wish I could go somewhere to hear him play.'

'Well, you never know what might happen.' Liz parked outside the cottage, leaning across Carla to open her door.

'Now,' she said, ushering her into the cottage and helping her out of her anorak, 'I have to make some phone calls, so the best thing will be for you to start straight away on your homework.'

'Okay. I've only got English tonight.'

'What a blessing. Well, I'll leave you to get on with it.' She went into the studio and turned up Sylvia's number.

The phone rang only four times. It was as if Sylvia had been by the phone waiting for someone to call her.

'Hello, Sylvia, it's Liz Frankland.'

'Liz, how lovely to hear from you.'

'How are you?'

'Oh, I'm coping. How is the band coming on?'

'That's what I'm phoning about, Sylvia. We've got a gig, a tea dance at the Old Town Hall in Ickringill.'

'Ickringill?'

'Yes, it's for the Darby and Joan Club.'

'Oh, they'll love that.'

Sylvia's response was typical of her. 'We're rather hoping you'll come along, Sylvia. It's ground floor access, and either Leah or I will take you there and bring you home again. What do you say to that?'

'How wonderful! Won't they mind, these Darby and Joan people?'

'No, they're quite happy for us to bring you, and this is the best bit. I've arranged 'All the Things You Are' for the band and two voices, soprano and baritone, as it was originally performed in the show, but without the verse, and we're going to play that for you.'

'Oh....' It was evident that Sylvia was having a tearful moment. Eventually, she managed to say, 'Liz, I'm so grateful, I don't know what else I can say.'

'Don't say anything, Sylvia. Just make a note in your diary on the third of March, and it will all happen.'

'Thank you, Liz. Thank you again.'

'You're welcome, Sylvia. Take care. 'Bye.'

'Goodbye, dear.'

Leah was next on the list. She knew about the gig, but it would be as well for her to know that her mum was happy.

'Hello, Liz.'

Liz made the decision to acquire a phone with a directory, or 'phone book', as Leah called it. At the very least, it would give warning when Simon called. 'Hi, Leah. I've just been on to the phone to your mum and given her the news.'

'I bet she was like a dog with two bones.'

'She's thrilled to bits. I told her one of us would bring her.'

'I'll do that, Liz. You'll have more than enough to do on the day. I must say, this whole thing's like a dream. First a new band, then the thing about my mum, you finding a new bloke.... How's that going?'

'It's making progress.' She told Leah about Simon's interruption and his phone call the next day.

'What a pathetic soul he is, and to think he can worm his way back into your affections....'

'I *think* that's what he was after. It still takes some believing. He even got sour about the fact I had someone here, as if he were accusing me of cheating on him.' Liz still couldn't believe it.

'There's no life after Simon the Terrible.'

'So he thinks.'

'Anyway, on to saner matters. When are you seeing Craig again?'

'Not for a while. I've got the session at the end of the week, and then Carla's having a sleepover here the following Friday.'

'Oh, I remember those things. What fun. Still, it gives you time to work up an appetite.'

'You've got a one-track mind, Leah. You're as bad as any man.'

'It was invented for enjoyment, I say. What's wrong with that?'

'Nothing at all, but I must go.'

'Okay. Love to Carla, and I look forward to seeing her on Thursday. 'Bye.'

''Bye.'

It was Craig's turn, so she tried his mobile number.

'Craig.'

'Craig, it's Liz. Is it a good time or a bad time?'

'It's always a good time when you ring me.'

'You really can say the right things when you try. Listen, I've just spoken to Sylvia, and she's thrilled to bits. Quite emotional, actually.'

'That makes it all worthwhile, doesn't it?' His response sounded genuine, and Liz had no doubt it was.

'That and other things. Also, I don't know if you had anything in mind, but I'm going to be in London from this Thursday to Saturday morning. I only heard today. It's because of a cancellation, apparently, and the next Friday, I'm hosting a return sleepover for Carla and her friend, so I'm afraid I'm being rather elusive as far as you're concerned.'

'Don't give it a moment's thought. I've been doing some homework, and I've learned that sleepovers are pretty important. In fact, they're an essential part of growing up.'

'I wouldn't put it quite so strongly, Craig, but I'm glad you're not too put out.'

'Not at all put out. Which hotel will you be using in London?'

'The same as before. Why?'

'Okay, I'll pick you up there on Friday and take you to dinner. The hotel restaurant's not all that brilliant, so I'll reserve a table elsewhere. You will book a double room, won't you?'

'Of course. I didn't realise you were going to be around.'

'Yes, these things can take us by surprise. Now, moving on from Friday night, have you any hard and fast plans in place for Tuesday, the fourteenth?'

She hesitated, preferring to avoid weeknights because of Carla. She said, 'No,' somewhat tentatively.

'Good, because I've booked a table for three at the Duke's Arms. I asked them to make it six-thirty, as early as they can.'

He'd lost her completely. 'For three? What's going on, Craig?'

'St Valentine's Day is what's going on, and I'm going to celebrate it by taking my two favourite people, you and Carla, to dinner.'

'What a lovely thing to do, Craig. Carla will be thrilled.'

'I hope you'll be quite chuffed, too.'

'Chuffed as blazes. Thank you, Craig.'

'I don't believe it,' said Liz, as Craig poured the last of the wine. 'You came two hundred miles to spend a night with me.'

He regarded her with mock-uncertainty. 'I thought that was normal behaviour,' he said. 'In all the best stories, the prince, or some such hero, rides vast distances on horseback and hacks through an impenetrable forest to be with his heart's desire.' He shrugged. 'Two hundred miles by high-speed rail is a mere bagatelle. In storybook terms, it's hardly worth dipping the quill in the inkpot.'

She smiled indulgently. 'When you told Leah and me back at the swimming pool, about this world of yours, we thought at first you were joking. Now, I know you're serious.'

'Seriously, would you like another drink, or shall we adjourn?'

' "Adjourn" sounds terribly discreet, doesn't it? Let's do that.'

Craig signalled the waiter, who appeared with the bill.

'Was everything to your satisfaction, sir?'

'Absolutely, thank you.' He paid in cash. 'That's fine. Will you ask someone to get us a taxi, please?'

The waiter looked at his tip and said, 'It will be a pleasure, sir.'

The taxi arrived within minutes, and they made the journey to the hotel.

'They've forecast snow flurries for tomorrow morning,' said Liz, 'but I don't expect it'll be enough to bring London to a standstill.'

'You northerners are very dismissive about us in the effete south and our relationship with snow. There are times when I feel quite scorned.'

'No, you don't.'

'But can you be sure of that?'

'If you're feeling hurt, I'll make it up to you later.'

'The glow is beginning to return,' he said, squeezing her hand in confirmation.

They arrived at the hotel, where Craig paid off the taxi and Liz picked up the key from reception.

They took the lift they'd used only recently to the second floor, where Liz opened the door to her room.

'I was very lonely last night,' she confessed, slipping into the bathroom.

'I'll try to be adequate company tonight,' he told her through the bathroom door as he began to undress.

'I'll hold you to that,' she said.

When she returned, she removed her stockings and hung them over a chair. He was doffing the last of his clothes, when she pulled her dress over her head and surprised him again.

'Do you never wear underwear nowadays?'

'It depends entirely on the company I'm in,' she said, unfastening her bra and draping it tidily. 'I left the rest in the bathroom.'

They lay together in each other's arms, confident that they would not be interrupted, and she returned his kisses, pausing after a while to whisper, 'What's it to be tonight? Byron? Keats? Shelley?'

'You do ask a lot. Hush and listen.' He kissed her and recited:

' "I wonder by my troth, what thou and I
Did, till we lov'd? Were we not weaned till then?
But suck'd on country pleasures, childishly?
Or snorted we in the sevearn sleepers den?
'T was so; but this, all pleasures fancies bee.
If ever any beauty I did see,
Which I desir'd, and got, 't was but a dreame of thee." '

'That wasn't Byron, was it?'

'No,' he said, kissing each of her breasts slowly and deliberately, 'it was Donne.'

'It works almost as well.'

'There are two more verses.'

'I don't think I could handle them just now.'

He continued to kiss her, moving gradually downward until she drew him back, clamping her legs round him in an exquisite mantrap.

'It's time for you to keep your word,' she said.

He kissed her and asked innocently, 'Which word was that?'

'That you would be adequate company tonight,' she prompted.

'I said I'd *try*.'

'Nevertheless,' she said, emphasising her words with kisses, 'I... mean... to... collect.'

'Help yourself.'

As she reached downward, she said breathlessly, 'I'm glad you didn't have to ride through wind and rain and hack your way through a forest. Most of all, though, I'm glad you came.'

———▸◄———

'Is it still snowing?'

'Off and on. Nothing serious.' Craig closed the curtain and climbed back into bed. 'Despite weather warnings couched in the most dramatic terms, it's unlikely that we'll be marooned in London.'

'Shame, although I do have to be back to pick up Carla.'

'She seems to enjoy staying with Gavin and Leah.'

'Yes, because they always spoil her to death, and then I have to work hard at being the cruel spoilsport.'

'I don't believe that for a minute.'

'Oh, no?' She narrowed her eyes to say, 'I'll have you know there's a stern side to me that you haven't seen.'

'In that case, I'd better deliver the bad news and get it out of the way.'

'What's the bad news? And before you speak, let me tell you that smothering me with kisses won't do you a scrap of good.'

'Okay, here it is from the hip.'

'I'm ready.'

'I've run out of romantic poetry that I can recite. I need the dots before I can go on.'

'In that case, we'll just have to do it without, so you can smother me with kisses after all.'

26

Carla was grappling with an array of choices.

'You can have anything you like,' Craig told her, 'as long as it's not alcoholic.'

'I don't want any of that,' she said decisively. 'I've seen what it does to Hannah.'

Liz looked up in surprise but said nothing. The waiter was similarly discreet.

Craig asked, 'How does fruit juice sound?'

'Lovely. Orange juice, please.'

'Excellent. You've made three decisions already. You've chosen your drink, starter and main course. Honestly, I've never had a St Valentine's date quite like it.' Turning to the waiter, he said, 'A bottle of the red Burgundy, bin twenty-nine, please.'

'Certainly, sir.'

Carla had the look of someone about to share a confidence. 'I told them at school what we were doing tonight,' she said, 'and nobody believed me, so I showed them my card.'

'Did someone send you a valentine?' Craig asked the question with studied innocence.

'You did,' said Carla. 'You know you did.'

'What makes you think it was from me?'

'You put a sticker on the back of the envelope, with your name and address on it.'

Liz was trying not to laugh. 'You're not cut out for a life of subterfuge, Craig,' she said. 'You put a sticker on mine as well.'

'I'm a slave to organisation,' he said, sounding as hopeless as he could.

'Did my dad send you a valentine, Mum?'

'Carla, you do choose your moment.'

'Sorry.'

'Anyway, Hannah's his valentine now.'

Carla screwed up her face in distaste. 'You should hear what Leah says about her.'

'I can imagine, but let's not talk about Hannah now, darling.'

'No,' agreed Carla, 'not when we're going to eat.'

'I wonder if they'll take something off the bill,' said Craig, 'for providing our own cabaret.'

'What's a cabaret?'

'It was an entertainment at a proper, old-fashioned night club, where people went to eat, drink, dance and listen to music late into the night.'

'In your cosy world,' said Liz. As an afterthought, she said, 'I've come to the conclusion that you probably have the right idea.'

'What idea's that, Mum?'

Before she could answer, the waiter arrived with the wine, which Craig tasted and declared excellent. The waiter poured some into their glasses and left them, to return immediately with Carla's orange juice.

'Why does Craig have the right idea, Mum?'

'I mean that he lives in a lovely, romantic world rich in beautiful music and an elegant lifestyle, where nothing remains wrong for long, and happiness always wins through.'

'Yes, he does.' Carla shrugged and tried her orange juice.

'Some things are obvious,' remarked Liz, 'even when you're ten.' Then, to move the conversation on, she asked, 'How's the Schumann coming along?'

'It's very early in the proceedings,' said Craig. 'I've only been to one rehearsal.'

'I think it's criminal.'

The waiter arrived with their starter course, and conversation was temporarily suspended.

When he'd gone, it came as no surprise when Carla asked, 'Who's a criminal?'

'No one, darling. I just think it's wrong that Craig has to help the orchestra learn a concerto, so that a guest pianist can come and enjoy the privilege of performing it.'

Carla looked uncertain, so Craig explained, 'It's a piece for piano, accompanied by an orchestra, and I have to play the piano part in orchestra rehearsals. Then, the BBC will broadcast the concert with a well-known pianist playing it. It makes sense, really. A guest performer, even one of Philip Henderson's questionable ability, will give the college orchestra a touch of celebrity.'

Carla appeared thoughtful, and said, 'I don't know which knife and fork to use.'

'These,' said Craig, pointing to the appropriate cutlery.

'Start on the outside,' said Liz, 'and work your way towards the middle with each course.'

'There's a lot to learn, isn't there?'

'I suppose there is,' said Craig, 'but you'll get the hang of it soon enough. The main thing is that you enjoy it.'

They all went on to enjoy both the meal and the evening, and they returned to the cottage before Carla's bedtime, so she was able to enjoy the occasion for a little longer.

When she'd gone up to bed, Liz said, 'It's been the most unusual St Valentine's Day I've ever known. Did you include Carla because it was a weekday? If you did, it was a lovely thought.'

'Only partly. When I told you about it in London, I said I was going to take my two favourite people to dinner, and I meant it. I couldn't consider not including her, and you must agree, she was entertaining tonight.'

'Entertaining and just a trifle embarrassing at times,' she agreed. 'She may have got the hang of multitasking, but she does need to work on tact and diplomacy as well.'

'How tactful were you at ten, Liz?'

'It's a fair question.' She considered it and said, 'I was probably no more tactful than Carla. Children don't think before they speak, and now I think of it, neither do a great many adults.'

He leaned towards her, and she joined him in a lazy, lingering kiss.

After a while, she said, 'Much as I would like you to stay, it's awkward with Carla here.'

'Be patient. All we have to do is wait for Carla to ask, "Mum, can Craig come for a sleepover?" '

She laughed and said, 'At her current rate of progress, it won't be long before she does.'

———◆I◆———

On Wednesday morning, it became known that Jason Hunter had succumbed to the flu bug.

'I shall have to cancel the orchestra rehearsal this afternoon,' said the harassed Vice Principal, 'and we've little enough time before the concert.'

'There's no need for that,' Craig told him. 'I'll take the rehearsal.'

'But you're playing the piano in the Schumann. How can you rehearse the orchestra as well?'

'It won't be the first time it's been done. In any case, I'll multitask. I know a little girl of ten who can do that. so it shouldn't be beyond me.'

The befuddled Vice Principal was left without an argument. 'Very well,' he said, 'if you think you can do it, you'd better go ahead.' He left the common room in a puzzled but more relieved state of mind.

'Oh he of little faith,' said Chris Ashton, Course Leader for BA (Honours). 'I suppose it's a bit out of his league.'

'More than a bit,' said Craig.

'What will you do for scores? They say Jason sleeps with them under his pillow.'

'They should be in the college library. I'll go and find it now.' He took the stairs to the first floor, where the library and practice rooms were situated, and it occurred to him, as it often did, that only an architect could put a library and listening rooms, both requiring peace and quiet, next to a suite of practice rooms.

The librarian, a matron of forbidding countenance, saw him enter, and asked with characteristic sharpness, 'What are you looking for, Mr Townsend?'

'Schumann's *Piano Concerto, op. 56 in A minor*, the full score thereof. Also Holst's ballet music *The Perfect Fool* and Hindemith's *Symphonic Metamorphosis of Themes by Carl Maria von Weber*, if it's not a lot to ask.'

'Just a minute, before you go rummaging.' She made her way to a section marked *Full Scores* and found all three within half a minute. Irascible she may have seemed to some, but as far as Craig was concerned, she was efficiency in support tights. 'How long do you want them for?'

'Until I know when Jason Hunter's likely to return to work, Miss Appleton.'

'All right, I'll book them out.'

'Thank you, Miss Appleton. May I say, I find you as charming as ever.'

'If you say so.'

As he left the library, he put a forefinger to his lips as a warning to two students who were about to give way to laughter.

———◆●◆———

First Orchestra rehearsal was held from three until five in the Recital Hall, and most of the students were there well before the starting time. Craig put the Holst score on the conductor's desk and waited until everyone was present. When he was satisfied, he said, 'Good afternoon, ladies and gentlemen. As you possibly know, Jason is unwell, so I'm going to take the rehearsal, beginning with the Holst. Ready, everyone?' With a wry smile to the band members, he added, 'This time, no counting in.' He started the piece, delighting in the bold trombone solo from Tyler, and Jessica's equally self-assured response on the timpani, and allowed them to play on for several bars before stopping them. 'Untidy, folks. It needs to be much more staccato. Once more, from the top.' He started the piece again, this time much better pleased with the articulation, and he allowed it to continue, communicating only by the occasional gesture. It was a gloriously exciting piece of music, and he could tell the students were enjoying it.

'Well done. That was excellent. Now for the hard bit.' He acknowledged their laughter and opened the full orchestra score of the Schumann concerto on the music desk of the piano. 'Let's see how far we can get.' He gave the downbeat for the opening chord and played the piano entry. It was going remarkably well until he had to stop them. It was a shame, because they'd been playing so well. 'That's great, folks. There's just one thing I'd like to tweak, and it's at rehearsal mark "M". The piano has that ecstatic, rising motif, but rather than everyone getting carried away, the woodwind need to play *secco*, almost without expression. Leave it to me to milk it. Okay?' Looking around, he said, 'If anyone's not familiar with an ecstatic, rising sensation, well, don't worry. You've a treat in store.' He let them laugh and said, 'Okay, from rehearsal mark "M", three, four and….' They resumed playing, and Craig was satisfied that he'd made his point as he played the rising motif followed by the cascade of arpeggios.

The rehearsal continued along the same lines, breaking eventually at ten minutes to five.

'Thank you all, ladies and gents. You've played extremely well.'

As one, the students applauded him, which was a nice gesture, and then they packed their instruments away and trooped out, offering such feedback as, 'Nice rehearsal, Craig' and 'Enjoyed it. Fantastic'. Tyler was more detailed in his observation. He picked up his trombone case and said, 'It's just a pity you can't conduct with your other end, Craig, You can do everything else.'

'I'm sure I could if I tried. I mean to say, you manage to talk through yours, and that has to be much harder than conducting with it.'

'Well, I'm not talking through my arse when I say this, Craig. It's just a pity you're not playing in the concert, and I'm not the only one who thinks so.'

———— ▸◂ ————

Twenty miles away, Leah was dressing her mother's thumb, having applied temporary stitches to stop it bleeding. 'I wish you'd call it a day and come to live with us, Mum. Gavin was saying only a few days ago that he worries about you being on your own.'

'He mustn't worry, and neither must you. This was sheer accident, an isolated injury.' She watched her daughter bandaging her hand and said, 'I must say, you're very good at this sort of thing.'

'I spent years giving first-aid to dance students. I had to be good at it.'

'Yes, and you attended to Liz's young man when he had cramp. He's ever so nice, isn't he?'

'Liz evidently thinks so.' Leah cut off a piece of sticking plaster and used it to fasten the end of the bandage.

'Oh? Has there been a development?'

'Yes, it all took off quite recently.' She smiled at her mother's inevitable interest in the relationship.

'I'm glad. That ex-husband of hers was a dead loss. I don't know what she saw in him.'

Leah resumed her seat. 'Not everyone gets it right first time, Mum. I had a few disasters, if you remember, before I met Gavin.'

'Yes.'

Leah could see that her mother's attention had wandered. 'What is it, Mum?'

'What, darling?'

'You were miles away. It must have been something important.'

'I was only thinking about Liz and her young man.'

'Craig,' prompted Leah.

'Yes, I was thinking about their band and how kind they've been to indulge a silly old woman with too many memories.'

Leah leaned forward to take her mother's uninjured hand. 'You're not a silly old woman, and those memories are special, not just for you, but for me as well, and anyone else who knew and loved my dad.'

It was as if Sylvia had not been listening. 'Yes,' she said, 'it's very kind of them to play 'All the Things You Are.'

'It is, but there's something else, isn't there? Is there another number that means as much to you, or maybe more? You've only to ask.'

'No, darling, I'm not asking for anything else. I'm very lucky they're doing that for me.'

'Mum, you're hiding something. I know you. Just remember that nothing is too much trouble for them or for us.'

'No, Leah, I have everything I need.'

Leah gave her a grown-up look. 'Call me if you change your mind.'

27

MARCH

A table had been reserved near the band for Sylvia, Leah, Gavin, Carla and either Liz or Craig, depending on which of them wasn't currently in front of the band. Elsewhere, tables lined the town hall floor, the chairs having been removed for the occasion.

As the band made their way to their seats, a woman on a neighbouring table said loudly, 'Eh, they don't look old enough to know owt at all.'

Leah shook minutely with suppressed laughter and stroked Carla's hand to reassure her.

When everyone was tuned and ready, Liz walked out in front of them to start their signature number 'Dancing Cheek to Cheek'. From the start, Sylvia was entranced, leaving her tea to grow cold. All that mattered to her was the music.

The applause died away, and Liz spoke to the audience. 'Good afternoon, ladies and gentlemen, and thank you to Ickringill Darby and Joan Club for your magnificent welcome. I'm Liz Frankland, one of the bandleaders, and I'll be introducing my colleague Craig Townsend after this next number. Let's start with a slow foxtrot, 'Red Sails in the Sunset'. She counted the band in, and the number began. After a while, Liz allowed herself a quick look at the audience, who seemed to be in shock, and she imagined that the event must have taken them by surprise.

Matthew stepped up to the microphone and sang the vocal refrain, prompting audible expressions of approval, which, in the circumstances, Liz found encouraging.

'Matthew Greenwood,' she told the audience as the applause

ended. 'You'll be hearing from him again. Meanwhile, let me introduce Craig Townsend.'

Craig took his place amid gentle applause. 'Let's have a waltz,' he said, 'and we can do no better than 'In a Sleepy Lagoon'.' He started the number and looked behind him, but the floor was still empty. Mouthing, 'Carry on' to the band, he stepped down and extended the hand of invitation to Liz, who joined him on the floor, to Carla's transparent delight. They used the whole floor, encouraging members of the audience as they came near, to join them, until there were several couples on the floor.

Relieved, Liz waited for the applause to fade, and said, 'Here's a lovely young lady come to sing for you. She's called Lauren Armitage, and she's going to join us in a lively quickstep, 'Exactly Like You'.'

This time, there was no need for Liz and Craig to give a lead. The members were ready to dance, and they did so enthusiastically to Lauren's vocal refrain.

Craig led the band in 'All I Do is Dream of You', and then it was time for Liz to announce 'The Very Thought of You'. As she spoke, she saw Sylvia's face, and remembered that it was one of her favourites. In no time at all, Craig was leading her on to the floor, followed by Leah and Gavin.

The afternoon was going better than they could have hoped, and it was soon time for 'All the Things You Are'. Matthew and Lauren took their places, and Liz started the number she'd arranged so carefully.

It was going beautifully, but when Liz took a look over her shoulder, there was no sign of Sylvia. She turned to scan the floor, which was now quite crowded, and eventually caught sight of her dancing with Craig. That she was enjoying the number was evident from her features, but unusually, she seemed to be talking to Craig, and that was most unlike her. She'd always maintained that a dance was no occasion for conversation, and Liz remembered her giving Leah and Gavin a gentle telling-off for the offence.

Eventually, the band took a break, giving Liz an opportunity to speak with Craig. 'What on earth,' she asked, 'was Sylvia chattering about during "All the Things You Are"? It was most unlike her.'

'She wasn't talking to me, Liz. Honestly, I think she must be losing her grip on reality. All the time, she was talking to her dear departed.'

They spoke to Leah when they could, and she provided the answer to the mystery. 'She talks to him all the time,' she said. 'She's convinced he can hear her, and who are we to disagree? For all we know, they might have a direct line.' She smiled. 'Anyway,' she said, 'be thankful she wasn't communicating with him in Morse code.'

Craig had to agree. 'That would really have scared me,' he admitted.

The second half was as successful as the first, with the two vocalists more popular than they could ever have imagined. Liz and Craig spoke to the band afterwards, thanking them for their excellent, but so far unpaid, efforts. Typically, it was Tyler who put the musicians' feelings into words.

'You've given us a new kind of music to enjoy,' he said. 'We're happy enough playing it.'

Everyone was happy. Leah was happy because Sylvia was happy, Gavin was happy because someone else had done all the work for a change, and Liz and Craig were happy because the event had been a success. Carla was simply happy to see Liz and Craig dance together.

As they left the Town Hall, Leah took Liz on one side to ask, 'Can we arrange to visit my mum together, you and I? There's something she's not told me, and I want to get to the bottom of it.'

With no idea of the nature of the problem or how she, of all people, might help, Liz could only agree, and with quite a heavy workload, she had to suggest a day nearer the end of the month.

———◆◄———

On the other end of the spectrum, Simon was being particularly difficult. More than three months had passed since his last excursion with Carla, and now he wanted to take her out on Sunday. Apart from the inconvenience, Liz could only wonder if he would still recognise his daughter after so long an interval, and she voiced her uncertainty.

'Don't be cheap, Liz. Life hasn't been easy.'

'And only you can ever have problems. Anyway, it'll have to be Saturday.'

'Why not Sunday?'

Liz transferred the receiver to her other hand. 'Because I am elsewhere on Sunday mornings, which means I can't sit here with Carla, waiting for you to arrive or, alternatively, to phone me with a pathetic excuse.'

'Of course, you do things with your other man on Sundays. I imagine that's, like, more important than Carla's happiness.'

Liz clenched her teeth to prevent herself shouting into the phone. 'There is no "other man". Not that it's any of your business, but he is the *only* man in my life, and secondly, nothing is more important to me than Carla's happiness. In fact, such an accusation from a father who hasn't bothered his arse to see his daughter for almost four months, who ignored her at Christmas, and who can't be trusted to keep an appointment, is too insulting for words.'

'Maybe I pitched it a bit strong—'

'Have you suddenly taken up baseball?'

'Liz, you're being unreasonable. I have things to do on Saturday.'

'Listen. If you want to see Carla on Sunday, and I warn you, it's unlikely that she'll be happy about it, I will bring her to you at a time convenient to me. All right?'

'All right, if that's how you want to play it.'

'You're so bloody unreliable, it's the only way it'll work.'

'It's not my fault, Liz. I told you, things are not good between Hannah and me.'

'That needn't concern me, Simon. In fact, you and Hannah can fly to the bloody moon for all I care.' She pushed the red button, knowing that her next job was to tell Carla she wouldn't be going to Ickringill on Sunday.

———◆◄———

As Liz had feared, the news was less than welcome to Carla, who nevertheless swallowed her disappointment and took the line that it would not happen every Sunday.

Liz and Carla duly arrived at Simon's house and rang the doorbell. Sounds of disagreement came from within, and Liz felt again that she'd betrayed Carla by agreeing to the meeting.

One of Hannah's sons opened the door and yelled, 'Mum!'

Hannah appeared. 'Oh,' she said, 'I didn't know you were coming.' She wandered back inside to say quite audibly, 'Simon, Glamour Puss and Little Miss Perfect are here. I wish you'd fucking told me they were coming.'

Simon came to the door looking careworn, 'Didn't you get my text? I'm sure I texted you to say I couldn't make it.'

Without a word, Liz took out her phone and showed him the empty text page. 'For what it's worth, Simon, "Glamour Puss" will be speaking to her solicitor on the subject of access. Goodbye. Come along, Carla. We have things to do with our Sunday.'

Carla waited until they were in the car before reacting. 'Yes!' Then, more casually, she said, 'I don't want to spend the day with them ever again. They don't like me, and he doesn't love me anymore. Anyway, Hannah gets drunk and takes drugs.' With a sideways look at Liz, she said, 'So does my dad sometimes.'

Liz felt a cold rush of blood. 'When have you had to spend the day with them, Carla?'

'Oh, a few times. He calls it "hanging out".'

'He would. I don't suppose there's an appropriate term for it in baseball. I thought he'd been taking you on picnics and things.'

Carla looked shamefaced and said, 'He did to begin with, but that was a long time ago. I just kept quiet about it. I didn't want to make trouble.'

'You can be sure of this, darling. I'm going to make trouble, *big* trouble. Anyway, how do you know they take drugs?'

'They talk about it, and they smoke funny cigarettes that Hannah makes herself.'

No wonder she looked so awful. 'I can't let you be exposed to that, Carla.'

'Well, anyway, I can go with you to the band rehearsal now.'

'Yes, let's both cheer up. We have that to look forward to.'

After a thoughtful silence, Carla said, 'I don't want to do anything with him and Horrible Hannah and her boys.'

'I'm going to speak to my solicitor about that, darling. If I have anything to do with it, you won't have to.'

———◆◆◆———

Band rehearsal proved to be an effective distraction, because Carla emerged at the end of the morning, her usual, cheerful self. Liz was less so, a fact that Craig was quick to notice.

'You're very serious, Liz. Is everything okay?'

'Yes, it was just a domestic disagreement. I'll tell you about it later. The awful thing is that it shoved something else to the back of my mind, something I should have told you earlier. I had a phone call from Frank Morrison yesterday.'

'Oh?'

'Yes, he had a suggestion to put to us.'

'To us?'

'Yes, about the band. Purely on Gavin's recommendation, he's suggesting a regular guest night at the Wool Exchange. He's spoken to a few committee members and, so far, the response has been favourable. After years of the same sort of thing, he thinks it'll put new life into the club's programme.'

'I think it's a brilliant idea.' He turned in his seat to speak to Carla. 'Don't you, Carla?'

'I'm not sure what he means, but yes.' Clearly, the wheels of thought were turning. 'Mum?'

'Yes?'

'Do you think Craig could come for a sleepover?'

Craig shook with suppressed laughter while Liz spoke to her daughter via the driving mirror. 'Yes, darling, I think he could.'

———◆◆◆———

Purely for the sake of common sense, Liz collected Leah, and they drove to Sylvia's house together.

'So Simon the Terrible is behaving true to form?'

'He is,' agreed Liz. 'He actually accused me of putting my relationship with Craig before Carla's happiness. Also, I learned

197

recently about Hannah's drink problem and the fact that she and Simon have been smoking cannabis or some such substance in front of Carla and filling the air she has to breathe with the foul stuff.'

'It's unbelievable.'

'At all events,' said Liz, 'I'm seeing the solicitor tomorrow. I'll stop him seeing Carla altogether if I can.'

Leah was shaking her head. 'I can't get over his brass neck, accusing you the way he did.'

'Not all that long ago, he thought he was going to worm his way back into our lives. I soon disabused him of that idea.'

'Has Bungee Boobs fallen out of favour?'

'It appears so, but I really couldn't care less.' Liz pulled up outside Sylvia's house. 'Let's concern ourselves with better things,' she said, getting out of the car.

'And there are so many,' said Leah, opening her mother's door. 'Mum, where are you?'

Sylvia opened the kitchen door. 'Oh, Leah, and Liz, too. How lovely. I'll put the kettle on,' she said, accepting kisses from them both.

'I'll do it, Mum.' Before Sylvia could argue, Leah was filling the kettle.

'It's lovely to see you both, and Martin and Wendy were here yesterday.'

Leah said, 'I don't think you've met my brother and his wife, Liz.'

'No, I haven't.'

'It'll be quite an experience when you do. Martin never says much. He has Asperger's syndrome, so it's only to be expected, but Wendy talks for both of them.'

'Wendy's a kind-hearted girl,' chided Sylvia.

'She is,' agreed Leah. 'She's a kind-hearted "girl" of about my age. How Martin and she got together is a story in itself, Liz. I'll tell you about it some time.'

'Yes, and I gather things have developed between you and Craig, Liz.' Sylvia hesitated. 'I have got his name right, haven't I?'

'You have, and yes, things have developed, as you say. He's a lovely man, and that's what I need just now.'

'Yes,' said Sylvia, 'a big improvement on your lamentable ex-husband, but I shan't say anything about him.'

'I think you just did, Mum,' said Leah, scalding the tea. 'Let's go to the sitting room. I'll bring the tea things in.'

When they were settled, Leah said, 'I think we're all agreed that the tea dance was a huge success.'

'Oh, yes,' said Sylvia.

'And that Liz's arrangement and the band's performance of "All the Things You Are" were as successful.'

'It was beautiful, Liz.'

'I'm also aware, Mum, that there's something else you'd dearly love to happen.'

Liz cringed inwardly. Leah was never less than direct.

'I can't think what you mean, dear.'

'I know you too well to believe that. I can only imagine it's something to do with my dad.'

Sylvia looked down at her hands. 'I don't want to put anyone to any more trouble,' she said. 'I wouldn't dream of it.'

'In that case, instead of dreaming of it, why don't you say what it is, and if it's too much trouble, I'm sure Liz will find a gentle way of telling you so.'

'Oh dear. Liz, you really will tell me if I'm asking too much, won't you?'

'Yes, Sylvia, but I'm on the edge of my seat with suspense.'

Sylvia levered herself out of her chair and went to the bookcase that contained photographs of Freddy and her. She took out a PoW letter and handed it to Liz. 'It was the last letter he wrote to me before the Germans marched everyone to Germany,' she said. 'They call it the "Long March" now. It's quite an understatement.'

Liz unfolded the letter, blinking at the microscopic writing. 'Excuse me a minute,' she said, taking her glasses from her bag.

'Freddy's writing was always tiny,' said Sylvia. 'It was so that he could put everything he wanted to say into the space allowed.'

Leah, who had already donned her glasses, joined Liz on the sofa, and they read the letter together. It was dated the 19th of November, 1944, and it began:

Dearest Sugar Plum,

Here is my combined Christmas and twenty-first birthday present to you.

Liz was vaguely conscious of Sylvia handing something to Leah, but the letter had now claimed her whole attention. It appeared to be in the form of a song with music and lyrics by Freddy. It was called 'You Make Everything Better', and Freddy was basically telling Sylvia how he felt about her and why.

Liz had reached the end of the song when Leah asked, 'Where do you keep your tissues, Mum?'

A box of tissues materialised through the veil of tears, and Liz and Leah each took one. Sylvia came to sit between them, and it was apparent, though not surprisingly, that she was similarly affected.

After a while, Sylvia asked, 'Have you got that cassette I gave you, Leah?'

Leah sniffed. 'Yes, it's here.'

'Freddy recorded it on the piano, Liz, but he never arranged it. He didn't even write it down. He considered arranging it for the Dalesmen, but we decided it was too private for public performance.'

'I can understand that,' said Liz.

'Of course, that was during Freddy's lifetime. Now, things are different and, if it's not putting too great a burden on you, because I know how busy you are, Liz, I should like.... I just feel that this song was so central to our relationship that.... Oh dear.'

Liz patted her hand. 'Let the words tumble out, Sylvia. We can rearrange them later. That's what I tell Carla.'

'I just think that if this song could be performed, it would be a huge part of Freddy that would live on.'

———— ◆◄ ————

Liz picked up Carla, and they arrived home. In her usual way, Carla checked the phone in the studio and reported back. 'There's a message for you, Mum.'

Liz picked up the phone, hoping earnestly that the caller might be anyone but Simon, and was delighted to hear Craig's voice.

'Liz,' he said, 'phone me on my mobile when you can. I'm free for most of the afternoon.'

She knew Craig's mobile number from regular use, so she dialled it immediately. It rang several times, and Liz wondered if she'd chosen the part of the afternoon when he wasn't free, but then he answered.

'Craig.'

'Hi, Craig, it's Liz. What's happened?'

'You'll never guess, so I'll tell you. Philip Henderson was in a collision with a removal van yesterday, and he's laid up in hospital. The principal's asked me to play the concerto in the concert.'

28

As it was a special occasion, and Carla was on holiday from school, Liz took her to the concert on the understanding that they would leave after Craig's performance. As well as taking into consideration the lateness of the hour, she felt that the Hindemith might be more than a trifle testing for a ten-year-old's sensitivities.

Carla was so excited by the time they reached Metcalfe Hall that, fearing an emergency, Liz insisted on taking her to the ladies' room before they took their seats.

Once seated, Carla stared around the Victorian concert hall, at the ornate, gilded plasterwork, the crystal chandeliers and the magnificent organ, and whispered, 'It's just like a palace.' It must have seemed so to a child on her first visit, and it occurred to Liz that such an impression could only add to the magic of an orchestral concert.

The BBC team finished adjusting the microphones, and an official, presumably from the BBC, made the announcement that the guest pianist Philip Henderson was indisposed, and that the piano solo would be played by Craig Townsend. At the mention of Craig's name, there was a cheer from the students in the auditorium, and Liz put her arms round Carla, fearful that the excitement might cause her to leap over the balcony.

The musicians were now taking their places. In no time at all, they warmed up their instruments and tuned to the oboe's 'A', reminding Liz of Dickens's account of the fiddler's preparations at Fezziwig's ball. 'Fifty stomach aches' described it well, but the cacophony only contributed to the excitement for Carla.

They finished tuning and sat in silence for the conductor's entrance. He bowed politely to acknowledge the applause and gave the upbeat for the start of Holst's Ballet Music from *The Perfect Fool*. Carla recognised Tyler and Jessica immediately, so that Liz's enjoyment was twofold, coming as it did from the music itself and the vicarious thrill of her daughter's obvious delight.

The Holst was just long enough for a child with no real experience of twentieth-century music, and it held her attention to the end. The applause was deservedly enthusiastic and, after it had died away, there was more excitement for Carla, when a student came on to the platform to raise the lid of the concert grand. For his pains, he received an ironic round of applause from his fellow students in the audience, but decided wisely against acknowledging the gesture.

With the orchestra silent again, Craig made his way to the piano, briefly acknowledging the applause, and Liz could feel Carla's thrill at seeing her hero in full evening dress.

Craig nodded to the conductor, who gave the downbeat that preceded the piano entry. Liz would never tire of the Schumann Concerto, and she listened, as spellbound as Carla, to the plaintive theme from the oboe, repeated by the piano, and then the ecstatic treatment of the themes as the movement continued.

At the exultant ending of the movement, Carla was about to clap, but Liz stopped her. 'There are two more movements, yet,' she said.

'Oh, good.'

They listened to the delicate, tentative second movement, and then, as it moved seamlessly into the finale, Liz whispered, 'The last movement.' It was as well to warn her.

Schumann had written the concerto during an eighteen-month period of clinical depression, and Liz thought of him marshalling his powers of concentration and creativity to produce this last movement that seemed to radiate joy and triumph.

The concerto reached its inevitable climax, and the audience, which included a large number of students from the college, erupted into cheering and applause. Craig's eleventh-hour substitution had been popular with the students, a fact they were quick to demonstrate. Also, had he looked up to the balcony, he would have seen two members of the audience applauding even more enthusiastically than the rest, so infectious was Carla's delight.

Craig took his applause, shook hands with the conductor and the leader, acknowledged the principal players, and left the platform.

The cheering and applause continued, and he returned, but instead of playing an encore, he nodded to the conductor, and they waved the whole orchestra to its feet to take its share of the applause.

Regretfully, Liz took Carla's hand and led her downstairs to the exit. 'You'll see Craig in the morning,' she said. 'We'll all have breakfast together.'

'Is he coming for a sleepover?' The excitement seemed never-ending.

'Yes,' said Liz, thankful they were alone.

———◆◄———

Carla went to bed, over-excited but deliriously happy. Downstairs, Liz opened a bottle of wine so that it could breathe before Craig arrived. In any case, she reflected, he would want to shower, so she needn't have worried.

Half-an-hour or so later, she heard his car arrive, and she went to open the door. She found him with his collar undone and the ends of his bow tie dangling.

'Before I can even consider ravishing you,' he said, kissing her, 'I must have a shower.'

'You were amazing tonight, but yes, it's upstairs, first off the landing.'

A stair creaked, and Carla came into the room. 'Craig, you were wonderful!'

'Oh, that makes it all the more worthwhile.' He bent to receive a kiss.

'Carla, I said you'd see Craig in the morning. You should be in bed.'

'I know. I couldn't help it.'

'I'll see you tomorrow, Carla. Unless your mum has other ideas, we could all go swimming. I brought my bathers just in case.'

'That sounds good to me.'

'Yes!'

'But first of all, you must sleep. If you need the bathroom, go now, because Craig's going to have a shower.'

'Okay. Night-night, Craig.'

'Night-night, Carla.'

'Night-night, Mum.'

'Night-night again, darling.'

Craig waited until he was sure Carla had finished with the bathroom, and then went up for his shower, leaving Liz to wonder once more about the direction her life was taking. In one week, she'd taken steps to deny Simon access to Carla, and now she was hosting a grown-up sleepover with a man who'd come to mean increasingly more to her than Simon ever had. She poured herself a glass of wine on the strength of it.

After a surprisingly short time, water stopped running through the pipes. Soon after that, Craig came downstairs in a fleece bathrobe.

'You were quick,' she said, pouring him a glass of wine.

'I don't linger, and I've been waiting to see you.'

'Come and join me.' She made room for him on the sofa. 'Carla wondered why you didn't play an encore.'

'It was a student concert. It wasn't about me.'

'That's what I told Carla. The students thought it was about you, though.'

'Yes, they're a supportive crowd.'

'For what it's worth, I thought you were truly wonderful, and if that isn't worth a kiss, I don't know what is.'

'Very remiss of me.' He put his glass down and said, 'Come, melt into my arms.' They kissed until Craig looked at the clock and said, 'This is where your "ex" phones up, isn't it? I'm not greatly impressed with his timekeeping.'

'It's not a regular fixture. Anyway, the next he'll know will be when he has a notice served on him.'

'What does that mean?'

'I'm getting a court order denying him access to Carla. He's made her unhappy once too often as well as exposing her to alcohol and drug abuse.' She told him about the aborted arrangement on Sunday and Carla's shocking disclosures. 'I've never been impressed by Hannah,' she said. 'She must have frightened scores of men away before she found Simon.'

'He does seem to have passed from the sublime to the hideous.'

'She calls me "Glamour Puss", although that doesn't worry me. What I really resent is that she calls Carla "Little Miss Perfect".'

'Not to her face, surely?'

'I'm not sure, but certainly within her hearing.'

'What a bitch she must be. Just think, though. They have each other, and we have each other, too. Let's do something to take the taste away.'

'That's a good idea. I'll shove the cork back into the bottle.'

'Yes, it doesn't taste very good in-between.'

'In between what?'

'Come upstairs and I'll show you.'

When they reached the landing, Liz peeped into Carla's room and closed the door gently. 'She's fast asleep,' she reported.

'Well, it is a sleepover.'

Liz undressed quickly and joined him in bed. 'Have you rediscovered any poems lately?'

'I've remembered one or two that I'd forgotten.' He took her in his arms and kissed her. 'I think the occasion calls for the assistance of Elizabeth Barrett Browning. Are you ready?'

'I think so.'

' "How do I love thee? Let me count the ways.
I love thee to the depth and breadth and height
My soul can reach, when feeling out of sight
For the ends of being and ideal grace.
I love thee to the level of every day's
Most quiet need, by sun and candle-light.
I love thee freely, as men strive for right.
I love thee purely, as they turn from praise.
O love thee with the passion put to use
In my old griefs, and with my childhood's faith.
I love thee with a love I seemed to lose
With my lost saints. I love thee with the breath,
Smiles, tears, of all my life; and if God choose,
I shall but love thee better after death." '

'Are you sure?'

'Absolutely positive.'

'Then so am I.'

He bent unhurriedly to kiss her. 'Mrs Browning put it better than I can, but I know how I feel, and I think you do, too.'

'I do. You *exude* it. I think that's the word, and I do the same. Have you noticed?'

'I couldn't help noticing.'

'I'd like to hear the sonnet again,' she said, 'but later.'

———◄►———

Leah knifed into the water and swam smoothly to the shallow end, where Liz, Craig and Carla were standing. 'Hello, you three. Fancy meeting you all here.'

'Craig came for a sleepover after his concert,' said Carla.

'I expect he needed it,' said Leah, smiling at Liz's discomfiture. Did the concert go well, Craig?'

'He was brilliant,' Carla told her.

'Need I say more?'

'No, Craig. Carla's said enough.'

'She certainly has,' said Liz.

With a look of martyrdom, Leah said, 'I suppose we should do a few lengths before we adjourn for coffee. I'll race you to the deep end, Carla.'

'You always let me win.'

'Let's make it a fast length, and then if you have any more secrets to disclose, you can tell me them before the others join us.' They did a shallow dive together and swam towards the deep end.

Liz and Craig completed several lengths and then they all went to change.

As usual, Craig was first to arrive at the cafeteria. He put down the tray and handed coffee to Leah and Liz, and orange juice to Carla.

'There's something that impresses me every time I see you swim, Leah,' he said, 'and it's that you're so graceful in the pool.'

'It's kind of you to mention it, Craig. It's really down to a life of ballet, I suppose, except that when I haven't been dancing, I've been in water. I had several operations on my right knee and, with each one, I had to spend time in the pool, strengthening my muscles. I don't recommend it.'

'The Royal Ballet School were preparing her for stardom,' Liz explained, 'but she was hit by a car, and that put paid to a career in ballet.'

'Oh Leah, I'm sorry. I'd no idea.' He wished he hadn't mentioned it.

'Such is life, Craig, and go easy on the sympathy. Liz and I shed enough tears at my Mum's.'

'What was that about?'

Leah picked up her coffee and said, 'You tell him, Liz.'

'Sylvia has the lyrics and a piano recording of a song Freddy wrote for her when he was a prisoner-of-war,' said Liz. 'It means an awful lot to her, and she's asked me to arrange it for the band.' She paused guiltily and said, 'I was going to tell you, and then all that unpleasantness I told you about started up.'

'My dad and Horrible Hannah,' prompted Carla, who was clearly in a sharing mood.

'Who's going to sing it?'

'Matthew. It's written by a man.'

'By a man,' echoed Leah, 'who had just witnessed the murder of two prisoners and seen his best friend beaten half to death. He wanted to do something decent and honourable, and to tell my mum how he felt…. Carla, have you got a tissue, darling?'

Carla passed her a packet of tissues.

'I'm working on it,' said Liz. 'I want it to be my best arrangement ever. It's as important as that.'

———— ►◄ ————

Liz had a phone call from Frank later that morning.

'The committee have given me the go-ahead to plan a regular guest evening,' he said. 'How does the second Saturday in May sound? It's the twelfth.'

29

Liz worked on Freddy's song in between attending to her bread-and-butter work, a schedule that led to a long working day. To begin with, she had to listen to the song and write it in manuscript before she could arrange it, although that wasn't a particularly arduous task as she enjoyed it. She'd learned that Freddy was a pianist of fairly modest ability, but his melody-writing and harmony were excellent, so that, even without her obligation to Sylvia, those elements were enough to drive her on, and she was often so engrossed in her work that she forgot the time. On one occasion, Carla came to the studio to say she was going to bed.

'Carla, I'm sorry. You poor, neglected child, come here.' Liz wrapped her arms round her. 'I love you, love you, love you, and as soon as I've finished this job, I'll be at your disposal, fit once more to be called your mum.'

'That's all right, Mum. It's for Sylvia, isn't it?'

'And Leah, and Freddy's memory.'

Carla looked at the score on the computer screen and asked, 'Will it soon be ready?'

Liz nodded. 'I'm hoping to have it ready for Sunday morning, so that we can start rehearsing it. I've already emailed the vocal part to Matthew.'

'Oh, good.' Carla's eyes were drooping.

'Night-night, darling. See you in the morning.'

'Night-night, Mum.'

Liz worked on with guilt as her companion, but with the rare luxury of an understanding and supportive daughter.

Craig noticed the difference on Sunday, when Liz and Carla arrived at his house. After welcoming Carla in the usual way, he said, 'Liz, your lovely features tell me you've been burning the midnight oil.'

'Do I look so awful?'

'Not in the least. In fact, most people wouldn't notice it, but I'm more finely attuned than most.'

'Yes,' she confessed, 'I've been working double shifts, I've neglected Carla, and I'm racked with guilt because of it.'

Craig turned to Carla and said in a confidential tone, 'I think we can make an allowance in this case, can't we, Carla?'

'Yes, there's nothing to be sorry about.'

Liz put her arm round her and said, 'I don't deserve you two.'

'Well, we think you do, so there.'

On the way to Ickringill, Craig nerved himself to ask, 'How's Sylvia's song coming along?'

'I've finished it, hence the lacklustre expression and the rings under my eyes. It's here, in my briefcase.'

'You're a marvel, Liz.'

'I should be inclined to suspend judgement until we've corrected any misprints and mistakes.'

When the musicians were assembled, at the club, Liz told them about the Cullington gig and gave out the parts of 'You Make Everything Better'. 'When you're all quite ready,' she said, 'I'll tell you the story of how the song came to be written.'

They finished tuning and waited for her to begin. They enjoyed Liz's stories.

'The man who wrote this song was a prisoner-of-war in Poland during the Second World War, doing dirty, heavy and dangerous work for the Germans, and living, I'm told, on black bread and weak cabbage soup. It would have been a miserable existence but for one thing. A girl in England had been asked to write to him and send him parcels. They'd never met, but a relationship developed through their letters that…. Well, let me just say that they were married in nineteen forty-five, and their marriage lasted until his death last year. The girl who wrote him those letters will be at the gig on the twelfth to hear her song performed for the first time. She's eighty-eight years old, but the song means as much to her now as it did when she read the lyrics for the first time at the age of twenty-one.'

They were silent until Matthew asked, 'Liz, what does "kriegie" mean? It says it here, in the verse.'

'Apparently, it's a slang abbreviation of the German word for "prisoner-of-war".'

'*Kriegsgefangener*,' confirmed Jessica. 'My great-granddad was a prisoner in Poland. They called themselves "kriegies". '

'The connection's closer than we thought. Right, everybody. A-one, a-two, a-one, two, three, four....' They played the introduction, and Matthew came in with the verse:

'Into ev'ry life, they say, a little rain must find its way....'

Liz wondered briefly about a song that connected a woman of eighty-eight, her sixty-year-old daughter, and a twenty-year-old percussionist. Music had remarkable qualities, but she already knew that. She dismissed the thought and concentrated on the song.

After a few tweaks, she pronounced herself happy with the band's performance. As usual, Matthew's rendering was excellent.

———◄►———

On the way home, Liz said, 'I've been very busy lately, as you know.'

'Yes, we've established that, and I'm concerned about it.'

'You're very sensitive, Craig. After this gig, do you mind if I take a back place? I'm quite happy to do some arrangements, but I'd rather not be just as active with the band. It was because of Sylvia that I mentioned the idea to you in the first place, and we're on the point of achieving that.'

A backward glance told Craig that Carla was fast asleep. 'As I see it,' he said, 'you have your own work to do, and the volume varies a great deal, doesn't it?'

'You can say that again.'

'I remember that from when I was arranging.'

'But it's not just the work.'

'I know,' he said, glancing again at Carla. 'There's being a parent as well. I don't know much about it, but it must be demanding for the conscientious.'

'I've felt so guilty this past week.'

'That's what I meant. I think you should do just as much or as little with the band as you feel comfortable doing. There's just one thing I'd like you to do before re-ordering your life.'

'What's that?'

'Will you show me how to conduct with my bum? The students are sure to demand it.'

Liz looked in the driving mirror to check that Carla was still asleep, and said, 'That'll be a pleasure, and best carried out, I would suggest, during a sleepover.'

30

Frank stood in front of the band, unusually in short jacket evening dress, and spoke into the microphone.

'Good evening and welcome, ladies and gentlemen,' he said. 'On this first-ever guest evening, I'm delighted to welcome Liz Frankland, Craig Townsend and the New Collegians Dance Orchestra.'

There was polite applause, and Liz and Craig took a bow before Craig returned to their table, leaving Liz to lead the band into their shortened version of 'Cheek to Cheek'.

At the end, the members, possibly surprised by the quality of the band's playing, applauded warmly.

'Thank you,' said Liz. 'Let's begin with a foxtrot, "Red Sails in the Sunset".' There was a murmur of approval, and Liz counted the band in, confident that the members, unlike those of the Darby and Joan Club, would need no urging to dance. She was right. When she turned to watch them, the floor was almost full, with Frank and Sarah, Leah and Gavin, and Craig and Sylvia among the rest.

Matthew came to the microphone for the vocal refrain, prompting new interest among the Exchange Club members. Their applause at the end of the number demonstrated to Liz beyond any doubt that it had been a success.

'Thank you, ladies and gentlemen. Please welcome my colleague Craig Townsend.' She left Craig in front of the band.

Craig addressed the members, telling them, 'I just had a quick chat with Frank, who told me that when the original New Albion Dance Orchestra played for the first time, their average age was around seventy.' He indicated the musicians behind him and said, 'Tonight, the average is nearer twenty, proof if ever it were needed of the evergreen quality of our music.' The observation earned a round of applause.

'Let's have a change of pace, now, with a lively number. It's "Exactly Like You", and here to sing it for us is the lovely Lauren.'

Liz sat with Sylvia, whose expression resembled that of a child enjoying a long-awaited treat.

'This is all so wonderful,' she said. 'I can't believe you've achieved all this in....'

'Eight months, and it's been the work of the students. They've been superb.'

'And Craig. He's a lovely young man.'

'I can't disagree with that, Sylvia.'

'He's a good dancer, too.' It was praise indeed.

'That doesn't surprise me.'

'Why do you say that, dear?'

'It's all part of the world he lives in.'

'What's that, darling? Come and sit on my good side so that I can hear you.'

Liz changed places obligingly and explained. 'He lives in a cosy world in which upsets and misunderstandings can be ironed out, and even the most threatening situation can be resolved. I found it hard to accept at first, but now I realise that he's got it right.'

Sylvia seemed unsurprised. 'Yes, he's quite right, you know. Freddy and I lived like that all our married life.'

'I imagine you did.'

'We'd lived through an awful time, worse for him than for me, and we decided that nothing could ever be as bad as the war years.'

'I'm sure.'

'You mustn't over-complicate your lives, you know. Just do things for the right motives and hope for the best, or you'll spend your life waiting for the next thing to go wrong or, at the very least, insuring against failure, and that's no way to live.'

It was sound advice, and Liz filed it away for future reference.

When the band broke for an interval, Craig went to the band room, and Liz took the opportunity to speak with Leah.

'I just hope your mum's not going to be too emotional when she hears the song. It would be awful if it upset her.'

'It won't upset her, Liz. She's bound to be emotional over something like this, but she got most of it out of her system at the tea dance, and she's loving this gig.' Leah looked around to make sure her mother was out of earshot, and said, 'One welcome development has come out of this evening already.'

'What's that?'

'In climbing the great staircase to the ballroom, she finally decided to accept our offer and come and live with us. She gave me quite a surprise, I don't mind telling you.'

'That is good news.'

'It's a relief,' said Gavin, joining them with more drinks.

'We had a little chat before the interval. I told her about Craig's lovely world, and she gave me some good advice.' She told them about their conversation.

'She's right, you know,' said Leah. 'They did live like that. I'll give you an example if you like.'

'We like,' said Liz. 'Tell us.'

'Okay. When they were first married, they spent five years trying to start a family, but without success, and then, in the end, they resorted to home-made superstition.'

Gavin smiled because he knew the story.

'Go on,' said Liz, 'tell me.'

'They were driving past Lady Hill. You probably know it. It's on the road between Leyburn and Hawes.'

'The hill with the tall pine trees?'

'That's right. Anyway, my dad said it set him in mind of an enchanted place, like the one in the Winnie-the-Pooh story. Well, for some reason, they decided to have a picnic on the summit. You can believe this or not – I could scarcely believe it at the time – but my mum told me this in a rare expansive and liberated moment. When they'd eaten, my dad decided that Lady Hill was the perfect place to conceive a child, so they had a spot of *al fresco*, and that was how I came to be born.'

'Brilliant.'

'She wouldn't want to be reminded of it now,' warned Leah.

'I wouldn't dream of it.'

'I was just thinking,' said Gavin with a thoughtful face, 'that's one place we've never—'

'Not on Lady Hill,' insisted Leah, 'and certainly not with the weather as cold as it is.'

He shrugged. 'I just had the impression it was a Hinchcliffe family tradition.'

Leah's expression convinced him otherwise.

'In that case, I'll just say that the band and the singers are sounding magnificent, Liz.'

'Thank you, Gavin.'

'I agree,' said Frank. 'I'm glad I suggested a guest night, although I say so as shouldn't.'

'I've decided to leave more of it to Craig from now on,' said Liz, 'and he's happy for me to do that.'

'It's quite an undertaking,' agreed Frank.

'Especially for a lone parent.'

Leah looked round. 'Hello, Mum. You found your way back, obviously.'

'It wasn't difficult. I'm not senile, you know.'

'I should say not,' said Frank, moving aside so that she could take her seat. 'You're the sprightliest one among us.'

'I wouldn't say that.' In an abrupt change of subject, she said, 'I'm looking forward to hearing Freddy's song. I hope no one thinks I'm being selfish.'

'Perish the thought. I'm dying to hear it.'

'The band's coming back,' said Liz. 'Craig's going to start the second half.'

The noise abated as Craig went to the microphone. 'Ladies and gentlemen,' he said, 'my colleague Liz recently arranged a wonderful song, possibly one of the greatest popular songs ever written. It's Jerome Kern and Oscar Hammerstein at their very best. It's "All the Things You Are", and here are Matthew and Lauren to sing it for you.'

For the second time in recent memory, Sylvia danced to the song, this time with Frank. Gavin and Sarah took to the floor, leaving Liz to compare notes with Leah.

'She's enjoying it,' said Liz, 'but she's not talking to your dad this time.'

'She got that out of her system at the tea dance, but she'll probably have a full-scale conversation with him when she gets home.'

The number ended, and the others returned to the table.

'That's an excellent arrangement, Liz,' said Frank.

'Yes,' agreed Sylvia, 'it's glorious.'

'Thank you both, but I'm needed at the front.' Liz made her way to the band.

She and Craig presented four more numbers before the time came for Liz to introduce the song for which Sylvia had waited so long.

'This is a very special number,' she told the members. 'Freddy Hinchcliffe wrote it when he was a prisoner-of-war in Poland, as a combined Christmas and twenty-first-birthday present for the girl whose letters had been making his life bearable, the girl he'd never met, but whom he was destined to marry. Tragically, Freddy passed away last year, but Sylvia Hinchcliffe is here tonight, and I hope she'll enjoy the first public performance of "You Make Ev'rything Better" by Freddy Hinchcliffe. Please welcome Matthew, who's going to sing it for Sylvia and for us.'

Matthew came to the microphone, and Liz started the number. After four bars' introduction, Matthew began to sing.

'Into ev'ry life, they say, a little rain must find its way,
To mask with temporary gloom all thoughts that otherwise illume.
A kriegie has his share of rain, although you'll not hear me complain.
I don't need a hat and coat. I've got the perfect antidote.'

Liz led the band into the foxtrot refrain.

'You make ev'rything better! No matter how gloomy the day,
A line from you makes the sky turn blue, and the sun finds an extra ray.
You put the "joy" into "joyful" and the "hope" into "hopeful" as well.
In the Hollywood vernacular, you're something quite spectacular!
You're ritzy! You're sensational! You're swell!

Yes, you make ev'rything better! You put a twinkle in the eye of despair;
You could even bring a smile to the Sphinx on the Nile,
An accomplishment, they tell me, that is rare.'

There were thirty-two bars by the band, providing a break for Tyler on trombone and Ryan on clarinet. Then it was Matthew's turn again with the vocal refrain.

Daffs in December

'A pickaxe feels like a feather, a shovel weighs nothing at all;
A letter with your name upon it rivals Shakespeare's greatest sonnet,
Making ev'ry task appear small.
Each paragraph acts like a tonic, ev'ry adverb, conjunction and phrase.
I must confess I feel quite heady ev'ry time I read "Dear Freddy",
And kisses leave me lost in a daze.

You make ev'rything better! You really show those stars how to shine,
You put to lowly shame the comet and its flame,
And the shooting star might just as well resign.
You make ev'rything better! It's a fact – believe me – it's true!
And that, by the by, is the reason why… I love you as much as I do!'

The band played out the number, there was a moment of silence, and then the members burst into applause. For a while, Liz was taken by surprise. She acknowledged Matthew, Tyler, Ryan and the band, and still the ovation continued. When, eventually, it receded, she looked across at Sylvia, whose face told her everything she needed to know. With a feeling of deep satisfaction, she handed over to Craig and re-joined Sylvia at the table.

THE END

www.ingramcontent.com/pod-product-compliance
Lightning Source LLC
Chambersburg PA
CBHW032143020726
47496CB00003B/683